Charles Rathbone Low

A Memoir of Lieutenant-General Sir Garnet J. Wolseley

Vol. 1

Charles Rathbone Low

A Memoir of Lieutenant-General Sir Garnet J. Wolseley
Vol. 1

ISBN/EAN: 9783337094379

Printed in Europe, USA, Canada, Australia, Japan

Cover: Foto ©Raphael Reischuk / pixelio.de

More available books at **www.hansebooks.com**

A MEMOIR

OF

LIEUTENANT-GENERAL

SIR GARNET J. WOLSELEY,

K.C.B., G.C.M.G., D.C.L., LL.D.

BY

CHARLES RATHBONE LOW,

I.N., F.R.G.S.

AUTHOR OF THE "HISTORY OF THE INDIAN NAVY," &c.

IN TWO VOLUMES.

VOL. I.

LONDON:

RICHARD BENTLEY & SON.

Publishers in Ordinary to Her Majesty the Queen.

1878.

CONTENTS

OF

THE FIRST VOLUME.

CHAPTER I.

THE BURMESE WAR.

CHAPTER II.

THE CRIMEAN WAR.

CHAPTER III.

THE INDIAN MUTINY.

CHAPTER IV

THE CHINA WAR.

CHAPTER V.

CANADIAN SERVICES.

PREFACE.

SOME explanation appears necessary in publishing the Biography of a man still living. On the 6th of May, 1874, immediately on the return of Sir Garnet Wolseley from Ashantee, I commenced to write this Memoir of his military services. The task was a difficult one, for Sir Garnet had lost all his papers and journals. During the Indian Mutiny they were stolen, and what remained to him were burnt at the great fire at the Pantechnicon, where all his furniture and effects were consumed. Thus, when I applied to him for assistance, he expressed his regret that he had no private papers whatever in his possession, but, with characteristic kindness, consented to give me all the information in his power. Thus, at numerous interviews, whenever he had a spare hour

from his duties at the War Office, as head of the
Auxiliary Forces, he told me

> "The story of his life,
> From year to year; the battles, sieges, fortunes
> That he had passed.
> He ran it through, even from his boyish days
> To the very moment that I bade him tell it."

As I was not unfamiliar with the military events of
the Wars in which he had participated, I was enabled
to put to him what lawyers call "leading questions,"
and these, as he frequently owned to me, assisted a
naturally retentive memory in reviving his recollec-
tions of the past. In this story of an eventful life, he

> "Spoke of most disastrous chances,
> Of moving accidents by flood and field;
> Of hair-breadth 'scapes i' the imminent deadly breach."

By correspondence and personal acquaintance with
officers of his staff, and others who had served under
his orders, I learned anecdotes illustrative of traits of
character, which will lend an additional interest to the
narrative. In this manner the book was written, and
Sir Garnet Wolseley, after perusal, testified to its
absolute veracity in a letter addressed to me. The
Memoir, especially the earlier portion, may, therefore,
almost be regarded as an Autobiography, though, owing
to the modesty of our hero, it required an assiduous
process of "pumping," based on despatches and the
information derived from comrades, to enable me to
make a connected narrative of the incidents of a

singularly stirring and eventful career. And here I would thank him for the unfailing good-nature he displayed during the ordeal, and his friends and brother officers for the assistance they so obligingly afforded to me.

The question of the publication of the Memoir in book form, slumbered until early in the present year, when war with Russia being imminent, and Sir Garnet having been placed under orders as Chief of the Staff to the Expeditionary Army, it was thought the present would be a favourable opportunity for publishing the military experiences of an officer whose name was in every one's mouth, as that of a General of established reputation, from whom great things were expected. The Press and periodicals of the day were full of speculations as to his chances of success, and the events of his past career, so far as they were known, were eagerly discussed, thus showing the public interest in him. The writer, accordingly, revised the work, and completed it up to date, including an account of the Natal Mission, derived from papers supplied by Sir Garnet Wolseley. However well or ill, from a literary point of view, the author may have acquitted himself, at least he claims for the book the merits of authenticity and completeness, and, as his hero's life has been a changeful scene of adventure, such as falls to the lot of few men in this prosaic age, no novel could be more exciting or full of incident.

In writing of one still among us, it would be unseemly to speak in the terms of eulogy warranted by the circumstances of his career, but, at least, it is allowable to quote despatches and the opinions of those who have served with him. As a young officer, wherever the danger was greatest and the fire hottest, there he was to be found. In Burmah he led two storming parties in one day, and was dangerously wounded at the moment of victory. In the Crimea he was once so severely wounded, that the surgeon passed him over for dead, and he was twice slightly wounded, while he was, perhaps, oftener in the trenches than any officer in the British Army. At the Relief of Lucknow he again led a storming party ; and, in the China Campaign, he was in the thick of the fire at the capture of the Taku Forts. The bare enumeration of the occasions on which he won " the bubble reputation," obviates the necessity of our dwelling on the fact that his courage was of the order that is absolutely destitute of fear, and these pages will show that his generosity, though less obtrusive, was equally remarkable, for he loved best to dwell on the gallantry of others, particularly of his humble comrades. More admirable than the fierce courage—"the rapture of the strife"—is the calm lofty spirit that retains its equanimity when failure appears certain and all men despair of success. That Sir Garnet Wolseley possessed this noblest and rarest of the attributes of those who claim to be leaders of men, is testified by those who served with him in the Red River and Ashantee Expeditions. A distinguished officer assured us that when, in the advance through the Canadian wilderness, every one resigned all hope of reaching Fort Garry, so many, and, seemingly, insurmountable were the natural obstacles, the Commander alone retained his sanguine anticipations of success, and nerved all hearts by his encouraging words and example. The same we know was the case in the Ashantee Campaign, when, at one time, it appeared that the task of reaching Coomassie and returning to the Coast within the limited period available for hostilities, was an impossibility. But his indomitable will removed all obstacles, and the Campaign was a brilliant success. We are accustomed to applaud such acts of heroism and devotion, when told of the warriors of Greece and Rome, but they are not less worthy of chronicle and admiration when narrated of our fellow countrymen and contemporaries. Moreover, the narrative of deeds such as we are about to recount, is useful as an example to the rising generation of young Englishmen, who will learn that the age of chivalry, notwithstanding Burke's magnificent lament, is not yet over, but will last as long as there are brave hearts to illustrate the page of our history, and generous instincts to applaud them.

Sir Garnet Wolseley carries self-reliance almost to a fault, if that is possible, though the absolute confidence he inspires in his staff, who rally round him as he passes from one triumph to another, willing tools in the hands of the master workman, shows that it is founded on just appreciation of his own powers. Swift to form his plans, he executes them with unfaltering tenacity of will, and the correctness of his judgments amounts almost to instinct, as appears in his conduct of affairs at crises during the Red River and Ashantee Expeditions.

Scarcely less remarkable than the aptitude in war, developed by experience in six campaigns, is the statesmanship and tact he displayed in the delicate task of inducing the people of Natal to surrender to the Crown their predominance in the Government of that Colony. This success, doubtless, led to his selection for the duty of evolving order and good government, out of the chaos and misrule of a Turkish province. That Sir Garnet Wolseley will succeed and add a fresh leaf to the laurels he has gained as a victorious Warrior and successful Administrator, no one can doubt who peruses this imperfect Memoir of one of England's greatest and most patriotic sons.

Chelsea, July, 1878.

SIR GARNET WOLSELEY.

CHAPTER I.

THE BURMESE WAR.

Introduction—Parentage—Early Life—The Burmese War—The Advance on Myat-toon's Position—Ensign Wolseley Leads the Storming Party on the 19th of March, 1853—Is Wounded—Returns to England.

SIR GARNET WOLSELEY is one of the foremost and most trusted of England's soldiers. In his conduct of the Ashantee Expedition, he presented a rare combination of dash and foresight, patience and energy, strategical skill and diplomatic sagacity. He made no false step from that day of October, 1873, when he landed at Cape Coast Castle, to find affairs in our Protectorate in a state of perplexity and confusion, to that day of the following March, when he embarked from the same fortress, a victor fresh from the field of his glory. During those few anxious months, he had driven across the Prah—a river which a native tradition declared no white man could cross and live—the army of the most warlike and ferocious tribe in Western Africa; he had worsted these savage warriors in every encounter on their own chosen battle ground—the impenetrable forest which afforded at every foot a vantage ground for the deadly foe lurking within its bounds—and these defeats he had inflicted under the eyes of their King, to whom discomfiture was an unknown humiliation; he had followed the panic-stricken columns to the banks of the Ordah, and forced them over that stream in headlong rout, converting a disciplined army into a demoralised mob; he had entered the capital, which, it was no idle boast to say, its savage but gallant defenders had kept inviolate from the foot of the invader for centuries; and, finally, after committing to the flames this "charnel house" of Western Africa—as he graphically described the Ashantee capital—and the palace of the monarch with its ghastly trophies of the skulls of his enemies slain in battle, he retired into British territory, his retreating columns followed only by the emissaries of the King. This wily, but astute, potentate—finding his empire crumbling under his eye, owing to the secession, one after another, of his tributary Kings, and, at length, humbled to the dust by the awful visitation that had befallen him, with the prospect of still further chastisement from another British column, commanded by Captain Glover (the dreaded "Golibar" of his

swarthy soldiery)—hastily despatched envoys to plead
with the victorious British general, for the peace he
had rejected under circumstances of treachery so
characteristic of his race.

But not only for the consummate skill with which
he conducted this Ashantee War does Sir Garnet
Wolseley merit the thanks of his countrymen, and the
commendation of military critics. He has seen much
and varied service during the quarter of a century he
has passed in that Army, whose marvellous roll of
achievements from Cressy to Abyssinia, he has still
further enriched by the names "Red River" and
" Ashantee;" and the galaxy of medals he wears on
his breast, attests the fact that, in every quarter of
the globe, and in every great, and almost every
"little" war, in which the British soldier has been
engaged since his entry into the Service, he has participated; while the official records of these campaigns
and sieges, show that he has earned the encomiums
of his commanding officers and the thanks of his
Government.

Sir Garnet Wolseley served as a subaltern officer in
the Burmese War of 1852-53, and showed in his " first
appearance" on that stage where soldiers achieve distinction—the field of battle—that he was made of the
stuff of which heroes are fashioned; again, in the
trenches before Sebastopol, which may be said to have
run with the blood of England's best and bravest, he
manifested, under the most trying circumstances, a
calm intrepidity which extorted the admiration of all

witnesses. He participated in some of the most
striking episodes of that terrible struggle, known as
the Indian Mutiny, which, doubtless, future historians
will regard as exhibiting in their strongest light the
patient endurance and stubborn valour of the British
soldier ; and again, the orders and despatches of the
General Commanding in the China War of 1860, show
the estimation in which he was regarded by his
military superiors.   In the Expeditions to the Red
River and the Gold Coast, when Sir Garnet Wolseley
was first entrusted with independent command, he
manifested talents for organisation and thorough practical knowledge of the art of war—of which he had
already exhibited a theoretical familiarity in his
" Soldiers' Pocket-Book"—and that peculiar aptitude
of inspiring confidence in those under his command,
which are among the chief attributes of military genius.
His successful conduct of these arduous operations
placed him in the foremost rank of that small band
of Generals from whom any Government, jealous only
of the honour of its country, without any regard to
aristocratic connections or political claims, would feel
bound to select the Commander of an army, in the
event of political complications embroiling this country
in an European war.

Sir Garnet Wolseley is the eldest son of the late
Major G. J. Wolseley, of the 25th King's Own Bor-
derers, and was born at Golden Bridge House, County
Dublin, on the 4th of June, 1833.

The family of Wolseley is one of the most ancient

in the County of Stafford, the manor of Wolseley having been in their possession before the Conquest. Among their progenitors was Sewardus, Lord Wisele, fifth in descent from whom was Robert, Lord of Wolseley in 1281; and Ralph, another descendant, was a Baron of the Exchequer in the reign of Edward IV. There are two baronetcies in the Wolseley family. The senior title was among the first creations of James I., and dates from the year 1628. Sir Charles Wolseley, the second Baronet, represented the County of Stafford in the Parliaments of Charles I. and Charles II.; he was also high in favour with the Protector, and was a man of much consideration in those times. Richard Wolseley, a younger son of the second English baronet, was a captain in the service of King William III., and had three sons, the eldest of whom, on the death of his uncle, succeeded as fifth baronet to the English title and estates. Captain Wolseley devised his Irish property to his youngest son, Richard, who, in 1744, was created baronet of "Mount Wolseley, Carlow," in Ireland. His eldest son, Sir Richard, succeeded to the title and estates; and the younger, William, Sir Garnet's grandfather, entered the army and became a captain in the 8th Hussars, in which regiment he served on the Continent. Subsequently he retired from the Service, took holy orders, and became Rector of Tullycorbet, County Monaghan.

Sir Garnet is not the first of his family who has won military fame, his ancestor, Colonel William Wolseley, having greatly distinguished himself during the Irish war, *temp.* William III. This officer, on the 29th of July, 1689, relieved the hardly pressed garrison of Enniskillen,* defended by Gustavus Hamilton, and advancing with the Enniskilleners, numbering about three thousand men, defeated the Irish Army, five thousand strong, with guns, commanded by Macarthy (Lord Mountcashel) at Newtown Butler. In those fanatical days, "the sword of the Lord and of Gideon" was the watchword alike among Protestants and Papists; no quarter was given by the stout colonists of Ulster, and one thousand five hundred of the enemy fell by the sword, and five hundred were driven into Lake Erne, where they perished miserably. Colonel Wolseley also commanded the Enniskilleners† at the

---

* Lord Macaulay (see his "History of England," Vol. III., p. 242) writes of Colonel Wolseley :—"Wolseley seems to have been in every respect well qualified for his post. He was a staunch Protestant, had distinguished himself among the Yorkshiremen who rose up for the Prince of Orange and a free Parliament, and had, if he is not belied, proved his zeal for liberty and true religion, by causing the Mayor of Scarborough, who had made a speech in favour of King James, to be brought into the market-place and well tossed there in a blanket. This vehement hatred of Popery was, in the estimation of the men of Enniskillen, the first of all qualifications of command; and Wolseley had other and more important qualifications. Though himself regularly used to war, he seems to have had a peculiar aptitude for the management of irregular troops."

† The Enniskilleners commanded by Colonel Wolseley, consisted of horse and foot, and are now known as the 6th Dragoons and 27th Regiment. They were raised, respectively, by Colonel Cole (afterwards Earl of Enniskillen) and Gustavus Hamilton, son of Sir

ever memorable battle of the Boyne, on the 1st of July, 1690, when the star of King William, of "pious, glorious, and immortal memory," rose in the ascendant, and that of his pusillanimous rival, James II., set for ever in defeat and ruin.

Sir Garnet Wolseley was educated at a day school near Dublin, and later had private tutors. As a boy he was remarkable for his studious habits, and, when a mere child, had read all the chief works on military history. It was always his own wish and that of his parents that he should enter the military profession, and his name was put down for a commission when fourteen years of age. His predilection for study was not confined to a liking for one branch of learning, and he was remarkable for aptitude in mathematical studies, and used regularly to go out four or five times a week surveying and acquiring a knowledge of the art of military engineering. He was also versed in fortification and astronomical science, and exhibited his versatility by the proficiency he acquired in such practical pursuits as carpentering and the use of the lathe. His aptitude for military engineering and fortification, and the practical knowledge

Frederick Hamilton, one of the Generals of Gustavus Adolphus, the great Protestant champion, who, for his great services as Governor of Enniskillen, at the Boyne, and the capture of Athlone, (which he effected by surprise,) was raised to the peerage as Baron Hamilton and Viscount Boyne. The author of this work hopes it may be considered a pardonable pride that induces him to note his descent from this nobleman, with whom Wolseley's ancestor was so closely associated, Richard, fourth Viscount Boyne, being his great-grandfather.

he acquired of these sciences, as well as of the cognate study of land surveying, was of great service to him during his career in the Crimea, where he performed the duties of Assistant-Engineer during the siege of Sebastopol, and afterwards was employed surveying in the Quartermaster-General's Department. A high historical authority has said that no " commander-in-chief is fit for his post who is not conversant with military engineering," and if we are to accept the *dictum*, then the successes achieved by Lord Napier in Abyssinia, and Sir Garnet Wolseley in the Red River and Ashantee campaigns, may be greatly attributed to their practical knowledge of the science of military engineering.

Sir Garnet Wolseley's military career commenced in March, 1852, when he was appointed Ensign in the 80th Regiment, at that time engaged in the Second Burmese War. As reinforcements were required for the Regiment, owing to the great losses it had sustained by disease more than at the hands of the enemy, he was ordered out from the depôt to the seat of war with a detachment of recruits.

Ensign Wolseley, therefore, had not been many months in the Army, before he saw his first shot fired in anger. He arrived at a time when the almost unbroken series of successes achieved by the British land and sea forces, was dimmed by a sad disaster— we refer to the failure at Donabew, which necessitated retributive operations, in which Mr. Wolseley first exhibited those soldierly qualities which have made his name renowned in our military annals.

A noted Burmese leader, Myat-toon by name—whom it was the fashion of despatch writers to style a "robber chieftain," though his countrymen, doubtless, regarded him as a self-sacrificing patriot—having established himself near Donabew, a force of three hundred men of the 67th Bengal Native Infantry, under Major Minchin, and a strong detachment of one hundred and eighty-five seamen, sixty-two Marines, and twenty-five officers of Her Majesty's ships 'Fox,' 'Sphinx,' and 'Winchester,' were despatched to disperse the enemy, the chief command being entrusted to Captain Loch, C.B., of the 'Winchester.' The combined force arrived at Donabew on the 2nd of February, and, on the following morning, Captain Loch, leaving forty-two men and five officers with the boats, marched inland with the remainder of the force. The march, through fifteen miles of jungle, was uninterrupted on that day; but, on the following morning, after they had advanced five miles, they came to a deep and broad nullah, from the opposite bank of which the enemy, concealed behind a breast-work, opened a heavy musketry fire. Captain Loch made repeated, but unavailing, efforts to cross the creek, and received a mortal wound; at length, when Mr. Kennedy, First Lieutenant of the 'Fox,' and many brave men had fallen, the force retired, the Grenadier Company of the 67th bringing up the rear, and, after a fatiguing march of twelve hours, reached Donabew.

General Godwin and the whole Army were eager to wipe out the stain of this disaster, and to that able soldier, the late Brigadier-General Sir John Cheape— an officer of the same distinguished corps that has produced Lord Napier of Magdala—was entrusted the honourable, but arduous, task. Every European soldier that could be spared from Rangoon, or elsewhere, was hurried up to Prome, and Ensign Wolseley, who had arrived in November with a detachment of about two hundred men of his Regiment, chiefly recruits, found himself under orders to embark from Rangoon. On the 18th of February, previous to Wolseley's arrival at Prome, Sir John Cheape had left that place, with eight hundred men, for the purpose of attacking Myat-toon's stronghold; and, four days later, quitted Henzadah, on the Irrawaddy, some thirty-five miles north of Donabew, and began the march inland, but owing to defective information, and a failure of supplies, he was obliged to fall back on the river, and reached Zooloom on the 28th of February. Thence, on the following day, the greater part of the force moved to Donabew, where they were joined, on the 6th of March, by reinforcements, consisting of one hundred and thirty men of the 80th Regiment, under the command of Major Holdich, with whom was En- sign Wolseley; three hundred of the 67th Native Infantry, under Lieutenant-Colonel Sturt; two mortars, with a detail of artillerymen, under Lieutenant Percival, R.A., and a large supply of Commissariat stores.

Again, on the 7th of March, the Brigadier-General started to beat up the quarters of Myat-toon, who had shown himself the most redoubtable of all the leaders of the "Golden Foot," as the monarch of Burmah styled himself. All the sick being left at Donabew, with a small party to garrison the place, the force now consisted of about six hundred Europeans, six hundred Natives, two guns of the light field battery, three rocket tubes, and two mortars, with a detachment of Ramghur Horse, and seventy Sappers. Being now assured that three days would bring them in front of Myat-toon's stronghold, they started in the following order, at two p.m., on the 7th, taking seven days provisions with them. The right wing, under Major Wigston, consisting of the detachments of Her Majesty's 18th and 80th Regiments, with the 4th Sikhs in front; then came the guns, followed by the Irregular Cavalry, rocket tubes, and mortars. The left wing, consisting of detachments of Her Majesty's 51st and the 67th Bengal Native Infantry, was under the command of Colonel Sturt.

The direction taken by the force was almost due west, and, about five p.m., the column reached the bank of a broad nullah, at least one hundred and thirty yards wide, seven miles distant from Donabew. Here the enemy opened a fire of jingals and musketry, but the guns came to the front and silenced them for a time. The troops passed the night behind a belt of jungle parallel with the nullah, and the rafts having been put together by the Sappers, the following day was occupied in crossing the guns and baggage, which operation was not concluded till late at night. The force marched on the 9th, but, about noon, it was said they were on the wrong road; the guide was accordingly flogged, sent to the rear, and another one called up to take his place. The new guide turned to the left, and, after a most tedious round, under a glaring sun, brought the wearied troops back to the identical spot from which they had started. After a halt of two hours, the column marched to a nullah at Kyomtano, where they encamped; during the night the Burmese showed themselves from the jungles on the left, but the guns opening on them, they soon disappeared; they then came down under cover of the fog, and fired into the camp at a point where the nullah was about fifty yards wide. On the following morning a bridge was extemporized by connecting the rafts with planks, and, with the assistance of an old boat found in the nullah, the greater part of the troops, and all the baggage, passed over. The bridge was then broken up, and the guns taken across on the rafts; the empty hackeries were also driven into the water, and floated across. Everything being now on the other side, the rafts were packed again by five p.m.

On the 11th, the force started at the usual hour (nine a.m.) and every one expected to reach Myat- toon's position that day. They had not proceeded two miles when the rear-guard were attacked by a strong party in the long grass, upon which Lieutenant John- son, commanding, charged into the jungle and dis-

persed the Burmese, with small loss. From this spot
the road lay through a thick forest, where the Burmese
had only to throw down a tree or two with their usual
skill in such matters, and a completely new road
would have to be cut round the obstacle. As they had
done this in several places, there was very hard work,
particularly for the Sappers, and the advance was
tedious. Shortly after entering the forest, a small
breastwork was taken, and, about two p.m., the Burmese disappeared from the front, and the road was
unobstructed. Two hours later, the force crossed a
piece of water, and soon the advance found that the
road turned into a footpath. Every one was now tired
out, and as the Artillery horses were staggering in
their harness, the General determined to encamp on
the spot, there being water a short distance a-head.
The hackeries, as they came up, were either pushed
right and left into the jungle, or remained on the road,
and the troops lay down on either side. Cholera made
its first appearance in camp this night.

Myat-toon's position was said to be only two miles
to the left, but there was no road to it. The guide,
who had committed himself on the 9th, and who was
now with the rear-guard, had pointed out a spot,
shortly after passing the first breastwork, where he
declared the road to Myat-toon's position diverged to
the left; and his statement afterwards proved to be
correct. The Commissioner, Captain Smith, informed
Sir John that he did not know the road, and had no
means of gaining information; but still the General

was determined to persevere. The force retraced its steps on the morning of the 12th, without rations having been served out, the rear of yesterday moving in front to-day. On passing the spot where the road branched off, there were serious thoughts of still advancing on Myat-toon ; but provisions were failing again, so it was thought prudent to return to Kyom-tano, about nine miles from Donabew, and wait for a supply. On the 13th, Colonel Sturt, with all the hackeries, and some eight hundred men, as also the sick and wounded, went into Donabew for provisions, and, until the 16th, when he returned with ten or twelve days' provisions, the column was put on half rations.

It would be difficult to exaggerate the difficulties and obstacles encountered on this march. When the small force had, with infinite toil, and suffering severe privations owing to the intense heat and want of water, taken up its position, and commenced to close in towards Myat-toon's stronghold, it was found that the approaches had to be made through a dense forest with thick jungle and heavy brushwood, through which it was necessary to cut every inch of the paths along which the hackeries, (or bullock-carts,) the guns, and the troops had to pass. This dangerous and fatiguing duty had to be performed under a hot sun, for throughout the entire time occupied by the operations, it was impossible to march until nine, a.m., on account of dense fogs, which rose about two in the morning. These fogs were, moreover, like "Scotch mists," and wet the men's clothes as effectually as rain, and as there was no such luxury as a change of clothing in the camp, the clothes had to dry on their wearers' backs, only to be drenched again on the succeeding night. There was not a single tent with the force, and the men bivouacked in the fog and dew all night, and marched and fought under the tropical sun all day. Thus, although all arms, from the General downwards, worked with untiring zeal and energy, the advance was very slow; and, at length, after several days' laborious marching across the creeks and through almost impervious forests, the unwillingness or treachery of his guides and the failure of provisions, forced Sir John Cheape, sorely against his will, to retrace his steps to Kyomtano.

The heat and hardships the troops had endured during this trying march, induced fever, dysentery, and worse than all, cholera; thirteen succumbed in one day, and many more perished from this fell disease, which is the invariable accompaniment of Indian campaigns in which the troops are much exposed.*

While halting at Kyomtano, Sir John Cheape ascertained that the jungle to the westward was quite impenetrable, and that there were only two routes to the position occupied by Myat-toon at Kyoukazeen, one to the southward, and the other to the northward by

---

* The 67th Native Infantry buried twenty-six men, the Sikhs thirty-one, the 18th Royal Irish, three colour-sergeants and ten men, the 80th about the same number, but the 51st had only a few cases. (See Sir John Cheape's Despatches, dated the 3rd and 13th of March.)

Nayoung-Goun.   As there was no choice between these routes as regarded distance, and the same obstacles and opposition were to be anticipated, Sir John resolved to adopt the northerly route.

In the life of young Wolseley had now arrived that most critical and anxious time for which every soldier most earnestly prays—the hour had struck in which he was to receive his "baptism of fire." Every man who has worn a sword, knows full well how many gallant hearts there are in both Services, who have prayed for this most honourable opportunity, but have been denied the distinction they would have earned had a hard fate been more propitious.   In his incomparable "Elegy," Gray sings how

"Hands that the rod of empire might have swayed,"

are bent only on the plough in the painful struggle, continued day by day, to gain a bare subsistence.   So, in some remote country town or cheap watering-place, may be seen gallant gentlemen on the Half-Pay or Retired List, who drag out their remaining years in obscurity, "unhonoured," as far as medals and decorations go, "unsung" by the muse of history, but who, had they been born under a luckier star, would have been immortalized in history as the possessors of qualities that we recognise in a Napoleon, a Wellington, and a Lee.

If Ensign Wolseley was fortunate in the circumstances of his military career, it is equally certain that he never missed an opportunity.   Whenever a chance offered for earning distinction, he eagerly grasped at it, and—being blessed with a sound constitution and an equable temperament, the *mens sana in corpore sano*, so much lauded by the Roman poet—was enabled to pass with unbroken health through the hardships of campaigns conducted in the most deadly climates of the world, or to return to duty after being wounded, and that he received some ghastly reminders of the hot work in which he participated, will soon appear.

As Sir John Cheape considered it desirable to give the enemy as little time as possible to strengthen still further the almost impregnable fortress they occupied, he directed Major Wigston, of the 18th Royal Irish, to occupy a position of importance some three miles in advance, so as to enable the main force to move early on the following morning, without waiting for the clearing of the fog, which always lay thick at that hour. Major Wigston, accordingly, marched at two p.m., on the 17th of March, with the right wing, consisting of his own Regiment, the 80th, (with which was Ensign Wolseley,) the 4th (or Major Armstrong's) Sikhs, a detail of Sappers, and some rockets. The road was found to be quite clear till within a mile of a breastwork, which was situated in the middle of the forest, and on the verge of a large lake; but the last mile was full of obstructions, such as felled trees and abattis, which had either to be removed, or, where this was a labour of time, a new path had to be made round the obstacles. The breastwork was carried in good style by the 18th Royal

Irish, who were leading, supported by the Sikhs, whose gallant commander particularly distinguished himself. Major Wigston bivouacked here for the night, and was undisturbed.

Sir John Cheape moved early on the morning of the 18th, with the left wing—consisting of the 51st Light Infantry and the 67th Bengal Native Infantry in front, followed by the guns—the entire force* carrying seven days' provisions, the remainder being left behind, together with the sick, at Kyomtano.

After going about two miles through forest, and passing breastworks from which only an occasional shot was fired, the guides, instead of proceeding further by the road which had been followed on the 11th, turned sharp off to the left, along a path bristling with obstructions and felled trees, so that it occupied two hours to perform the distance of one mile.

---

* From the "East India Army Magazine and Military Register," it appears that the following was the exact strength of the force engaged :—

EUROPEANS.

Bengal Artillery,	4 officers and 64 non-commissioned officers and men.			
Madras ,,		11	,,	,,
H.M. 18th R. Irish	9 ,,	200	,,	,,
H.M. 51st Regt.	6 ,,	200	,,	,,
H.M. 80th Regt.	3 ,,	130	,,	,,

NATIVES.

Madras Sappers	1 ,,	33	,,	,,
67th B.N.I.	8 ,,	380	,,	,,
4th Sikhs	3 ,,	190	,,	,,

Total force engaged, 605 Europeans and 22 officers; 608 Sepoys and 12 officers.

As they drew nearer to Myat-toon's stronghold, it was found that his dispositions for defence exhibited considerable skill, and were admirably adapted to the nature of his position. The entire country, or rather forest, was defended with strong works, such as stockades, abattis, stakes or fences, according as the nature of the ground seemed to require, while the presence of the enemy was constantly made apparent by a straggling and worrying fire on every side.

They had not proceeded more than a mile from their mid-day halting place when a sharp fire opened from the left; but the troops, advancing with great gallantry, carried a breastwork. In this affair the 51st Light Infanty, and the 67th Native Infantry, distinguished themselves, Captain Singleton, of the 51st, leading the advance. Ensign Boileau, of the 67th, was killed while gallantly attacking the enemy on the left flank. The Burmese, who numbered one thousand, suffered severely ; and unfortunately, Myat-toon, who commanded in person, effected his escape to his main position about midway between the Bassein river and the Irrawaddy.

Sir John Cheape lost no time in following up the enemy; but, after proceeding along the road for about a mile, thought it advisable to halt at a piece of water, the surrounding jungle being reported as full of the Burmese. At eight p.m. the General fired three rockets as a signal to Commander Rennie, I.N., who, with eighty blue-jackets from his ship, the Hono""ble Company's steam-frigate 'Zenobia,' and

Captain Fytche, with his Native levies, were acting in co-operation in the neighbourhood, and the shots were replied to by guns. All that night cholera raged in the camp, and the position of affairs looked very gloomy.

At seven a.m. of the 19th of March the force moved, the right wing leading, with the 80th as the advance guard, followed by the Sappers clearing the road; the left wing being in rear of the artillery. This eventful day was not to close without some warm work, in which young Wolseley was destined to play a prominent part.

A storming party was told off, consisting of the 80th Regiment, supported by the 18th Royal Irish and the 4th Sikhs. On coming opposite the enemy's left flank, the firing commenced, and the rockets were advanced and opened fire. The Sappers worked away at the path, which was much entangled with wood, and the guns were shortly got into position and opened; the enemy, however, were not idle, but commenced a heavy fire, under which both the senior officers, Majors Wigston and Armstrong, and many men, were wounded. "On reaching the front," says the General in his dispatch, "I found that Major Armstrong was also wounded, as well as many other officers and men, and that the fire of the enemy on the path leading up to the breastwork was so heavy, that our advanced party had not succeeded in carrying it; the most strenuous exertions were made, and Lieutenant Johnson, the only remaining officer of the 4th Sikh Local Regiment, persevered most bravely, but it only increased the loss. The 80th and Sikhs then went on in the hope of getting round the extreme right of the enemy. The jungle, however, was so thick, and the abattis so strong, that our men got dispersed, and could not get through it."

Ensign Wolseley's personal share in this first effort to storm the enemy's works was cut short, doubtless fortunately for himself, by a *contretemps.* He speaks with admiration of his associate in the perilous honour of leading the stormers, young Allan Johnson of the 4th Sikhs. He himself being well in advance of his men, had reached within twenty yards of the breast-work, when, suddenly, the earth gave way under him, and he found himself precipitated into a covered pit, technically known as a *trou de loup* having pointed stakes at the bottom, with which, among other obstructions, the Burmese had studded the narrow entrance to their position. When his men were beaten back, he was in great danger of being killed by the enemy; but after a time, he managed to rejoin the detachment, which had fallen back and got scattered. The task alloted to the 80th, was certainly a very trying one for a body of men consisting almost entirely of recruits who had never before been under fire; to carry an almost inaccessible position, held by a numerous and invisible enemy, was a duty that was calculated to put to the test the steadiness of veteran soldiers.

The General now determined to try the 18th Royal Irish, but the fire of musketry and grape was so heavy, that they also fell back having sustained loss, including Lieutenant Cockburn,* who was wounded. Although it was difficult, from the dense smoke, and under so heavy a fire, to discern exactly what was between the assailants and the breastwork, the General —who was now joined by Major (now General Sir) Edward A. Holdich, of the 80th, who succeeded to the command of the right wing on Major Wigston being wounded—at length ascertained that there was no water, and no obstacle that could not be easily surmounted, if only the troops could pass through the enemy's fire, a distance of some thirty yards. The "assembly" was, accordingly, sounded, with a view of getting together as many men of the right wing as could be collected.

In the meantime, Major Reid, of the Bengal Artillery, brought up, in the most gallant manner, his 24-pounder howitzer, which was dragged through the bushes by the hand, (chiefly by men of the 51st Regiment, who volunteered their services,) and opened with canister within twenty-five yards of the enemy, with deadly effect. The gun was, however, in a much exposed position, and Major Reid was almost immediately wounded, upon which the command devolved upon Lieutenant Ashe, who kept up the fire with spirit.

"Finding," says the General, "the right wing much weakened from the loss they had sustained, and the number of men it was necessary to employ as

---

* This gallant young officer died shortly after of his wound.

skirmishers on the banks of the nullah for the purpose of keeping down the enemy's fire, I ordered a
reinforcement from the left wing; they were joined by
the men of the right wing that had been collected by
Major Holdich, and who were led by Ensign Wolseley,
and the whole advanced in a manner that nothing
could check. The fire was severe, and I am grieved
to say that gallant young officer, Lieutenant Taylor, 9th
Madras Native Infantry, doing duty with Her Majesty's
51st Light Infantry, fell mortally wounded. Ensign
Wolseley, Her Majesty's 80th Regiment, was also struck
down, as well as many other gallant soldiers; but the
breastwork was at once carried; and the enemy fled
in confusion, the few who stood being shot or bayo-
netted on the entrance of our men."

In this second attempt to storm the enemy's position, which ended in a complete and glorious success,
the chief honours were borne off by Lieutenant
Taylor, who fell a sacrifice to his gallantry, and
Ensign Wolseley, who nearly shared a like fate,
though, happily for his country, a merciful Providence
bore him through that terrible fire to increase her
renown on many battle fields. Taylor led the men of
the 51st, and when Major Holdich called for volunteers of his own regiment, Wolseley immediately
responded, and, though much shaken by his accident,
offered to lead the storming party. In a few minutes
he had hastily collected such of his men as
were within call, and was ready for a second attempt.
The two young officers, without a moment's hesita-

tion, made a rush up the path leading over the breastwork, which was so narrow that but two men could advance together. Almost at the same moment, while well in advance of their men, and racing for the honour of being first in the enemy's works, they were both shot down, and, strange to say, were wounded exactly in the same spot. A large iron jingall ball struck Wolseley on the left thigh, tearing away the muscle and surrounding flesh. Feeling the blood flowing from the wound, with great presence of mind he pressed his fingers on the veins, and so slightly staunched the bleeding. Fortunately, in his case, the artery, which was laid bare, was not severed, whereas, with poor Taylor the artery had been cut, and so he bled to death in a few minutes before assistance could come.

As Wolseley lay helpless on his back, he, with unabated resolution, waved his sword, and cheered on his men, and though some of them offered to carry him to the rear, he refused, and lay there until the position was gained by the gallant fellows, who emulated the example of their youthful leader.*

Mr. Wolseley received the most prompt attention

---

* Speaking of his own men, Wolseley says that, after he received his wound, Sergeant Quin greatly distinguished himself by the intrepid manner in which he led the detachment. This gallant soldier, who afterwards served in the 78th Highlanders, was offered a commission for his bravery on this occasion, which, however, he declined. The General wrote in his despatch :—"Lieutenant Trevor, of the Engineers, with Corporal Livingstone, and Private Preston, of Her Majesty's 51st King's Own Light Infantry, first entered the enemy's

at the hands of Assistant-Surgeon Murphy, who immediately applied a tournaquet to the wound, and to his
skill and care he attributes, under Providence, his recovery. For six months he had a soldier in constant
attendance upon him, as there was great danger of his
bleeding to death. During all that time his constitu-
tional strength was severely taxed, owing to the sup-
puration, which was constant and profuse, and he was
given to understand that his condition was one of
grave anxiety, for had the sloughing extended to the
artery, which was much apprehended, nothing could
have saved his life. But, thanks to a sound constitution, unimpaired by youthful excesses and hard living,
he gradually gained strength, and though he had to use
crutches for some time after his arrival in England, no
permanent injury was sustained either to his general
health or to the limb affected.

In the captured works were found the two guns
which fell into the enemy's hands on the 4th of the
previous month. They had been well served to the
last, and in attempting to carry off one of them, twelve
Burmese were killed by a well directed discharge from a
9-pounder gun. The enemy sustained heavy loss in
killed and wounded. His whole force and means were
concentrated in this position, and the General was of

breastwork, the two former each shooting down one of the enemy
opposing their entrance. The lead devolved on them and on Sergeant
Preston, of Her Majesty's King's Own Light Infantry, and Sergeant-
Major Quin, of Her Majesty's 80th, when Lieutenant Taylor, Ensign
Wolseley, and Colour-Sergeant Donahoe fell in the advance."

opinion that he must have had about four thousand men in the breastworks, which extended some twelve hundred yards in length. Myat-toon, the Burmese leader, escaped with about two hundred followers, and owing to the active assistance of Captains Tarleton, R.N. and Rennie, I.N., by one p.m. of the 21st, a sufficient number of boats were ready in the nullah, for the conveyance of the artillery, and the sick and wounded, Ensign Wolseley being of the party. The whole were shipped on board the steamer on the following morning, and arrived at Donabew the same day. Mr. Wolseley, with all the bad cases of the sick and wounded, was then transhipped to the 'Phlegethon,' which was despatched to Rangoon.

On the evening of the 24th of March, the whole force had arrived at Donabew, and thus ended the last service of importance of the Burmese war. The loss in killed and wounded during the operations, between the 27th of February and the 19th of March, were two European officers* killed, and twelve wounded; one

* The following were the officers killed and wounded :—Killed : Lieutenant Taylor, 9th Madras Native Infantry, Ensign Boileau, 67th Bengal Native Infantry. Wounded : Bengal Artillery, Major Reid, severely. Madras Artillery, Lieutenant Magrath, slightly. Bengal Engineers, Lieutenant Trevor, slightly. Her Majesty's 18th Royal Irish, Major Wigston, severely, Lieutenant Cockburn, mortally, and Lieutenant Woodwright, slightly. Her Majesty's 80th Regiment, Lieutenant Wilkinson, severely, Ensign Wolseley, severely, and Assistant-Surgeon Murphy, slightly. 67th Bengal Native Infantry, Lieutenant Clarke, severely. 4th Sikhs, Major Armstrong, severely, and Lieutenant Rawlins, severely.

Native officer killed and one wounded; eighteen non-commissioned officers and rank and file killed, and ninety-three wounded. Of these casualties, eleven were killed, and nine officers and seventy-five men were wounded, in the action of the 19th of March.

The conspicuous gallantry of the 51st Light Infantry, on this occasion, as on every other from the capture of Bassein in the previous May, extorted the warm commendation of the General; and not less praise-worthy were the efforts of the 18th and 80th Regiments, which had borne their share of the dangers of this war, from the day they stormed the Dagon Pagoda, and on this occasion they bore the first brunt of a fire, pronounced by Sir John Cheape—a veteran soldier who had conducted the engineering operations at the second siege of Mooltan in 1849, and was present at the "crowning mercy" of Goojerat—to be "the most galling he had ever seen." Myat-toon, styled a robber, and for whose head a reward of one thousand rupees was offered, though he asserted that he had a commission from his sovereign, displayed military capacity of a high order in the choice of his position, the manner in which he strengthened it, and the resolution with which he withstood the assaults of a disciplined force with guns. He inflicted on the first Expedition the severest check and the heaviest loss we had experienced throughout the war, and was not routed by Sir John Cheape until the gallant band under his command had lost a large proportion of their numbers, and then confessedly only by a final desperate effort; though the arena of the encounter was in a remote jungle, where special correspondents, unknown in those days, had not penetrated, it is certain that British heroism has not often received a brighter illustration than in the stubborn efforts, at length crowned with victory, made by that handful of soldiers.*

This service, which was the last performed by Sir John Cheape, was also the first seen by young Wolseley, who received here a scar which he will carry to his grave, the first of those honourable mementos of valour and patriotism. It was a service that merited the Victoria Cross ; and had the order " For Valour," been instituted in those days, most surely Ensign Wolseley would have added the magic letters V.C., after the numerous other distinctions he is entitled to bear. Doubtless he would have appreciated the honour as highly as another gallant soldier under whom he served in India during our desperate struggle with the mutinous Bengal Army. We refer to Sir James Outram who coveted beyond any earthly distinction the Victoria Cross, which he had fairly earned during

---

* The Burmese War cost the Indian Government two millions of money, though the great sacrifice of life was a high price to pay, even for the fertile province of Pegu. Between January, 1852, and May, 1853, no less than fifty-four officers, and one thousand three hundred and fifty-three European soldiers, and two thousand Sepoys, died from the effects of climate and disease alone, exclusive of the large number who fell in action during the military operations. The military and naval forces engaged in Burmah received a medal and six months batta, together with some prize money which was not distributed until ten years later.

the memorable advance on Lucknow, in September, 1857, when he acted simply as leader of the handful of volunteer cavalry; but though recommended for the Cross for repeated acts of personal gallantry, by Colonel Vincent Eyre, commanding the cavalry and artillery brigade, the honour was never conferred, much to the mortification of this *chevalier sans peur et sans reproche.*

An officer of the 80th Regiment, who at the forcing of Myat-toon's position, received a severe wound in the arm, gives some interesting anecdotes of our hero.

When Mr. Wolseley accompanied his regiment from Rangoon to take part in the operations against Myat-toon, a soldier who was bathing with some comrades in the Irrawaddy, was carried away by the current. Seeing the man in imminent danger of drowning, young Wolseley plunged into the stream, which ran with great velocity, but, notwithstanding all his exertions, the unfortunate soldier perished.

In the severe fighting on the 19th of March, Ensign Wolseley, says Mr. W——, seeing his men hang back, headed the advance guard, which consisted of only three or four men; it was then that he fell into the pit as mentioned in the preceding chapter, and to this circumstance he doubtless owed his preservation from death. After Wolseley made his retreat under a hot fire, and returned to his regiment, Mr. W—— was severely wounded in the arm; and Wolseley bound up the wound, and attended him when, owing to the heat of the sun and loss of blood, he became faint. When volunteers were called for by Major Holdich, Wolseley, in company with Taylor, headed the second storming party, and received his severe wound in the leg. On seeing him go down, Lieutenant W——, who had lent him the only shirt he had besides the one on his back, mentally ejaculated, " There goes my change of linen !" for he never expected to see any more of either his friend or his garment, a loss almost equally to be deplored in a campaign when an officer's kit consisted of little more than the shirt and bit of soap, considered sufficient by Sir Charles Napier. The two officers, with the other wounded, remained all night in the stockade, and, on the following morning, were put into a canoe and escorted down the river to a place of safety. The sailors prematurely set fire to the stockade, and Sir John Cheape and others narrowly escaped death. It was owing to his remembrance of this circumstance that Sir Garnet Wolseley, during his Ashantee campaign, issued an order that no stockades or other entrenchments were to be fired before instructions had been given by himself, or some other responsible authority.

As it was apparent, on Ensign Wolseley's arrival at Rangoon, that his wound was of so serious a nature as to render his return home necessary, in May he embarked for England in the 'Lady Jocelyn,' steamer. The voyage home was performed without any noteworthy incident beyond the circumstance that during the four months of the passage, he suffered greatly from his wound, and was only convalescent and out of danger shortly before his arrival in England. In the Autumn of 1853, Wolseley proceeded to Dublin to stay with his family, and, on having sufficiently recovered his health, proceeded to Paris, accompanied by a brother officer. He did not rejoin his old Regiment, but was posted to a lieutenancy, without purchase, in the 90th Light Infantry, with which his name and fame are identified, although the officers of the 80th have cause to remember with pride that he made his *début* in the arena of arms in their Regiment.

CHAPTER II.

THE CRIMEAN WAR.

THE Winter of 1853 was a momentous period. Already were audible the distant mutterings of the storm brewing on the Turkish frontier, which was destined soon to break over Europe and deluge a remote corner of the Continent with the blood of the bravest of three great Powers.

It was the eve of the Crimean War, a memorable contest in which was broken the spell of a forty years' peace, and which was destined to be the precursor of an era of conflict, which there is too much reason to fear has not yet been closed. Within the quarter of a century since passed, how many and vast have been the changes that have occurred, and how stupendous the conflicts we have witnessed! An Empire has been founded, and a petty Kingdom has risen to the rank of a great Power; our ally of Crimean days has been humbled to the dust by her ancient foe, and a great nation—whose boast it was that Europe could only be at peace when she was satisfied, has expelled from her soil the dynasty of her mightiest soldier, and, after having drunk to the dregs, the bitter cup of defeat, spoliation, and dismemberment, which she undertook, " with a light heart," to force upon a neighbour who had once suffered all these humiliations at her hands—has risen Phœnix-like from her ashes, under the ægis of the same form of government which produced a Hoche and a Dumouriez to lead her armies to victory.

The first Power to take upon itself the great responsibility of breaking the long peace was Russia, or, rather, its autocratic ruler, the Czar Nicholas ; but, had our Government displayed the firmness and resolution of Lord Palmerston in 1836, on the question of the evacuation of the fortresses on the Danube after the payment of the indemnity for the Turkish War of 1828, the Crimean War would have been an unwritten page of history, and this Empire would have been saved a loss of *prestige*, no less than of tens of thousands of lives, and one hundred millions of treasure.

The combined British and French Expedition sailed from Varna on the 3rd of September, 1854, and landed, without meeting any opposition, at Old Fort, near Eupatoria, on the 14th of that month. The troops at

this time numbered fifty-eight thousand* men, of
whom twenty-five thousand were English, and thirty-
three thousand French. The former were under the
orders of Lord Raglan, a tried veteran who had won
the good opinion of his former chief, Wellington;
and our Allies were commanded by Marshal St.
Arnaud, who, dying soon after the Alma, gave place
to General Canrobert. The fleet of war-ships and
transports formed the most mighty Armada the world
had seen; but, on the element where Britain and Gaul
had so often fiercely contended, there was none to
oppose them, and the laurels won by our sailors were
gained on shore in the trenches before Sebastopol, or
at the bombardments of Kertch and Kinburn.

On the 19th of September, the Allied Army quitted
their encampment at Kalamita Bay, and, after a weary
march, bivouacked on the right bank of the Bulganak.
That night many brave men slept their last sleep,
for, ere the morrow's sun had set, was fought and
won the victory of the Alma. Six days later Balak-

* According to Major Reilly, R.A., C.B., the number of the Allied
Force was sixty-one thousand four hundred, with one hundred and
thirty-two guns. The British siege train consisted of eight companies
of Artillery, with sixty-five pieces of ordnance, with about five hundred
and twenty rounds per piece. To assist in the operations of the siege,
a Naval Brigade of seven hundred and thirty-two seamen, and thirty-
five officers, under Captain Lushington, was landed, with fifty guns,
only twelve of which were at first got up to the front. Reinforcements
continued to arrive, and at the first bombardment, on the 17th of
October, of the seventy-three pieces of ordnance, the Royal Artillery
manned forty-three, and the Navy thirty.

lava surrendered after the memorable and much discussed flank march, and the siege of Sebastopol was undertaken.

On the 10th of October, the first parallel, about one thousand yards in extent, was traced at a distance of one thousand three hundred and fifty yards from the Russian works; and, soon after dark, a working party of one thousand two hundred men of the Line, under Captain (now Lieutenant-General Sir Frederick) Chapman, R.E., commenced work along the whole extent.* At half-past six a.m. of the 17th of October, the whole of the French and English batteries, the latter mounting seventy-three guns and mortars, commenced to bombard the Russian works, which replied with spirit, the number of guns opposed to the British batteries alone being no less than one hundred and nine. The Fleet also attacked the forts on the sea face at one p.m., but, after most gallant exertions, withdrew towards dusk, having suffered more injury than they inflicted. At this time the Malakhoff had been reduced to a ruin, and the Redan was completely silenced, but unfortunately, although the troops were told off to storm, the attempt was not made. With wonderful energy and resource, the Russians repaired and strengthened their works, and, in a few days, possessed an artillery fully double that of the Allies.

On the 25th of October was fought the Battle of

---

* See "Journal of the Military Operations, conducted by the Corps of Royal Engineers." Part I. By Captain (now Sir Howard) Elphinstone, R.E.

Balaklava, and, on the following day, the Russians made their first sortie on a large scale, but were driven back with great loss. The 5th of November will ever be a glorious anniversary, for on that day took place the most sanguinary and hardly-fought battle of the war. The obstinate valour and bull-dog pertinacity of our soldiers never received a brighter illustration than in the desperate hand-to-hand conflict at Inkerman.

As it was now apparent that the siege would be prolonged, probably, throughout the Winter, preparations were made to withstand the onslaught of enemies far more dreaded than the Muscovite. Cold, the bitter cold of an almost Arctic winter, attacked the soldier without, while disease, the result of privation, gnawed at his vitals.

After the Battle of Inkerman, Lord Raglan made urgent requests for reinforcements to fill up the gaps caused by that sanguinary struggle and the demands of the siege. At this time that gallant soldier and ex-Governor-General of India, Viscount Hardinge, was Commander-in-Chief, and his Lordship had determined very wisely to abolish an exemption enjoyed by Light Infantry Regiments and the Rifle Brigade, by which they were relieved from service in the East. The 52nd and 43rd had gone out to India, and the 90th were warned for service there in the following year. However, Lord Raglan's demand for every soldier that could be spared, shook the expressed determination of the Horse Guards' Chief that the 90th should go nowhere, not even to the Crimea, until they had first served in India; and, yielding to the inevitable, that Regiment, then quartered in Dublin, was ordered to embark forthwith for the seat of war. Lieutenant Wolseley was so disgusted by the prohibitory order regarding service in the Crimea, that he and a brother officer, Captain Barnston, had made all arrangements to exchange into a corps before Sebastopol, when the orders arrived for immediate embarkation. Mr. Wolseley describes how they were at church when the colonel received telegraphic news of Inkerman, accompanied by the peremptory orders of the Field-Marshal Commanding-in-Chief. And so our hero, who had by this time quite recovered from his wound, was again placed in a position to win that distinction for which every soldier sighs.

The Regiment sailed from Dublin on the 19th of November, 1854, and, landing at Balaklava on the 4th of December, immediately proceeded to the front. The first object that greeted Wolseley's eyes as he stepped out of the boat on to the inhospitable shores of the Crimea, was a firelock which lay half in and half out of the water. Lifting it up, he found it marked "G Company," and identified it as one of the Miniè rifles that lately belonged to his own company. In those days when "Brown Bess," with her well-known proclivity of "shooting round corners," was the arm with which the British soldier was marshalled for battle, only a small proportion, about twenty men of each company, were supplied with the Miniè rifle; and, as the demand for these weapons during the Crimean War was greater than the supply, the 90th gave up their rifles, and placed their trust once more in " Brown Bess." Probably this arose from their being destined for India, where, we suppose, our experiences during the Afghan War had failed to teach the authorities how infinitely superior was the native " juzail" to that antiquated, but, in the eyes of martinets of the old school, infallible weapon. The 90th, accordingly, landed at Balaklava armed with the musket, and, on the following day, marched down to the trenches.

The mismanagement which was so conspicuous in almost every military department, was apparent at this early stage of the Crimean experiences of the 90th Regiment.

The distance from Balaklava, the base of operations, to the camps by way of the Col de Balaklava—which was the road we were forced to adopt in preference to the Woronzoff Road, after the Russians occupied the Turkish redoubts on the 25th of October—was about nine miles, and, until the construction of a tramway, the road was quite unformed, and without any metalling. The traffic was stated to be equal to that along Piccadilly, but yet to form and macadamize such a road, the working party consisted at first of four hundred, and subsequently only of one hundred and fifty sickly Turks, some of them too weak even to dig, and none working more than four hours a-day. Besides the difficulty of procuring labour, the road itself passed through a rich, alluvial soil, while the stones, which were only procurable about three-quarters of a mile distant, had to be carried by manual labour, the transport being insufficient to supply the troops with provisions. Such was the road along which the 90th Regiment marched when proceeding to the front, and such their first experience of service before Sebastopol.

Their arrival, and that of other reinforcements, must have been hailed with joy by the troops investing this fortress, if that could be called an investment in which the enemy's forces were literally surrounding the position of the allies and blockading the base of supplies at Balaklava.* Before the landing of these reinforcements, the French Army mustered thirty-nine thousand four hundred and fifty men, while the British who held an extent of ground, including the Right and Left Attacks, of nine miles, numbered about twenty-two thousand three hundred and sixty-nine effectives, there being no less than ten thousand and ninety sick on the 30th of November, 1854. When we contrast the numerical inferiority of the Allies with the strength of the Russians, we cannot but be filled with admiration at the constancy and courage that animated every man, from Canrobert and Raglan to the drummer and private in the ranks. Prince Menschikoff had under his orders, after the arrival of the 4th Corps d'Armée and other reinforcements, an army of eighty-two thousand men, and though, according to what Fluellen would call

* In the last days of December, the Russians withdrew from the valley of the Tchernaya, and abandoned the old Turkish redoubts, con centrating their troops in Sebastopol.

"the true disciplincs of the wars," the investing force
should be double or treble that of the besieged, the
latter was more numerous, and possessed a more
powerful artillery. At this time the Allied Generals
had it in contemplation to storm Sebastopol as soon as
the new armament of the French and English Attacks*
had been completed. The latter, which was divided
into the " Right Attack," under Major (the late General
Sir) J. W. Gordon, and the " Left Attack,' directed by
Captain (now General Sir) F. E. Chapman, was to be
armed with ninety-six pieces of ordnance, exclusive of
the armament proposed for the defence of the position
above Inkerman; and it was decided—after the rejection of Sir John Burgoyne's proposal† that the

* " The English Left Attack begins," says Mr. H. Russell, Correspondent of the *Times*, " on the rise of the ridge which springs up from
the right of a ravine, as we face Sebastopol, and the advanced works
in front of it run close up to the Garden Battery and to the Redan.
The Attack itself faces these two Russian batteries, and is directly
opposite the pile of Government offices and dockyard buildings.
Between our Left Attack and our Right Attack is another deep ravine,
along the right side of which the Woronzoff road zigzags into Sebastopol.
On the ridge, on the right side of this ravine, is our Right Attack,
and on the right and rear of it is the Sea Service Mortar Battery. To
the right-front of this attack are the works of the Round Tower,
flanked by the Mamelon on the right. To the right of the Right
Attack, springing from the plateau between the 4th and Light
Divisions, there is another deep ravine called the Middle Picket
Ravine, and the French works on their Right Attack begin at the fall
of the hill, at the right of this ravine, and thence spread away to
the right of Inkerman."

† See Sir John Burgoyne's Memoranda of the 23rd and 25th of
November, 1854. Unfortunately, for the public service, the same
fortune attended the proposals made by this sagacious veteran in his

English attack should be directed exclusively against the Malakhoff Tower—that the British fire was to be directed "as much as possible to the proper right of the salient of the Redan."

The 90th arrived in the lines before Sebastopol on the 5th of December, and, on the following morning, went down to the trenches. In those days staff officers did not come up to the standard now exacted at Sandhurst, and Wolseley recounts how when his Regiment was ordered to the front, no staff-officer appeared to show them the way to the trenches. However, they managed to find their way down, and proceeding to the foremost rifle-pits, four or five companies, including Wolseley's, at once became engaged with the enemy, who opposed their rifles to the antiquated British musket. Presently the Russians opened fire with shot and shell, when the order came for the 90th to cease firing.

The first serious fighting that took place after Mr. Wolseley's arrival before Sebastopol, was on the night of the 11th of December, when the Russians made sorties against both the English and the French positions, and, again, on the 20th of December against the English lines. In this second sortie they managed to penetrate as far as the second parallel, on the Left Attack, but only obtained temporary possession of the third parallel on the Right Attack. Had the enemy

Memoranda of the 11th and 20th of December, to the effect that the operations of the allies should be directed against the quarter of Sebastopol containing the dockyards and arsenals, which side, when once in the possession of the Allies, would give them the command of the head of the harbour, so that their ships could be destroyed.

been in sufficient force, they could have penetrated to the first parallel—for the entire guard of the trenches of the Right Attack did not exceed six hundred men—and might have succeeded in spiking the guns; henceforward, to guard against the possibility of a surprise rifle-pits were dug some distance in front of the third parallel, and occupied by sentries in the manner practised by the Russians. The remainder of this eventful year passed without any incident of note, and so 1855 was ushered in.

Since his arrival before Sebastopol, Lieutenant Wolseley had been employed with his Regiment in trench duty, but was soon selected for the post of Acting-Engineer, the number of officers of that distinguished corps being unequal to the severe work entailed upon them by the protracted siege. He was posted, accordingly, to the Right Attack on the 30th of December, and did duty for the first time as Assistant-Engineer on the 4th of January, 1855. On that day he was employed in "Gordon's Battery," and the working party, consisting of only thirty-one men and twenty-eight sappers, "finished laying two platforms, relaid the sleepers of a third, and cleared out the drains in the third parallel."

On the 1st of January, 1855, the effective of the British Army, according to Returns furnished at the time to Lord Raglan, numbered only one thousand and forty-five officers and twenty-one thousand nine hundred and seventy-three men. The French Army, meanwhile, had received considerable reinforcements, and mustered at the same date about sixty-seven thousand men. Their arrangements were also further advanced than ours. Their batteries were armed, their trenches had approached to within one hundred and eighty yards of the Flagstaff Bastion, and they expected soon to be in readiness to assault Sebastopol in conjunction with their Allies. On our side, however, the insufficient number of workmen had retarded the construction of the defensive and offensive works, and the engineering operations were greatly hindered for want of such essentials as timber for the platforms and magazines, which could not be removed from Balaklava where it was stored, owing to the limited supply of transport.

Throughout the siege the Engineers had to carry on their duties under the greatest difficulties, and, generally without obtaining that support which was essential to the success of their operations. Irrespective of the inclemency of the weather, and the rocky nature of the soil, which rendered the construction of siege-works a task of great labour, the Engineers had to make up for their numerical paucity by increased exertions. The term of duty for Engineer officers was never less than twelve, and sometimes even twenty-four hours; and, after returning from the trenches, they had to write the Report of the day's proceedings. Although skilled labour was in great demand for the construction of wharves, hospitals, and store-houses at Balaklava, also for the road to the front, and the hutting of the troops and horses, as well as to carry on the siege and defensive works, yet the total effective force of Engineers on the 1st of January, was only twenty-eight officers and three hundred and ninety-five non-commissioned officers and men.

Between New Year's Day and the 13th of January, the weather was very unfavourable. At times the snow-storms and heavy drifts rendered it necessary to suspend the works entirely, and on the 13th of January, the frost set in with so much severity that it was difficult to make any impression on the ground even with a pickaxe. The snow lay on the plain from twelve to eighteen inches in depth, and the drifts were in some places dangerous. Owing to the disappearance of all fuel, even roots were eagerly grubbed up by the starving soldiers, and sold at a high price. The appearance of the camp was cold, dreary, and miserable; and no blazing fires could to seen to cheer the men or dry their clothes on their return from the trenches or other fatigue duty.

Owing to this great scarcity of wood, the sufferings of the troops on the exposed plateau of Sebastopol were much aggravated; and when a large supply of charcoal arrived at Balaklava, as no means of transport was available other than by manual labour, the Turks employed in the trenches were withdrawn from the Engineers, and the siege works in consequence suffered.*

During the latter half of January the British Attacks

* See Part II. of the "Journal of the Operations conducted by the Corps of Royal Engineers." By Major-General Sir Harry D. Jones, K.C.B., R.E.

had been so feebly guarded, owing to sickness, that " the
covering party for the entire Right Attack, upwards of
a mile in extent, never had exceeded, during this period
of the siege, three hundred and fifty men, and, on the
night of the 21st of January, it mustered only two
hundred and ninety men. The guards for the other
attacks were equally small." As, according to Sir
John Jones, the eminent Engineer officer of the
Peninsular War, " the guard of the trenches ought
never to be less than three-fourths of the garrison,"
and allowing one half of the besieged, or between
thirty-six thousand and forty thousand men, to have
been opposed to the British Attacks, it follows that the
guard instead of being three-fourths, was less than
one-twentieth of the strength opposed to it. Such
were the adverse circumstances under which this unparalleled siege was prosecuted ! Fortunately the
Russians were deficient in enterprize.

The guard being so small, it often happened that
all repairs of importance had to be performed by the
Sappers alone ;* but when, on the 21st of January, a
French Division relieved the Light and Second Divisions
from the guard of the extreme right flank, they were
enabled to furnish more adequate parties for the protection of the batteries and the assistance of the
Engineers.

* Between the 16th and the 21st of January, the number of workmen in the Right Attack never exceeded thirty-nine. According to
M. de Bazancourt's *L'Expédition de la Crimée :—* " The French employed daily four thousand men on the works, and sometimes the
number exceeded six thousand."

The duty in the trenches* was also very severe, and the enemy, by frequent sorties during the night, kept the troops on duty constantly on the alert.

The effective strength of the British Army before Sebastopol on the 1st of February, 1855, had dwindled to one thousand one hundred and ninety-eight officers, and eighteen thousand and twenty-one men of all arms, a force totally inadequate to undertake its part in the siege operations which the allied commanders had decided to prosecute. Pending, therefore, the arrival of the reinforcements, the Engineers employed the first few days of February in expediting the transport of their siege *matériel.* They transferred one hundred thousand sandbags to the French, prepared the platforms and magazines required for the two batteries on the right, and carefully reconnoitred the ground along which approaches could be effected towards the Redan and Malakhoff. On the 8th of February, Major-General Jones, R.E., (the late Sir Harry Jones, K.C.B.), who had led the stormers at San Sebastian, and recently successfully conducted the engineering operations in the Baltic, landed in the Crimea, and took over the charge of his branch of the service from Majors J. W. Gordon and F. Chapman, R.E., who, subject to the advice of Sir John Burgoyne, had from the 20th of October up to that date, under the most trying circumstances, and with the most in-

* In the month of January, Wolseley was on day duty in the trenches, on the 4th, 14th, and 24th; and on night duty on the 7th, 10th, 16th, 20th, and 27th.

efficient means in men and *matériel,* carried on the engineering works of this memorable siege.

Two days before the arrival of General Jones, Lieutenant Wolseley, whose talent for sketching and for topographical studies, was well known, was requested to prepare for the General a plan of the position of Inkerman, including the trenches. It was required to be done in water-colours; but so intense was the cold that the water froze on his brush, and he had to use charcoal to melt the ice and keep the water from freezing. He succeeded in completing the survey, and preparing the plan to the complete satisfaction of the General.

The engineering work now commenced was in accordance with the plan laid down in the paper of the 2nd of February, as proposed by the French Engineers, consequent upon the Council of War* held on the previous day; this plan embraced an attack upon the Malakhoff and Mamelon, as recommended by Sir John Burgoyne. At this period the weather was very severe and unfavourable for siege operations, so that little progress could be made. The trenches were knee deep

* About the middle of January, the late Marshal Niel, a distinguished Engineer officer, and high in the confidence of the French Emperor, arrived on a special mission at the French head-quarters; and, immediately after, the Engineers-in-Chief of the Allied Armies held several conferences to consider the course it was most desirable to pursue. On the 26th of January, General Bizot, commanding the French Engineers, prepared a paper showing a proposed plan of attack, which was submitted to Generals Niel and Sir John Burgoyne. This Memorandum, as well as that of Sir John, in reply, dated the 30th of January, are published in Sir Harry Jones's work.

in snow, which, when a shower of rain came on, was converted into liquid mud, employing the men in clearing it out from the trenches, or cutting drains as outlets for the water.

At this time occurred a singular circumstance in connection with Lieutenant Wolseley's promotion to a captaincy. He was gazetted to his Company in December 1854, but fourteen days after, the authorities, considering him too young—he was exactly twenty-one and a half years of age—cancelled the promotion they themselves had authorised. Considering this as a slur cast upon him, Mr. Wolseley at once wrote expressing his intention to resign his commission unless he was immediately reinstated, and fortunately for his country, the order was rescinded. Some time afterwards, Captain Wolseley learned the true cause of this extraordinary freak of the authorities; and it was this. The father of an officer of the 77th, went to the Horse Guards, and asked why his son, who was older than Captain Wolseley had not been promoted to his Company. The answer the anxious parent received was, that his son was too young, and that Captain Wolseley's promotion was an exception to the rule, *because he rose from the ranks.* Subsequently finding out the blunder they had committed, and that Wolseley had *not* risen from the ranks, the said authorities cancelled his promotion, only to reinstate him as before mentioned, and so ended this *Comedy of Errors.*

On the night of the 3rd of February, Captain Wolseley was employed with a working party of fifty men and four Sappers; he was again on duty on the 7th of February,* and the working party, which since the beginning of the month, had been greatly strengthened, was divided into two reliefs, and was under the command of himself and an Engineer officer. During that day the men were engaged in improving the trench of the right communication, building banquettes on it, and getting more cover on the left of the advanced work; while the Sappers widened the rocky parts of the trenches, and excavated for the mortar magazine, and the Turks cleared up the 21-gun battery and carried gabions from the park. The night of the 11th was very stormy, and so inclement was the weather that no work was done in the Left Attack. Captain Wolseley, who was in sole charge of a small party of men in his (the Right) Attack, was busily employed, but on applying to the field officer on duty for a larger number of men, his request was refused on the ground of the inclemency of the weather.

On the 13th of February, Captain H. C. Owen, R.E. arrived from England, and was appointed to duty with the Right Attack. On the first occasion of his proceeding to the trenches, which was in company with

---

* The day duty was generally from eight or nine a.m. to four or six p.m.; and the night duty from seven p.m. to four a.m. During the month of February, Captain Wolseley was on duty in the trenches— day, 7th, 15th, 22nd; night, 3rd, 11th, 18th. The working party on this night, the 7th of February, which may be considered of an average strength, was constituted as follows:—Line, first relief, one hundred and thirty-four men; second relief, one hundred and forty men. Sappers, four brigades, or thirty-two men. Turks, fifty-two men.

Captain Wolseley, the gallant officer proposed that they should proceed at once to trace out a new battery, the work then in hand. Wolseley vainly tried to dissuade him, as it was still light and the attempt might draw the enemy's fire upon them. However Captain Owen was full of ardour, and Wolseley was not the man to throw cold water on any adventure, however risky; so they set to work. But, speedily, the Russians opened fire from all the surrounding rifle-pits; two men were killed, and Wolseley's coat was pierced by a ball. So the work was postponed till nightfall, when it was successfully accomplished.

On the 15th of February, when Captain Wolseley was on duty with Captain Craigie, R.E., the weather being more favourable, the working parties were increased to four hundred men (besides one hundred French troops employed at No. 9 battery) and six brigades of Sappers, or forty-eight men; and on the 18th and 22nd, when an almost equal number were employed, the work in the trenches progressed rapidly. On their part the Russians were not idle in their works facing the Right Attack. On the night of the 22nd, they threw up a redoubt* (Selinghinsk) which the French attacked on the night of the 23rd of February,†

* These, with other works, were afterwards known by the name of "Ouvrages Blancs," from the colour of the earth, which being white, made them very conspicuous throughout the siege.

† During the month of February, the Russians assumed the offensive at Eupatoria, which had been fortified, but their attack of the 17th of February, though made with nearly forty thousand men, was repulsed with considerable loss. While the hostile cannon were

but were repulsed with great loss; and, on the 28th, they commenced a redoubt (Volhynian) in advance.

Early in March, upwards of three thousand yards of parallel and approach had been made in the Right Attack; and, in the Left, upwards of four thousand two hundred yards. All this had been done on very rocky ground,* with the enemy's works only six hundred yards distant at the nearest point.

On the night of the 10th of March, the Russians established themselves upon the Mamelon, which we had neglected to occupy, erecting thereon heavy batteries, with trenches, rifle pits, and screens running

replying to each other on the plateau of Sebastopol, smooth-tongued envoys were discussing "points" at Vienna, which, however, were only taken up to be dropped. During this month a railway was constructed between Balaklava and the trenches, thereby greatly facilitating the transport of war *matériel*. A Council of War was held on the 6th of March, and, on the 8th, Sir John Burgoyne prepared two Memoranda, one on the plan of operations then agreed on, and the other on the circumstances of the operations against Sebastopol. General Bizot's paper of the 28th of February, and Sir John Burgoyne's Memoranda, may be found in Sir H. Jones's work.

* The country was intersected with deep ravines, whose sides being nearly inaccessible, afforded an additional strength to the place by breaking the Attacks into distinct portions, and interfering with the communications of the besieging force. It was also extremely difficult to establish enfilading batteries, owing to the gullies and ravines. The French works at this time extended from our left to the sea at Quarantine Bay, and upon our right from the ravine of the Careening Creek to the causeway across the Inkerman Valley; this latter formed the first parallel, and a second had been made in advance of it. The total extent of the first parallel, French and English, from Quarantine Bay to the extreme right on the Inkerman Heights, was eleven thousand yards, or six and a quarter miles.

down to the foot of the hill within one hundred yards
of the French parallel. These works, from their commanding position on the right flank of the English
Attack, seriously retarded the operations of our Engineers, and a line of the same description was thrown
up between the Mamelon and Great Redan opposite
the English works. This completely altered the position of affairs, and lengthened the duration of the siege.

Captain Craigie, R.E., the Engineer officer in charge
of the trenches on the 13th of March, was killed in a
somewhat singular manner. Captain Wolseley, on
relieving him, asked if anything particular was going
on. "No," said Craigie, "matters are much as usual."
And so, bidding each other " good night," they parted,
he to return to his quarters, and Wolseley to take
charge of the trenches. At this time an Artillery duel
was in progress, but the Russian practice was wild
and their shells mostly burst short, causing the officers
and men much diversion. They were in the middle of
their merriment, greeting each discharge with roars
of laughter, when a sergeant came running back, saying that Captain Craigie* was killed. He was several
hundred yards in rear of the batteries, and was in the
act of giving a light to a sapper from his pipe, when
one of these erratic shells killed him instantly.

---

* Of this officer, Major Gordon, R.E., says :—"Throughout the
whole of the operations of the Army in the Crimea, this officer has
never once been absent from his post. Oftener on duty in the trenches
than any other officer of his rank, he never even during the worst of
the Winter, allowed a murmur to escape his lips."

On the morning of the 17th of March,* when Captain Wolseley, accompanied by Captain King of the Engineers, went on duty, it was discovered that the enemy had formed new rifle pits in front of the French on our right, which enfiladed the British new right advance. As it was impossible to employ the working party† of one hundred and fifty men, application was made to the officers commanding the Royal Artillery and Naval Brigade batteries, to open fire on these pits. The former fired only a few shots, but the sailors made such good practice with their 8-inch guns, that they knocked over the parapet, and sent the occupants flying out of the pits. A good day's work was then begun, under the directions of Captains Wolseley and King, "improving cover in right advanced parallel; forming magazine in 21-gun battery; a new 10-inch mortar battery, No. 7; altering line of fire of 8-inch gun in 21-gun battery, and bringing two 24-pounders to bear on Russian rifle pits. The working party of the Line also filled eight hundred and twenty sandbags and cleared drains."

The Russians‡ continued to receive reinforcements,

* Captain Wolseley was on duty during this month; day duty, 10th and 17th; night duty, 13th, 19th, and 30th.

† The total number of men employed in the trenches at this time, was two thousand one hundred, from which were furnished the working parties, as well as the guards necessary for the defence of the batteries and parallels.

‡ The Russian Infantry in Sebastopol, in April, numbered thirty-six thousand six hundred. There were besides, near the town, thirty-five thousand four hundred; at Eupatoria, thirty-four thousand six

while their supply of guns was practically inexhaustible; their fire on the Right Attack during the latter part of March, was officially described as " very heavy," and among the casualties was Major J. W. Gordon, second in command of the siege operations, who was severely wounded on the night of the 22nd, when the Russians made a determined sortie, not inaptly styled " Inkerman on a small scale," but were repulsed. During the early part of April, the Engineers were very busy preparing for the bombardment, which had been decided on by the Allied Commanders. On the 3rd, when Captain Wolseley was on duty, the enemy kept up a heavy fire, one of the casualties being Captain Bainbrigge, R.E., who was killed during the night by the explosion of a shell. At this time, Captains Stanton and Armit, R.E., being respectively in charge of the Right and Left Attacks, Major Chapman, replacing Major Gordon, being in command of the whole, Major-General Jones notified, in General Orders of the 4th of April, his " great satisfaction with the manner in which the works were executed, reflecting great credit upon them. and the other Assistant-Engineers employed under them."

On the morning of the 9th of April, the whole of the Allied Artillery opened fire. The British batteries, which at the first bombardment mounted seventy-three guns and mortars, were now armed with twenty 13-

hundred; and in ·other parts thirteen thousand. Total, including fifteen thousand cavalry, and eight thousand artillery, one hundred and forty-two thousand six hundred men.

inch, and sixteen 10-inch mortars, and eighty-seven guns, giving a total of one hundred and twenty-three pieces of ordnance,—of which forty-nine were manned by the Naval Brigade, and seventy-four by the Royal Artillery. The French, on their part, opened fire with three hundred and three pieces on the left, and fifty on the right.

The morning of the 9th of April broke in thick fog and drizzling rain, but shortly before half-past five the mist partially rolled away, permitting the outlines of the Redan and Malakhoff to be seen. Exactly an hour later, the first gun was fired from the British batteries, and, in a few seconds, the whole of both Attacks, with the exception of one battery, were in action; shortly afterwards the French opened fire, and the south side of Sebastopol, from the sea to Inkerman, was encircled in what Prince Gortschakoff well called, a *feu d'enfer*. The Russians appeared to be taken by surprise, but, about six o'clock, their batteries began to reply; though at no time of the day was their fire heavy or effective. The continuous rain and bad weather made the work very laborious, some of the platforms being under water and all very slippery. At dusk the fire on both sides ceased, with the exception of an occasional shell from the mortars. On the following day all our batteries opened fire at daylight, the Russians replying with spirit. Some heavy rain fell during the early morning, but, about ten, the weather cleared up, and the sun shone bright and warm. The fire of the Mamelon was soon checked, and that of the

Malakhoff Tower slackened; but, according to the report of the Engineer officers of the Right Attack, " our fire made no material impression upon the Redan and Garden Batteries, by which alone it was answered. Much damage was done to the embrasures, magazines, traverses, &c., by the enemy's fire, which can, however, be easily repaired. The Sappers behaved very well in repairing the embrasures, and even reconstructing them, under fire."

Lieutenant Graves,* R.E., who, with Captains Owen, R.E., and Wolseley, was on duty, was wounded, and Wolseley himself had a narrow escape. The Russian fire had been very heavy, and the Artillery officers reported an embrasure as unserviceable. This, of course, it was the duty of the Engineer officers to repair, but, from the proximity and precision of fire of the Russian batteries, it was a service of extreme hazard, for directly a man showed himself above the parapet, he became a mark for the Russian gunners. However, Graves and Wolseley, with two or three Sappers, set to work to repair an embrasure, and while they were building up one cheek with gabions, a round shot from the enemy carried away the other cheek, to which Wolseley had his back turned, killing a Sapper. At the time he was holding on to a handspike, prizing up one sandbag to put another under it, and it was, in racing parlance, " a near thing" for him; indeed, he received a slight

---

* This gallant young officer was killed by a rifle bullet, on the 18th of June, in the Assault on the Redan.

wound from the *débris* scattered by the round shot,
though he did not report himself as wounded, it being
a point of honour among the Engineers not to leave
their post until disabled.

On the night of the 12th, Wolseley was again on
duty, the working party consisting of three hundred
Linesmen and forty-one Sappers; much was done in
effecting repairs, laying platforms, and other necessary
work. Though our batteries had kept up a hot fire
all day, little permanent effect was visible; and, so
inexhaustible were the Russian resources, that fresh
guns opened fire from embrasures whose guns had
been dismounted or silenced. When next on duty,
the night of the 15th of April, with a working party
of three hundred men and thirty-two Sappers, the
enemy were very active, and Lieutenant-Colonel
Tylden, R.E., in charge of the Right Attack, reported :—" Captain Wolseley, Assistant-Engineer, who
was in charge of the working party in the advanced
trenches, retired the party from the most advanced
part between twelve and one, finding it impossible to
keep* the men at work under the fire the enemy
poured in." Our loss on this occasion was heavy,
being three officers killed, and one officer and twenty
rank and file wounded.

The following incident, which happened on this
night, is one of many such during the siege :—Captain
Wolseley was with Captain (now Lieutenant-General)
E. Stanton, R.E., who was sitting behind the Engineer park giving orders to two Sappers standing at

attention before him. Suddenly a round shot took
one man's head off, and drove his jaw bone into the
other man's face, to which it adhered, bespattering
the party with blood. Men got into the way of considering these incidents as almost common-place, and
scarcely noteworthy, but, though such horrors bred a
feeling of indifference to danger and death, few could
lay claim to the possession of such imperturbable
sang-froid as Captain W. Peel, R.N , of Her Majesty's
ship 'Diamond,' then serving on shore in the Naval
Brigade. Wolseley, who saw much of Peel and his
sailors, confesses that he never saw any man so in-
different in the presence of seemingly *certain* death
as this gallant sailor, and gives the following instance,
among others, of this characteristic. He was walking
one day during the bombardment with Captain Peel,
in rear of the line of batteries, when a 13-inch shell,
hurtling through the air, lit on the entrance of a magazine and crushed it in. Just for a passing second,
Wolseley stood still, paralysed as it were, while he
waited for the whole party to be blown to atoms, a
fate which seemed imminent. But Peel's undaunted
heart quailed not even for that infinitesimal portion of
time, and he dashed into the magazine, full as it was
of powder, without a moment's hesitation or a thought
of danger. A second later and Wolseley was by his
side, and they were engaged pulling down the sandbags, which guarded the entrance, and were all on
fire, and soon the magazine was built up again.

The subject of this Memoir has, however, a more

modest opinion of his courage than other people who know him well, and have seen him under fire. A distinguished officer of Engineers, who served in the trenches with Captain Wolseley, perhaps on more occasions than any other man, and therefore had more ample opportunities of observing his bearing under the most trying circumstances, declared to us that he considered him " the bravest man he ever knew." He also mentioned that he was noted for always turning his face towards an approaching Russian shell; and on being interrogated as to his reason for doing so, replied, that in the event of his being killed it could not be said of him, that he turned his back on the enemy, or fell while running away from a shell. Such little traits as these give the clue to a man's character.

After eight days' incessant firing, the second bombardment ceased on the 17th of April, without any decisive result having been achieved, and, though the Mamelon and Malakhoff suffered considerably, the guns destroyed, or silenced, by day, were replaced at night. On our side, twenty-six pieces of ordnance were disabled, and our expenditure of ammunition amounted to forty-seven thousand eight hundred and fifty-four rounds, of which upwards of fifteen thousand were shell.*

* During the bombardment the Artillery lost five killed and eighty-six wounded; and the Naval Brigade, which suffered more severely, owing to their practice of not retiring behind the parapet after firing, lost two officers and twenty-four men killed, and six officers and ninety-two wounded.

On the 19th of April, the 77th Regiment, led by Colonel Egerton, carried, by assault, the rifle pits in advance of the Right Attack. These they most gallantly maintained, notwithstanding a determined attempt by the enemy to recover the ground. In this affair, the gallant leader and Captain Lemprière were killed, and, of the Engineer officers on duty, Captain Owen, R.E., lost a leg, and Lieutenant Baynes received a wound, from the effects of which he died in a few days. Ten rank and file were also killed, and four other officers and fifty men wounded. The dearly-won pits were always known throughout the siege, as "Egerton's Pits," in compliment to the gallant colonel of the 77th.

During the month of May,* the Russians, who had increased the number of rifle pits and screens in front of the Right Attack, and connected them by lines of trenches, thus forming a regular parallel, made two determined sorties on the advanced parallel of the Right Attack, which, as Lord Raglan reported, " were on each occasion most nobly met, and repulsed with considerable loss owing chiefly to the judicious arrangements of Colonel Trollope." On the 18th of May, Lord Raglan, accompanied by General de la Marmora, in command of the newly arrived Piedmontese Division of seventeen thousand men, and General Jones, in-

† During this month, Captain Wolseley was on duty : day, 1st, 5th, 14th, and 18th ; night, 25th, 28th, and 31st. On the three last occasions he was the only Engineer officer with the working parties, which numbered one hundred and fifty men, and twenty Sappers.

spected the works of the Left Attack; and, on the 18th, when Captain Wolseley was on duty, those of the Right Attack. On the following day, General Canrobert resigned the command of the French Army to General Pelissier, who had earned great distinction on the 22nd and 23rd of May, by his pertinacity and valour. The working parties of the Right Attack having completed the new communication with the right of the third parallel, the troops were able to circulate freely without being exposed to the musketry fire from the enemy's works in advance of the Mamelon.

On the 28th of May, it was decided, at a meeting held at General Pelissier's head-quarters, that, after the Russian works had been bombarded, the French should assault the Mamelon, and the "Ouvrages Blancs" which supported it, and the English, the Quarries in front of the Redan; and, on the 31st, General Jones handed to Lord Raglan a Memorandum of the proposed attack, which was approved by his Lordship, and communicated to Generals Pennefather and Codrington, from whose Divisions the assaulting columns were to be drawn.

On the 6th of June, when the third bombardment took place, the English batteries mounted one hundred and fifty-four mortars and guns. Of these, there were in the Right Attack fifty-five pieces, twenty-two of which were manned by the Naval Brigade; and ninety-nine in the Left Attack, of which thirty-six were worked by the sailors. The whole fire of the right of the Right Attack was to be directed on the Mamelon and the Malakhoff, whilst the left of the Right, and the Left Attack engaged the Redan and Barrack Battery. The English batteries opened fire at half-past two p.m. of the 6th of June, on the Russian works, which stood out in bold relief under a cloudless sky, offering a strong contrast to the dismal circumstances of the last bombardment. The enemy replied vigorously at first, but about half-past four the Mamelon and Malakhoff were almost silenced, and at dusk, when our fire, except from the mortars, ceased, the Russian works showed unmistakable evidences of the severe handling they had undergone. Our batteries reopened on the 7th, and, on that evening, was delivered the memorable assault on the Quarries by our troops, and that on the Mamelon by our Allies.

All that day a heavy cannonade was kept up; but, at six o'clock, when the French and English assaulting columns were formed in the trenches, it burst forth with an intensity literally unparalleled. Major Reilly, R.A., says, " The sailors and gunners, rivalling each other in their exertions, worked the heavy guns and mortars with almost incredible rapidity. For the hour that it lasted, the fire was the heaviest during the siege."* The Russians had massed men on the Redan, evidently anticipating an assault, and so tremendous was the fire directed on that work, that "the shells

* During the day the Royal Artillery had forty-seven killed and wounded, and the sailors forty; being the heaviest loss on one day during the siege.

could be seen plunging and cutting gaps in the ranks, blowing the bodies of their victims into the air."

At half-past six the French captured the Mamelon, aud the " Ouvrages Blancs," which had been rendered almost untenable by the fire from our batteries, but, advancing towards the Malakhoff, were driven back. The Mamelon was now retaken by the enemy, but, after a renewed fire from the British batteries, once more changed hands.

A few minutes after the French had attacked the Mamelon, the British columns advanced on the Quarries and the Russian trench leading to the Karabelnaia Ravine. The column consisted of detachments of the Light and Second Divisions, who were supported at night by the 62nd Regiment. The command of these troops was entrusted to General Shirley, of the 88th, who was acting general officer of the trenches ; and Lieutenant-Colonel Campbell of Wolseley's Regiment, the 90th, led the storming party, and remained in the Quarries all night in command of the troops. On the Engineer officers of the Right Attack, however, devolved, according to custom, the honourable and deadly duty or " showing the way" to the storming column, and also of forming the lodgment after the enemy's works were won, and the communication from the parallel in our occupation, a trying and perilous task, as it would have to be completed in the open and under the enemy's fire. Colonel Tylden, R.E., an officer who had been assiduous in his duties during the siege, advised as to the attack and distribution of the troops, but the

Engineer officers who actually accompanied the assaulting columns, were Captains Browne, R.E.,* and
Wolseley; and Lieutenants Elphinstone, R.E.,† Lowry,
R.E., and Anderson, 96th Regiment. Already one
officer of the corps, Captain Dawson, R.E., who had
been in charge of the engineering duties during the
day, had fallen, but he was not destined to be the only
Engineer officer sacrificed on the altar of duty and
patriotism in this memorable struggle.

The Quarries were carried with a rush, though the
Russians made three desperate attempts to retake them‡
during the night, and, again, soon after daylight on the
following morning, and it was in resisting these repeated efforts on the part of the enemy that the Army
sustained its chief loss. Among the officers who thus
fell, was Lieutenant Lowry, R.E., who was killed by a
round shot whilst gallantly cheering on the men.
Notwithstanding the frequency of the endeavours of
the Russians to regain possession of the Quarries, and
the interruptions to which these attacks gave rise, the
Engineers made a lodgment of gabions and barrels,
and also established the communication with their
advanced sap, which, says Lord Raglan, "redounds to
the credit of Colonel Tylden, and that of the officers

* Now Major-General J. F. M. Browne, C.B. On the 24th of
August this officer was severely wounded in the shoulder by a rifle-
bullet.

† Now Colonel Sir Howard Elphinstone, V.C., K.C.B., C.M.G.

‡ The Engineer officer in charge of the Right Attack, says :—"The
enemy actually expelled us three times and removed some of our
gabions, which were immediately retaken."

and men employed as the working party; and I cannot," adds the Field-Marshal, "miss the opportunity to express my approbation of the conduct of the Sappers throughout the operations."*

* Colonel Tylden, in his Report of the Engineering operations of the 7th, which is derived from materials supplied to him chiefly by Captain Browne, the officer in immediate command, says:—" The Quarries, and the adjoining trenches in front of the left of the Right Attack, were stormed and carried yesterday evening about seven p.m., by a party of four hundred men from the Light and Second Divisions. A good lodgment has been formed on our right of the Quarries, and the communication thereto from the left advanced sap has been made good. Our troops are at present in occupation of the Quarry lodgment covering their left, extending from thence to the right, along the reverse of the enemy's trench to his salient rifle-pit at the centre. The whole of these works of the enemy have been appropriated for our use. The enemy's resistance was energetic and determined, evinced not only in his defence of the Quarries, but in the repeated efforts he made during the night to retake his trenches, by turning their right, as well as by direct attacks. A reserve of six hundred men formed the immediate support of the assaulting party, and a working party of eight hundred men, detailed for the forming of the lodgment, communications, &c., were divided into four different parties, each for a special part of the work. Three of these parties I brought forward in readiness to commence work directly the enemy's trenches were taken; but such was the vigour of the enemy's resistance, and his numbers, that the assaulting party and their reserve were insufficient to hold the captured trenches, and I quite concurred in the necessity of those portions of the working party who were armed being appropriated for this purpose. The last portion, two hundred and fifty men, I kept in reserve in the right ravine communication, notwithstanding that their services were more than once urgently required as an armed party in front; and as soon as the advance had been reinforced and regularly posted, I brought this party forward, and with them made the lodgment and communication."

Colonel Tylden eulogised the services of Captain Browne and Lieutenant Elphinstone, and says the former " speaks in high terms of the conduct of Captain Wolseley, 90th Regiment, Assistant-Engineer, who was employed in forming the communication to the lodgment." Captain Browne,* who was the senior Engineer officer accompanying the assaulting column, after passing a high encomium on the gallant young Lowry, proceeds :—" I beg to report most favourably on the conduct of Lieutenant Elphinstone, R.E., and of Captain Wolseley, 90th Regiment, Assistant-Engineer, who was employed in forming the lodgment and communication. Lieutenant Anderson, 96th Regiment, Assistant-Engineer, was unfortunately wounded in the leg early in the evening." But the highest honour a soldier can receive, next to the approval of his country and his sovereign, was in reserve for Captain Wolseley, who was specially mentioned in the despatch of the Field-Marshal Commanding-in-Chief,† as one of the

* By the courtesy of General Browne when Deputy Adjutant-General at the Horse Guards, we have been enabled to peruse the originals of the reports of the Engineer officers of the Right Attack throughout the siege, including those of Sir Garnet Wolseley.

† In a General Order to the troops, of the 8th of June, Lord Raglan says: "The Commander of the Forces hastens to congratulate the Army upon the achievements of last night. The attack was vigorously conducted and nobly executed, and although no detailed Report has yet been made, he considers it due to the officers and men engaged in the assault on the Quarries to thank them for their gallant exertions, and to assure them that he will not fail to represent them to the Government, for Her Majesty's information, in the terms that their conduct so fully justifies. He laments most deeply the loss of those

officers, " who distinguished themselves on this occasion."

The casualties on the 7th of June were proportionately heavy as the result attained was glorious. Ten officers and one hundred and seventeen rank and file were killed, and thirty-six officers and four hundred and eighty-six men were wounded, besides eighteen missing. Of the six Engineer officers engaged during the 6th and 7th of June, two were killed, and one was wounded.

Captain Wolseley's personal share in the dangers and glories of this memorable day was arduous, and no officer was exposed for an equal length of time, or to a similar extent, to the perils incident to a bombardment and an assault. The cause of his having this double share of duty, entailing a corresponding increase of fatigue and exposure, we will now detail, as well as his experience of the assault of the Quarries. For twenty-four hours before the time named for the attack on the Russian works, all the officers detailed for service were kept off duty, so as to be fresh for the perilous work in store for them. Among them, of course, was Wolseley; but in the morning, Captain Dawson, who had gone on duty for the first time that day, was killed by a round shot, and he was ordered to take his place. Wolseley was, therefore, all day hard at work as the only Engineer officer of the Right Attack, and the bombardment was in full progress,

who have fallen upon this memorable occasion, and sympathises most sincerely in the sufferings of the wounded."

requiring all his energies, besides entailing that great mental wear which is incidental to the performance of duties under such a terrific fire as raged on that day. When evening came, and the hour named for the assault arrived, most men would have had enough of it, but not so Wolseley; and though he had never quitted the trenches, when the hour struck—big with the fate of so many gallant hearts throbbing with eager expectancy, while they waited for the signal to quit the protection of their batteries to run the gauntlet of the open space ploughed by the death-dealing shells and bullets—Captain Wolseley took his place with the small band of Engineer officers, whose perilous duty it was to accompany the assaulting column.

There were two communications to be made—one between the parallel on the right and the Quarries, which he was directed to carry out; and the second direct between the Quarries and the parallel in rear, under the direction of Lieutenant Lowry. The difficulty of doing much towards effecting the lodgment and communications was enhanced by the fact that of the eight hundred men detailed as a working party, only two hundred and fifty were actually available, the remainder being engaged with the enemy. And so it was throughout this unparalleled siege; the British Army was expected to perform, and, as a matter of history, *did* actually perform duties that required the exertions of a force at least treble their numbers. It was a *dictum* of Nelson's that a British sailor was equal to three Frenchmen, and the saying certainly holds good of the relative value of the British soldier and his Russian foeman.

Wolseley began working the lateral communication too soon, and the enemy's fire was so hot, that the party was driven back with loss. Just then he was sent to take the place of poor Lowry, and proceeded to make the direct communication on the open,* between "Egerton's rifle-pits" and the captured works. While so engaged, he lost one-third of his working party, and on the three occasions when the enemy expelled our soldiers from the Quarries, only in turn to be themselves driven out, he entered the Quarries with the victorious column. Not often has more desperate hand-to-hand fighting taken place than on that eventful night, and Wolseley's *penchant* for such work was amply gratified. That the position was retained in the end was perfectly marvellous, considering the persistent attacks made by the Russians with overwhelming numbers. Between these assaults he busied himself with building up, on the reverse side of the Quarries, a little parapet composed of anything he could lay his hands on, among the chief ingredients being the bodies of the fallen, friends or foes indiscriminately, the latter thus affording in death the welcome protection they would have denied while living. Just before daybreak, Wolseley saw a dense column of

---

* Gunner and Driver Thomas Arthur received the Victoria Cross for " carrying barrels of infantry ammunition for the 7th Fusiliers several times during the evening across the open." On this very " open," Captain Wolseley and the other Engineer officers and Sappers were engaged throughout the night.

Russians " so long that he could not see the end of it," issue from out of their works with the object of making a final dash to recover the lost Quarries; and had they known the real position of affairs they might have accomplished their purpose, temporarily at least. Our soldiers were so overcome with fatigue by the night's fighting and hard work, that it was in vain the officers made the utmost efforts to rouse them from their sleep to resist the enemy. British officers have seldom failed to do their duty under the most trying circumstances, and they did not belie this characteristic of the race on this occasion. Finding their efforts useless, the officers, to the number of twenty, with some few non-commissioned officers and men, certainly not more than sixty, opened fire, the former with their pistols, on the advancing column; at the same time the bugler sounded, and the little band shouted and cheered to their utmost capacity. Never did the famous British cheer stand in such good stead to British throats as on this occasion. The Russian soldiers, remembering the bloody repulses they had already suffered, first wavered and finally refused to advance. Wolseley saw the officers by turns imploring and threatening them, but all in vain; they could not be induced to proceed, and the British officers redoubling their efforts, the Russians gave up the task as hopeless and retired, and so ended their last effort to regain the Quarries. But it is the opinion of officers present, that had the Russians shown any enterprise they might have easily overcome the only opposition that awaited them, as there was no force in the Quarries capable of an effective resistance.*

It will not be surprising that after his indefatigable exertions both by word of mouth and example, Captain Wolseley completely lost his voice, and could not speak above a low whisper; also that when he was relieved in the morning, so overpowered was he with the exertions of the past twenty-four hours, and the strain upon his faculties, that he fell down from fatigue outside the Quarries, and lay there among a number of dead bodies, himself having the appearance of one numbered with the dead. So thought an officer of his Regiment, who, passing by, found his friend lying on a heap of slain covered with blood. Though he had not reported himself wounded, Wolseley had been hit on the thigh by a bullet from a canister shot which tore his trousers, and caused considerable loss of blood. He received this wound just as he got outside the parapet on his way to the Quarries to relieve Lieutenant Lowry. His friend of the 90th roused him with much difficulty, and then assisted him to the camp at the Middle Ravine, a distance, allowing for the zigzag road, of

---

* This is not the only instance in war where a bold face has changed the position of affairs as effectually as a large reinforcement could have done. A notable instance occurs to one's memory when, after the first day of the sanguinary struggle at Ferozeshuhar, in 1846, a fresh Sikh Army of twenty thousand men, with a powerful artillery, feared to attack the small British force led by Lords Gough and Hardinge, which decimated by Sikh shot, and worn out by their unparalleled exertions, must have succumbed to a determined attack. But the pusillanimous leader of this force, Lall Singh, if we remember right, mistaking the audacity that comes from despair for the assurance of victory, after a brief cannonade, retreated with his whole force.

over two miles. The kind Samaritan had almost to carry our hero, who was so fatigued that he fell down many times, and had to be roused up again, just as a man might who was intoxicated. It must have been a relief to them both, as it was a cause of thankfulness to Wolseley, when they met Major (now Lieutenant-General) Maxwell, who dismounted and lent him his horse, on which, with assistance, he rode the remainder of the way, often nearly tumbling off with fatigue. His position was all the more trying, as he had completely lost his voice, so that when he mustered up sufficient energy to speak, he was totally inaudible. And so concluded what Wolseley himself emphatically declares was " the hardest day's work he ever did in his life."

" It may be said," writes Major-General Sir Harry Jones, " that until the 7th of June, when the Quarries, Mamelon, and ' Ouvrages Blancs' had been captured and lodgments made in them, the Allies had scarcely gained an advantage over the enemy since October, 1854, a period of seven months." By the capture of these works, the besiegers were placed in a more favourable position for carrying on ulterior operations, while every man in the Allied Armies was inspired with increased spirit and energy, for they regarded these important successes as only the prelude to the fall of the great stronghold that had so long defied their utmost efforts, and attributed them chiefly to the substitution of Pelissier, emphatically a fighting general, for the more easy-going Canrobert. Considering the great strength of the enemy, it is surprising the want of energy they displayed. This numerical superiority rendered it necessary to be prepared with strong reserves to repel an assault on the trenches by a powerful column; but to do this effectually would have been a task of great difficulty, there being no cover for troops in the immediate rear of the trenches, while the distance to the nearest camp was too great to afford any hope that a body of men could arrive in time to render immediate support. As this circumstance necessitated a stronger guard than is usual at an ordinary siege, the Engineers were unable to obtain the complement of men necessary to carry on the required works. After the success of the 7th of June, Lord Raglan and General Pelissier determined to press on the siege with redoubled energy, and preparations were made for a fourth bombardment, and the assault of the enemy's works extending from the Redan to Careening Bay. Two days after the capture of the Quarries, Captain Wolseley was again on duty,* accompanied by Lieutenant Darrah, R.E. The working party was, as usual, divided into two reliefs, consisting respectively of four hundred and two hundred men, with three brigades of Sappers, or twenty-four men. Captain Wolseley says in his Report:—"I had a special working party of four hundred men, fifty of whom, with half brigade of Sappers, repaired the embrasures in the 21-gun battery; one hundred men,

* During the month of June he was on duty as follows : day duty, 4th, 7th, 12th, 21st, and 28th ; night duty, 7th, 9th, 14th, 17th, 23rd, and 26th.

with a brigade of Sappers, revetted all the embrasures in Nos. 9, 12, and 14 Batteries; fifty men, with half brigade of Sappers, were employed mending and placing in a fighting condition the old third parallel and Left Advance ; the remaining two hundred men, with a brigade of Sappers, were engaged in the Quarries and the communication to them. They completed a rifle-screen overlooking the Woronzoff Ravine on our left. At two, a.m., the battery parties were relieved by one hundred and fifty men from the guard of the trenches, and the Quarry party by fifty men. All the batteries were placed in admirable repair, and our new lodgment considerably strengthened. The Russians were found to be working outside the proper right of the Redan." The Russian fire during the day had been very heavy, and our casualties proportionately great. Thus we had lost three officers and seven rank and file killed, and thirty-eight officers and men wounded, a severe loss for what might be called an " off day."

A good many casualties were also caused on the 12th, when Captain Wolseley was on duty, " by shells from a 2-gun battery under the Garden Batteries, which likewise annoyed the parties in the Quarries during the forenoon," so that they had to be withdrawn. " In the afternoon," continues his Report, " some of the enemy's riflemen climbed up among the rocks on the opposite side of the Woronzoff Ravine under the advanced trenches of the Left Attack, and caused us some annoyance." The working parties of four hundred men, besides Sappers, employed on the night of the 14th of

June, "worked well, but were annoyed by shells from the Garden Batteries, and grape and canister from the salient gun in the Redan, which caused about ten casualties. The enemy were heard working through the night inside the Redan." During this time, while our Engineers worked hard preparing for the attack which it was hoped and anticipated would decide the fate of Sebastopol, the Russians were also busied strengthening the Redan, large parties of troops being seen bringing up gabions and pieces of timber.

Between the 14th and 18th of June, the Engineers were employed improving the lodgment in the Quarries. The Russians had, before our occupation, entrenched this position with great care; emplacements for field guns had been prepared, and about twenty yards in advance of them, large cubical boxes, filled with powder, had been buried in the ground, to be exploded by the pressure of a single man passing over them. Fortunately no accident had been occasioned by them during the assault, though two or three subsequently exploded, when several men were wounded.

At daylight on the morning of the 17th of June, the British batteries* opened fire for the fourth general bombardment of the defences of Sebastopol, the fleet

---

* In the Right Attack were mounted sixty-two pieces of ordnance; and in the Left Attack one hundred and four. Total one hundred and sixty-six guns and mortars. The following was the calibre of these pieces : eight 10-inch guns, eight 68-pounders, forty-six 8-inch guns, forty-nine 32-pounders, thirty 13-inch mortars, seventeen 10-inch mortars, and eight 8-inch mortars.

also co-operating against the sea defences. The Royal Artillery were directed, as they had been throughout the siege, by Major-General (now Sir Richard) Dacres; and the Naval Brigade by Captain Sir Stephen Lushington, K.C.B., who, on his promotion to flag rank, was succeeded, on the 21st of July, by Captain Honourable (now Admiral Sir) Henry Keppel.

Our efforts were chiefly directed against the Redan and its flanking works, although the British gunners afforded powerful aid with the mortars of the Right Attack against the Malakhoff Tower. The Russians replied from both these works with a steady fire. The French battery of the Mamelon, assisted by our mortars, told with great effect against the Malakhoff, which was silenced about nine o'clock, sending only an occasional shot during the rest of the day. The Redan almost ceased firing an hour before noon, but caused a considerable number of casualties in the Quarries by its fire from Coehorns and showers of hand grenades.* But though the Redan presented a shattered appearance, it was only temporarily silenced, for at night fresh guns were mounted wherever they were disabled by our fire during the day. In the evening, Captain Wolseley, accompanied by Lieutenants Graves and Murray, both of whom fell in the assault on the Redan on the following day, went on duty with a working party of four hundred men and twelve Sappers.

* "Account of the Artillery Operations before Sebastopol," by Major M. N. Reilly, C.B.

The responsibility of the engineering duties, even upon an "off day," devolving upon a young officer in his twenty-second year, may be gathered from the report of the day's work:—"One hundred and forty men and two Sappers, with Major Campbell of the 46th Regiment, were employed carrying materials; one hundred and twenty men with Lieutenant Graves, one hundred men and two Sappers with Lieutenant Murray. All these parties were employed carrying materials to the places assigned for them; twenty men and four Sappers revetting embrasures in 21-gun battery; twenty men and four Sappers revetting embrasures in Nos. 9, 13, and 14 batteries. These parties worked until two o'clock, a.m., after which none were employed. There were three considerable fires in the town in the rear of the Flagstaff Battery. The enemy were working all night at the Redan, and seemed to be strengthening the abattis in its front."

The night of the 17th passed without anything remarkable occurring; a heavy fire was kept up on the works from the mortars, and at daylight all the guns joined in the bombardment. It had been arranged at a meeting held at Lord Raglan's head-quarters on the 15th, that the assault should not take place until the obstacles in advance of the works had been destroyed, and the works themselves, which had been strengthened during the night, subjected for three hours to a heavy fire. The assault was, accordingly, fixed for the 18th of June, a singular choice, for though the anniversary of Waterloo is a day the memories of which must always exercise an inspiriting effect on British soldiers, the influence must be correspondingly depressing, not to say exasperating, to our Allies when acting in concert with us. However this may be, at the last moment the French General made a change in the plan, which exercised a potent influence for evil on the result. Late in the evening of the 17th, General Pelissier, after having explained to his Generals who were to command the several columns, the details of his plan of attack, sent word to Lord Raglan that he should assault the works at three on the following morning. Though Lord Raglan had worked with the utmost loyalty with the French Commander-in-Chief, this disarrangement at the last moment of a plan adopted after much discussion, boded ill for the success of the movement of the morrow, and never did the evils of a divided command receive a more impressive and disastrous illustration.

Before three a.m., Lord Raglan was at the signal post, accompanied by the Head-Quarter Staff, Generals Jones and Dacres and their respective staffs, Colonel Warde, commanding Siege Train, and Captain Lushington, R.N., commanding Naval Brigade. Captain Wolseley was also there, having charge of the third parallel of batteries, in which Lord Raglan and staff were assembled. From this position he witnessed one of the most gallant attempts to carry an enemy's works, and at the same time one of the most sanguinary repulses of which we have any record in the annals of war.

No sooner had the three assaulting columns *
shown themselves beyond the trenches than they
were assailed by a most murderous fire of grape
and musketry, such as Lord Raglan declared he had
never witnessed before. The superiority of the fire of
the Allied batteries on the previous 17th, had led the
Allied Commanders, as Lord Raglan wrote in his despatch, " to conclude that the Russian Artillery was, in
great measure, subdued," whereas it appears, from
Prince Gortschakoff's voluminous Report to the Emperor
Alexander, that the Russians expected and were fully

---

* The following were the arrangements for the assault. The English
were formed into three columns, drawn from the Light, Second, and
Fourth Divisons, under Lieutenant-General Sir George Brown. The
right column was to attack the left face of the Redan, between the
flanking batteries; the centre, the salient angle; while the left was to
move upon the re-entering angle formed by the right face and flank of
the work; the first and last preceding the centre column. Each
column was to consist of one thousand seven hundred and fifty men,
of whom four hundred were for the assault, a working party of four
hundred to cover them in case of a lodgment and to reverse the work,
eight hundred men as a support, and one hundred riflemen preceding
the assaulting column to keep down the enemy's fire. On a given
signal the columns advanced, each preceded by covering parties of the
Rifle Brigade, and by sailors carrying ladders, and fifty soldiers with
wool-bags. The ladder-men consisted of four parties of sixty sailors each,
of whom only two, or one hundred and twenty men were engaged : of
these fourteen were killed, and forty-seven wounded, being more than
one half. Among the wounded was the gallant Peel, who volunteered
to lead his men, and himself carried the first ladder; and Mr. Midship-
man Wood, now Colonel Evelyn Wood, V.C., 90th Regiment, who
has since played a prominent part under Wolseley during the Ashantee
War.

prepared to meet the assault with a determined resistance.

Those in advance were either killed or wounded, and the remainder found it impossible to proceed. The Light and Fourth Divisions were the chief sufferers. Major-General Sir John Campbell, who led the Left Attack, Colonel Shadforth, of the 67th, who commanded the storming party under that General, and Colonel Yea, of the 7th Fusiliers, who led the right column, were killed. While the direct attack upon the Redan was in progress, Major-General W. Eyre* moved down the Ravine, separating the left of the British from the right of the French advanced works, and made a demonstration on the head of the Dockyard Creek. This service was performed with the utmost gallantry, and, notwithstanding that they were exposed to a most galling fire, his troops maintained themselves in the position they had taken up during the day, and, in the evening, withdrew unmolested, leaving a post at the Cemetery, which had been one of the objects of the attack.

The French were not more fortunate than ourselves in the result of their operations. Generals Mayran and Brunet, commanding Divisions, were killed, and though the *enciente* of the Malakhoff was entered, and the French eagles planted on the Russian works, the enemy brought up powerful reserves, and Marshal Pelissier ordered a retreat. The French loss, in

* The late Major-General Sir William Eyre, whose son was killed in the Ashantee War.

killed alone, was thirty-nine officers and one thousand five hundred and forty-four men.

In this disastrous affair the Russians,* no less than the Allies, lost heavily. Our casualties were, twenty-one officers and two hundred and thirty men killed; seventy officers† and one thousand and fifty men wounded; two officers and twenty men missing; total casualties, exclusive of the Naval Brigade, ninety-three officers and one thousand three hundred and eighty men. The Engineers suffered heavily on this occasion. Three officers, Captain Jesse and Lieutenants Graves and Murray, were killed; and Major-General Jones, Major Bourchier (Brigade-Major), and Colonel Tylden, Director of the Right Attack, were wounded. The latter officer, who had taken part in the Engineering operations from the commencement of the siege, was shot through both legs while directing the assault of the Redan, and died from the effects of these wounds on his passage to Malta in the following August. Captain Wolseley was near General Jones when he received his wound. He was standing at the time in

* Prince Gortschakoff gives the Russian loss as follows : two superior officers, fourteen subaltern officers, and seven hundred and eighty-one men killed ; four superior officers, forty-three subaltern officers, and three thousand, one hundred and thirty-two men wounded; five superior officers, twenty-nine subaltern officers, and eight hundred and fifteen men contused ; fourteen superior officers, fifty-seven subaltern officers, and eight hundred and seventy-nine men slightly wounded, but not sufficiently to quit the ranks.

† Among the wounded were General Eyre, Colonel (now General Sir) Daniel Lysons, of the 23rd Royal Welsh Fusiliers ; and Colonels Johnstone, 33rd ; Gwilt, 34th ; and Cobbe, 4th Regiments.

rear of Lord Raglan, with whom General Jones was in
conversation, when the latter, whose head was over the
parapet, received a bullet wound in the temple, which,
with his white hair, was all dabbled with blood.
Almost at the same time another officer received a
severe wound.   Wolseley was in conversation with
Captains Beresford and Browne of the 88th, when a
round shot carried off the arm of the latter, covering a
new jacket Wolseley had put on that morning with
blood.   Captain Browne jumped up from the ground,
and actually did not know of the loss he had experienced.   To Wolseley's hurried question, "What's
the matter?" he replied, "Nothing."

So exposed was the position occupied by Lord
Raglan, that officers and soldiers as they passed, cried
out to his staff, "If you want Lord Raglan to be killed,
you'll let him stop there."

The disastrous failure of the 18th of June told
severely on the already failing health of Lord Raglan,
and though he was assured of the sympathy of his
Sovereign,* he grieved over the loss of so many gallant
officers and men, and expired on the 28th of June, four
days after the death of General Estcourt, his Adjutant-
General.   His death, which was unexpected, evoked
expressions of regret and sympathy from all quarters,

* Her Majesty, on receiving news of the repulse, telegraphed the
following message, which was read to the troops by order of the Commander-in-Chief.   "I have Her Majesty's commands to express her
grief that so much bravery should not have been rewarded with
success ; and to assure her brave troops that Her Majesty's confidence
in them is entire."

and Pelissier issued a General Order to the French Army, in which he spoke of the "calm and stoic grandeur of the character" of the late Field-Marshal. Thus, one by one, all the chief actors of this tremendous drama, had been removed. Nicholas, Menschikoff, St. Arnaud, and finally, Raglan, all were gone; while the world watched with breathless interest, the struggle progressing in that hitherto obscure peninsula.

Lord Raglan was succeeded in the chief command by Lieutenant-General Simpson,* his "Chief of the Staff," although there was present with the Army a soldier who had served with distinction in almost every war in which our troops had been engaged from the Battle of Corunna to Chillianwallah; while at the Alma and Balaklava he had showed that he possessed military capacity of a high order. But the "seniority" system, which had been the curse of this war, placing in the highest commands, officers whose sole claim to lead our soldiers rested on the accident of birth, or service forty years before in the Peninsula, prevailed at this critical emergency, and General Simpson was requested, by the Ministry at home, to retain the chief command. The return to England of Sir George Brown and General Pennefather necessitated other changes, and General Codrington succeeded the former, and General Barnard the latter officer, in the command of the Light and Second Divisions respectively.

* General Simpson was a Peninsular officer, and served as second in command to Sir Charles Napier in his famous campaign in Scinde. Both Napier and Lord Ellenborough entertained a high estimate of the capacity of General Simpson, though he scarcely justified their opinion.

Captain Wolseley was on duty in the trenches on the 21st of June, and again on the 23rd, 26th, and 28th of June; but nothing of exceptional importance occurred, except a violent storm on the 23rd, which caused great damage to the batteries and trenches, which were inundated with water. After the assault of the 18th, he and the other Engineer officers were employed in effecting the necessary repairs to the parapets and platforms consequent upon the damage they had sustained; a trench was also dug from the left of the Quarries to the edge of the Woronzoff Ravine, and a Russian trench was altered so as to afford cover to our advanced pickets. The parapets of the fourth parallel were improved, and a battery for three guns (No. 14) was constructed.

The enemy, on their side, were busily employed in retrenching the Redan, and strengthening the fronts between the Malakhoff and Careening Bay. Large convoys were seen daily entering the town from the north, bringing in supplies and munitions to any extent. As the siege progressed, the place increased in strength; and never, perhaps, was an investment carried on under such disadvantages, but still the determination of the Allied Commanders to prosecute the enterprise to a successful conclusion never faltered; like Cato, whose only cry was "Delenda est Carthago," the British and French Generals, rendered more obstinate by resistance, resolved that the great stronghold in the Chersonesus must fall.

During the month of July, the efforts of the Engineers were directed towards working up to the enemy's entrenchments. The French, considering that the state of the Russian works from the Malakhoff to Careening Bay, presented smaller difficulties against entering the town on this side, and that there were fewer obstacles to overcome before reaching the gorge of the Malakhoff Tower, decided to make their great attack on this side, while not abandoning the intention previously entertained of assaulting the Great Redan and works on the town side.

Meanwhile, our troops, situated as they were between the two Attacks of the French, and exposed to heavy artillery fire on both flanks, also from the Garden, Malakhoff, and intervening batteries, including that of the Redan, could make but little progress in their Attack. The enemy, guided by the genius of Todleben, did not fail to profit by the time thus afforded them for strengthening their works, and strong parties were constantly to be seen employed upon the Malakhoff and retrenchments in rear of the Little Redan, extending towards the Great Harbour; thus they formed, in this part, an interior and second line of defence, which every day presented a more formidable appearance.

Captain Wolseley was on duty on the 1st of July,* each relief of the working party numbering four hundred men and twenty-four Sappers, and the works were carried on under a heavy fire, the enemy shell-

* During this month Captain Wolseley was on day duty 1st, 6th, 12th, 15th, and 22nd; night duty, 3rd, 8th, 15th, 19th, and 22nd.

ing the Quarries and the new fourth parallel. On the 8th of July, when he was on night duty in the trenches, the working party numbered nine hundred and fifty men, besides twenty Sappers; on this occasion Lieutenant Graham, of the Engineers, was severely wounded. He says in his Report, the original of which is lying before me :—" Lieutenant Graham having been, unfortunately, struck in the face with some stones from a round shot, and, consequently, forced to leave his party on the Left advanced sap, the officer of the 62nd Regiment, who commanded the party, withdrew his men, telling the Sapper then in charge, that he considered it too dangerous for Linesmen. The enemy kept up a continual fire of shell and grape, and then a number of light balls, which greatly interrupted our work."

The Engineers of the Right Attack completed battery No. 18, for six mortars, and commenced No. 19. They also converted, for the occupation of our troops, the Russian trench nearest the third parallel, a work of great labour, many parts being of rock, and requiring the addition of earth to form a parapet ; and extended the right of the advanced works in front of the Quarries, to form a junction with this trench, which now became a fourth parallel, a perilous and difficult task, owing to the numerous light balls, which burnt nearly half-an-hour. Traverses were thrown up in the Quarries to protect the working parties and guard of the trenches, from the fire of the Garden batteries and Bastion du Mât. The casualties were heavy, owing to the proximity of the British works to the Redan, from which the enemy maintained a vertical fire from mortars, and discharges of grape and grenades.

As this cannonade continued day and night, causing great loss to our troops, and hindering the prosecution of the Engineering works, all our batteries that bore upon the Redan opened fire on the 10th of July, which had the desired effect.

The Engineers now being more free from annoyance, extended the fifth parallel as far as the small Quarry, and ran out a sap from its left. The works were pushed on with the utmost alacrity, and at no time of the siege were the Engineer officers harder worked, Wolseley being the only one on duty, on the 12th of July, to direct the two reliefs of the working party, each of which numbered four hundred men, with twenty-four Sappers. In conjunction with Major Stanton and Lieutenant Somerville, he was on duty, for twenty-four hours on the 15th of July. During the afternoon, the enemy opened a very heavy, well-directed fire on the right of the fifth parallel, and the working party was obliged to be partially withdrawn. Most of the damage was, however, made good during the night; but the labour was very great in consequence of the party having to carry the earth some distance, and there were several casualties from grape and case-shot fired from the left of the Redan.

The night of the 19th, when Wolseley was again on duty, passed off more quietly, and the working parties were enabled to do a fair average of work. The para-

pets and batteries were put in a thorough state of repair
during the latter part of July, and the platforms for the
guns were removed to batteries more in advance, while
new communications were made from the third parallel
and the Quarries to Battery No. 19. At this time,
orders were issued by General Simpson, that the night-
guard in the trenches of the Left Attack was to be
increased to one thousand four hundred men, and in the
Right Attack to two thousand four hundred, under a
General of the day, and three field-officers. Of this
number, six hundred were to work, if required by the
Engineer officers, from four to eight a.m., when they
were to return to camp, if they could be spared; the
remainder were to furnish working parties during the
day. There was also to be a special working party of
four hundred men, independently of the guard, who
were to return to camp at daybreak.

On the 22nd of July, Major Stanton and Captain
Wolseley were on duty for twenty-four hours.* There
were no less than one thousand and fifty men at work
in the trenches under their orders, besides fifty-two
Sappers and sixteen carpenters, and the work was very
heavy. During the day, the Right Attack kept up a
fire on the Redan for some hours with mortars, and a
shell from the enemy, falling among a heap of carcasses

* The officer commanding the Royal Engineers in his Remarks on
the progress of the siege, says :—" The young officers of Engineers and
of the Sappers lately joined from England, suffer very much from the
heat. They soon fall ill with fever. This makes the duty in the
trenches very severe upon those who are able to bear the fatigue."

in the new batteries of the Right Attack, ignited about fifty of them, and the gabions being very dry, they also were set on fire; but the flames were extinguished by earth being shovelled over them. Again, during the day and night of the 22nd, when Wolseley was on duty for twenty-four hours, there was hot work, and his exertions, under constant fire from cohorns, and grape, and shell, were too much even for his constitution. He had been suffering for some time from dysentery, but with that devotion to duty which had characterised him since he joined the besieging force in December of the previous year, he battled against his ailment, and could not be induced to go on the sick list. This arduous and prolonged duty of twenty-four hours, however, quite incapacitated him for further exertion, and the medical authorities directed his removal to Balaklava, thence to proceed on board ship for a period of a fortnight at least, or until the restoration of his health had been established. But Wolseley could not be persuaded to remain beyond a week, and returned to duty not much better than when he quitted the scene of his labours.

The Home Ministry, impatient at the delay in the capture of Sebastopol, and urged by political considerations, telegraphed instructions to the Commander-in-chief, forthwith to " hold a Council with General Pelissier and the Admirals, to consider the actual state of the siege, the chances of arriving at the destruction, or the capture of the southern side of the town, and what it will be possible to do failing these two alternatives."

Accordingly, on the 15th of August, it was decided that the necessary batteries being on the eve of completion, the fifth bombardment should be opened on the 17th of August, without waiting for two hundred mortars which were on their way from France, and fifty from England, the batteries for which were nearly ready. The Russians, meantime, maintained a heavy fire of shot, shell and grape, causing numerous casualties in the guard of the trenches and working parties.

On the 16th of August, Prince Gortschakoff made a desperate assault on the lines of the French and Sardinians on the Tchernaya,* in the hope of raising the siege, but was driven back with a loss of five thousand men, that of the victors being one-fifth of the number.

Captain Wolseley was in charge of the trenches, with a working party of four hundred men and twenty Sappers, on the night of the 16th of August, and on the following morning, when the fifth bombardment of Sebastopol commenced. He says—"The enemy appeared to be working at, and in the neighbourhood of the 6-gun Battery to their left of the Karabelnaia Ravine. Their vertical fire was heavier than usual, as they fired salvoes from three mortars on the left flank of the Redan. Upon a signal of three mortar shells from No. 13 Battery, fire was opened this morning at daybreak from all our batteries." During the night there were thirty-nine casualties in the Right Attack.

---

* The Black River, or river of the Tchernaya, after leaving the valley of Baidar, runs from east to west through numerous ravines, and falls into Sebastopol roads.

At this time, the British batteries mounted one hundred and eighty-six pieces of ordnance, of which seventy-seven were in the Right Attack, and one hundred and nine in the Left Attack. Our gunners directed their fire chiefly against the Redan and Malakhoff, so as to enable the saps to advance, and soon obtained a decided superiority over the Malakhoff; but so heavy was the fire from the Town, Garden, and Barrack batteries, that our advanced batteries in the Left Attack were partially destroyed, and at noon the detachments were withdrawn. During the day, the casualties in the Royal Artillery were thirty officers and men, and in the Naval Brigade, twenty-four.

At daybreak on the 18th of August, fire was re-opened on the enemy's works from all the batteries, with the exception of the advanced batteries of the Left Attack, until the morning of the 19th, when the Redan being much damaged, and the Malakhoff almost silent, orders were issued to cease firing.*

During the 21st of August, Captain Wolseley was on duty with two reliefs of three hundred men each, besides a strong body of Sappers and carpenters, the latter being engaged in making platforms and placing frames for magazines. The men worked well and much progress was made, though under a brisk fire from the

---

* During the forty-eight hours between the morning of the 17th, and six a.m. of the 19th of August, the British batteries had expended no less than twenty-six thousand two hundred and seventy rounds of ammunition, of which eleven thousand, two hundred and forty-three were 10 and 13-inch shell, the total weight being eighty-one tons.

enemy.   He was again on duty on the night of the 23rd
of August, when they were on the *qui vive,* as the
Russians made a sortie upon the French in front of the
Malakhoff.   On the previous evening a sap was commenced from the fifth parallel in advance upon the
capital* of the Redan.   Fifty-eight yards were executed
without interruption from the enemy, and during the
night of the 23rd, Wolseley managed to execute about
fourteen more yards, but under a heavy fire from the
Redan.   In consequence of their proximity to this
work, there were fifty-two casualties among our men
on this day.

Captain Wolseley was on duty in the trenches, with
a working party of eight hundred men from five a.m.
to seven p.m. on the 27th of August, when, under
orders from General Simpson, a heavy fire was opened
by the batteries† of both Attacks on the salient angle
of the Redan.   Of the effect of this fire, Wolseley says
in his Report :—" The salient of the Redan was considerably injured towards the evening by our fire.   The
enemy's fire during the day was heavier than usual,
and they kept up a continual fire upon the several
working parties."

Preparations for the final assault were pushed forward with much energy, and the Engineer staff were

* The capital is the centre line which divides a bastion into two
equal parts.

† The return of guns and mortars in position on the 27th of August,
signed by Colonel St. George, commanding the siege train, showed
that there were seventy-seven pieces of ordnance in the Right Attack,
and one hundred and twenty in the Left Attack.

worked to the utmost, making up by their good will and indomitable perseverance for their numerical inferiority. The time since the repulse of the 18th of June had been utilised by the Allies, and an incredible amount of work had been performed. The French had a very difficult task before them, but by dint of perseverance, and regardless of great loss of life, aided by the powerful and well directed fire of our artillery, they succeeded in establishing themselves close to the crest of the counterscarp of the Malakhoff, the key of the position. Scarcely less difficult was the task our troops undertook in their advance against the Redan, while, owing to the features of the ground, the fire from the Malakhoff and the Bastion du Mât could not be silenced by counter batteries on the glacis, or by enfilade fire from distant batteries.

During the month of August, the Russians, rendered desperate by the sight of the iron ring which was growing in strength day by day, made repeated efforts to break through the toils thus encircling them within its fatal embrace. Frequent sorties were made all through the month, and the fighting in that confined and blood-stained arena became fast and furious. The genius of a second Homer—"whose verses," says Bacon, "have a slide and easiness more than the verses of other poets,"—would be worthily taxed in describing the numberless heroic deeds of our gallant soldiers and their Allies. Failing the pen of " the blind old bard of Scio's rocky isle," we will, in homely prose, depict an event in the life of our hero who, like Achilles in his ardour for the fight, was "impiger, iracundus, inexorabils, acer." In any future epic having for its theme this war of the giants, the achievements of the Allied Army might be compared with that of the Grecian host beleaguering the classic city on the banks of the Scamander; while the Russians in their valour and the obstinacy of their defence, would worthily fill the *rôle* of their Trojan prototypes. Again some of our leaders would compare not unfavourably with the Homeric heroes. Raglan, whose "antique heroism" at the Alma extorted the admiration of St. Arnaud, was an Agamemnon, the "king of men," and no braver warriors landed from the Grecian ships than Gordon and Lysons, Peel, whose fire-eating proclivities were insatiable, and Hewett, of Lancaster battery renown, and Blake and Yea, who fell in "the imminent deadly breach," and Egerton, Cathcart, and the three Campbells—Sir Colin, Sir John, and the young Colonel of the 90th—and numberless others whose self-sacrificing devotion will live for all time in the memory of their countrymen.

However, to our account of an event in Wolseley's life which, at length, after his many narrow escapes, incapacitated him from taking part in the closing scene of the struggle in which he had been engaged since the preceding December. At eight p.m. on the night of the 30th of August, Wolseley, accompanied by Lieutenant Dumaresq, R.E., proceeded on duty, and had charge of the advanced flying sap, which he was directed to carry on as far towards the Redan as the time at his disposal before daylight, and the endurance of his working party of four hundred men and twenty Sappers, would permit. The work progressed as satisfactorily as could be expected, but there was very little earth, and most of the gabions had to be filled with rubble and stone as substitutes. However, he managed to place sixty gabions when the moon rose, and her unwelcome light put a stop to all further proceedings for that night, when, taking advantage of this enforced period of idleness, he proceeded to make a sketch of the ground in order to give his successor an idea of the topography, so that he might carry on the work in hand. Wolseley was thus engaged, when suddenly the Russians made a sortie, and he found himself surrounded by the uncouth visages and strange forms of the soldiery of the Czar, who looked more formidable by the pale and uncertain moonlight. The sortie was made under circumstances and at an hour to call for the exercise of that promptitude and presence of mind which the great Napoleon once described as " two o'clock in the morning courage," and said he rarely found even among the bravest of his soldiers. This serious state of affairs had arisen through the neglect of the field-officer in command, who could not be induced to cover the working party properly, notwithstanding the repeated representations of Captain Wolseley, who begged him to take a rifle-pit that was annoying his men, and showed how it might be done with most advantage. However, this officer would not do as he was requested, and as the Russians kept firing volleys from it all night, Wolseley's men had to work lying down. As a further consequence, the front was not protected by sentries, so that a sortie or surprise of some sort was just what might have been anticipated. As we have seen, there was a sortie, and the surprise was complete, but Wolseley was equal to the occasion.

In a moment the working party of one hundred and fifty men, finding themselves surrounded, cast down their tools or arms and bolted to a man. In vain the officers did all they could to stop the stampede. Wolseley seized by the belt one man who was in the act of flying, but was instantly knocked down by another fellow who took this irregular method of releasing his comrade. On recovering his feet, Wolseley found there was nothing between himself and the Russians but the gabions, which they were pulling down with all celerity. Looking about him with the intent of making an effort to rally his men, he found that he was alone; all had fled, the officers, recognising the futility of resistance without their men, being the last to retire. Another moment's hesitation on Wolseley's part and it would have been too late for him to secure his own safety, and he had barely time to spring over the work and run back to the nearest parallel about one hundred and fifty yards in the rear. British soldiers do not often, or for any length of time, forget themselves; and the same men who, taken by surprise, had just fled in panic from the face of their enemies, rallied in a few minutes, and, led by their officers, drove the Russians pell mell out of the advanced sap.*

* "At about half-past twelve a.m. a party of the enemy, apparently

The field-officer whose negligence had caused this unfortunate business, now asked Captain Wolseley, " What was to be done?"

" I will do nothing," replied Wolseley, " until you have carried the rifle-pit I requested you to take before."

A gallant officer, Captain Pechell,* of the 77th, who was standing by, hearing this colloquy, said, " I will take the rifle-pit." And this he did with a small party of his own men, who carried it with a rush.

about twenty or twenty-five in number, made an attack on the advance up the little ravine from the fifth parallel. The working party retired in great confusion, in spite of repeated attempts on Captain Wolseley's part to rally them, and the Russians threw down about fifty gabions into the trench ; they then retreated, keeping up a fire of musketry, which caused considerable loss. The guns also from the batteries below the Malakhoff opened and caused numerous casualties by stones. Amongst the wounded, I regret to say, was Captain Wolseley, who was severely cut in the face and leg by stones. The guard of the trenches was very strong in the fifth parallel, and there were abundance of men near the entrance to the sap ; but the attack was so sudden, that unless the working party themselves repulsed the enemy, the mischief done to the trench could not be prevented. Captain Wolseley had placed about fifty gabions, and was proceeding to fill them when the attack took place, all of which, and a considerable quantity besides, were overturned into the trench by the enemy. No more work was done there, on account of the precision of the artillery fire from the Malakhoff batteries, and also the incessant fire of musketry, as the enemy only retired about two hundred yards down the ravine. The casualties among the working party were very great, amounting to twelve out of sixty-five, and these in a very short space of time." (See Official Narrative)

* Two nights afterwards this promising officer was killed when retaking this same pit.

The Russians had not only pulled up some of the gabions, which had been filled at such great cost of time and labour, but they had rolled others down the hill; Wolseley, therefore, taking with him a strong party of men, recovered most of these gabions, and was engaged in the task of putting up and refilling them when he received his wound. He was at the end of the sap talking to two Sappers, who were assisting him to fill with stones one of the gabions; one hand was stretched back, and the other was resting on a spike of the gabion, when a round shot dashed into the middle of the group. He had just time to call " Look out !" when down went both the Sappers, while he felt himself hurled to the ground with resistless force. The round shot had struck the gabion, which was full of stones, and scattering its contents with terrific violence, instantaneously killed. the poor fellows by his side, the head of one man being taken off while the other was disembowelled. As for himself, he lay senseless until a sergeant of Sappers picked him up, and, after a time, he rallied sufficiently to avail himself of the assistance of this man and of Prince Victor Hohenlohe,* who, coming up, helped him to walk towards the doctor's hut in the trenches. He just managed to totter so far, and

* His Serene Highness is a sailor who has shown high courage at the hotly-contested boat action at Fatshan Creek in China, in May, 1857, as well as in the batteries before Sebastopol. When, after the lapse of many years, Prince Victor again met Sir Garnet at a public dinner, after his return from the Gold Coast, he reminded the successful General of the circumstances of their last meeting.

was laid down outside the hut in a semi-unconscious state.

Prince Victor called the attention of the surgeon to his newly arrived patient, and the reply was, after a hasty glance, for he was too busy just then to examine him, " He's a dead 'un."

This roused up the wounded officer, who, though half-unconscious, seemed to regard the remark in the light of a reflection; and turning himself as he lay there all smothered in blood, he made answer, " I am worth a good many dead men yet." This remark caused the doctor, who fancied from his appearance that his injuries were mortal, to turn his attention to Captain Wolseley, and from the nature of the wounds, and the shock to the system their number and extent would have caused in most cases, it seemed as if the surgeon had only been a little premature in his rough and ready diagnosis.

Wolseley's head and body presented a shocking appearance. His features were not distinguishable as those of a human being, while blood flowed from innumerable wounds caused by the stones with which he had been struck. Sharp fragments were imbedded all over his face, and his left cheek had been almost cut completely away. The doctor fancied, after probing the wound, that his jawbone was shattered, but Wolseley made him pull out the substance in his mouth, when a large stone came away. The surgeon then lifted up and stitched the cheek. Both his eyes were completely closed, and the injury to one of them was so serious that the sight has been permanently lost. Not a square inch of his face but what was battered and cut about, while his body was wounded all over, just as if he had been peppered with small shot. He had received also a severe wound on his right leg, so that both limbs had now been injured, the wound in left thigh, received in Burmah, rendering him slightly lame. For many years afterwards the wound on the shin, received on this 30th of August, caused him much suffering, and, when on duty in Canada, nearly ten years after the event, he was under the necessity of returning to England for medical advice regarding the bone which was exfoliating. Considering the extent of his wounds, which in many cases would have caused collapse, or induced erysipelas or other *sequelæ*, Captain Wolseley's recovery must be chiefly attributed to his wonderful constitution, and, in a scarcely less degree, to his strong vitality and buoyant courage.

After the surgeon had dressed his wounds, Captain Wolseley was placed on a stretcher, and carried by four soldiers to St. George's Monastery, situated on the sea-coast not far from Balaklava, and there he passed some weeks in a cave, as the sight of both eyes was too much injured to subject them to the light. While he was pent up in this gloomy cavern, meditating on the sad prospect of being totally blind for the remainder of his days, news arrived of the fall of Sebastopol. The great Russian stronghold which had, for so many weary months, defied the utmost efforts of two Great Powers, was, at length, carried by assault on the 8th of Sep-

tember, and Captain Wolseley had the additional mortification of feeling that all his devotion and suffering
had not received the reward he most coveted—that of
participating in the storm of the Russian stronghold.*

The Siege of Sebastopol stands in many respects
without example in the annals of war. The Russian
works extended for nearly fifteen miles, while the
besiegers' trenches were no less than fifty-two miles in
length, and comprised one hundred and nine batteries,
armed with eight hundred and six pieces. The expenditure of ammunition during the siege, according to
the estimate of our Artillery officers, nearly amounted
to one million five hundred thousand rounds. The
trenches were open three hundred and thirty-four days,
and the batteries, in the most advanced of which were
placed guns and mortars of a calibre seldom before
used in siege operations, were open for three hundred
and twenty-seven days. The Russians opposed to the

---

* Our loss on the 8th of September was twenty-nine officers, thirty-
six sergeants, and three hundred and twenty rank and file killed;
one hundred and twenty-four officers, one thousand seven hundred
and sixty-two non-commissioned officers and men wounded; and one
officer and one hundred and seventy-five men missing; total loss, two
thousand four hundred and forty-seven. The French lost five general
officers killed, four wounded, and six contused; twenty-four superior
officers killed, twenty wounded, and two missing; one hundred and
sixteen subaltern officers killed, two hundred and twenty-four
wounded, and eight missing; also one thousand four hundred and
eighty-nine non-commissioned officers and men were killed, four
thousand two hundred and fifty-nine wounded, and one thousand four
hundred missing; grand total, seven thousand five hundred and fifty-
one.

Allies an army numerically superior, intrenched behind formidable defences, mounting no less than one thousand one hundred cannon, and protected by the guns of their fleet.

Immediately on learning the news of the fall of Sebastopol, Captain Wolseley resigned his post of Assistant-Engineer, and his name was removed from the list from the 7th of November. He had been ordered to England for the recovery of his health and to seek the best medical advice for his eyes, the sight of both of which it was feared was permanently lost.

Sir Harry Jones, in a confidential Memorandum to the Secretary of State for War, brought to his Lordship's notice the names of the officers whom he recommended for promotion, among them being that of Captain Wolseley. Throughout the siege the duties of the trenches fell with great severity on the Engineer officers, of whom the General said he "could not speak too highly in praise of the zeal and intelligence they displayed;" day and night they were constantly under fire in the most advanced positions, directing the working parties, and it is surprising that any of those who, like Wolseley, served continuously for many months escaped with their lives.

The total number of non-commissioned officers and men of the Royal Engineers employed throughout the siege, amounted to only nine hundred and thirty-five; of these two hundred and eighteen were killed or died, and one hundred and nineteen became non-effective from various causes, leaving five hundred and ninety-eight in the Crimea on the 9th of September. During the same time, sixty-nine officers of the Royal Engineers, and nineteen other officers acting as Assistant-Engineers, served with the corps; of the former, eighteen were killed or died, (exclusive of Lieutenant H. G. Teesdale, who died of wounds received at the Alma,) and fourteen were wounded, while two Assistant-Engineers were killed and six wounded.*

During the nine months he served uninterruptedly before Sebastopol—with the exception of a week's sick leave at Balaklava—Captain Wolseley, was, perhaps, as often on duty in the trenches as any officer in the British Army; while as one of the Engineer officers of the Right Attack, he was in the post of the greatest danger, as evidenced by the fact that of the fourteen officers killed at the siege, twelve belonged to the Right Attack, or were killed when doing duty there.†

---

* The total loss of the British Army in the Crimea was one hundred and fifty-seven officers, one hundred and sixty-one non-commissioned officers, and two thousand four hundred and thirty-seven drummers and rank and file, killed in action ; and eighty-six officers, eighty-five non-commissioned officers, and one thousand eight hundred and forty-eight drummers and rank and file, died of wounds. The wounded numbered five hundred and seventy-seven officers, six hundred and forty-five sergeants, and ten thousand one hundred and fifty-five men ; the missing, thirteen officers, twenty-three sergeants, and four hundred and sixty-eight men. The Naval Brigade, out of a total force of one hundred and thirty-five officers and four thousand three hundred and thirty-four seamen and marines, had five officers and ninety-five men killed, and thirty-eight officers and four hundred and thirty-seven men wounded.

† The reason is obvious why the mortality in the Right Attack was

The preceding pages show the nature of the duty performed by Captain Wolseley during those eight months. In the dreary Winter of 1854-55, he, in common with every officer and man, suffered the pangs of hunger and cold, but though for weeks his diet was an insufficient allowance of unwholesome biscuit, and still more unwholesome water, he cheerfully performed his tour of duty in the trenches, and faced the Russian fire and the biting cold of an Arctic Winter, which proved fatal to so many gallant officers and men. While the

greater than in the Left. The Right Attack was on the slope of the Redan, while a ravine intervened between the Russian batteries and the Left Attack. The following are the names of the twenty Engineer and Assistant-Engineer officers who were killed before Sebastopol, or died of their wounds, or of illness contracted during the operations, with the dates of their deaths. Captain A. D. Craigie, 13th of March ; Lieutenant E. Bainbrigge, 4th of April; Captain J. F. Crofton, (wounded 12th of April) died 15th of April ; Captain F. W. King, (wounded 17th of April) died 22nd of April; Lieutenant C. E. Baynes, (wounded 19th of April) died 7th of May ; Lieutenant J. S. Carter, (Left Attack) 2nd of May ; Captain J. F. Dawson, 7th of June ; Lieutenant J. G. Lowry, 7th of June ; Brevet-Colonel R. Tylden, (shot through both legs on 18th of June) died in August ; Captain W. H. Jesse, 18th of June ; Lieutenant J. Murray, 18th of June ; Lieutenant J. M. Graves, 18th of June ; Captain Anderson, (31st Regiment) 5th of September ; Major S. Chapman, (Left Attack, 20th Regiment) wounded on the 8th of September, died 20th of September. Died of disease, or by accident—Brigadier-General V. B. Tylden, of cholera, on the 22nd of September, 1854 ; Lieutenant-Colonel Alexander, of apoplexy, 19th of October, 1854 ; Captain W. M. Inglis, drowned in 'Prince' on the 14th of November, 1854 ; Captain Belson, of typhus fever, on the 5th of August, 1855 ; Lieutentant Somerville, of typhus fever, on the 3rd of September ; Major Ranken, killed by the fall of a wall on the 27th of February, 1856.

Army was perishing from want and cold in the trenches, ship after ship arrived at Balaklava, stowed with boots too small for use, and great-coats that would not button : and when officers, even at head-quarters, were fain to be thankful for mouldy biscuit, preserved meats and vegetables were rotting on the quays of Balaklava. Routine and red-tapeism reigned supreme, and the world wondered at the astounding display of mismanagement in every department of our complicated military machine. The one satisfactory feature was the valour and patience of our soldiers, who doggedly fought on, and never murmured when affairs looked their blackest.

It was a point of honour among the Engineer officers and Sappers to bear up against sickness, and hold out as long as they could stand on their legs; and Wolseley, though he frequently suffered from illness and over-work, with the exception of a brief interval in July, remained at his post until severe wounds incapacitated him for further duty. Speaking of the officers and men of the Royal Engineers, he has expressed an opinion that, " he never saw men work like them," and considers their conduct in this unparalleled siege, as " beyond all praise."

During its progress, Captain Wolseley was wounded severely on the 30th of August, and slightly on the 10th of April and 7th of June. On the 15th of February his coat was pierced by a ball ; on the 10th of April a round shot struck the embrasure at which he was working, and his trousers were cut ; and, on the 7th of June, a ball passed through his forage cap from

the peak to the back, knocking it off his head.   It may
be said, without exaggeration, that he bore a charmed
life, for, at the termination of the siege, of three messes
of four members each to which he had belonged, he
was the only officer remaining in the Crimea, all the
others being either killed or forced to leave through
wounds.

Captain Wolseley was about to return to England
for the recovery of his health, when he was offered an
appointment in the Quartermaster-General's* Department.   As there was a great improvement in the sight
of one of his eyes, though he regarded that of the other
as hopelessly gone, he resolved to remain in the
Crimea, and, accordingly, accepted the offer.   He was
employed on the Quartermaster-General's staff, in
conjunction with two other officers of the 90th Light
Infantry, Major Barnston, (who, in December, 1857,
died of wounds received at the Relief of Lucknow, of
whom Wolseley speaks as "the best officer he ever
knew,") and Captain Crealock, whose gallantry on the
disastrous 8th of September, and in the China Campaign of 1860, and whose skill as an accomplished
artist, have made his name famous.   Captain Wolseley
and Major Barnston were attached, for surveying
duties, to a French Army of twenty thousand men and
a small force of English Cavalry, which had taken up a

---

* Sir Richard Airey, who had been Quartermaster-General throughout the War, was succeeded in November by Colonel Percy Herbert,
who had been head of that Department in Sir De Lacy Evans'
Division.

position in the valley of the Belbec, menacing the left flank of the Russians, who, after the fall of the south side of Sebastopol, occupied a line extending from the Star Fort to the extreme left on the Mackenzie Heights. At this time the Allies had in the Crimea an army of about two hundred and ten thousand men, of which the British portion numbered, on the 16th of October, fifty-six thousand men,* of whom only four thousand five hundred were ineffective through wounds or sickness.

While employed with the French *corps d'armée* in the valley of the Belbec on surveying duties, Captain Wolseley had many narrow escapes of being captured. Every morning, he and Major Barnston would leave the French camp on their expeditions, either alone, or escorted by a few troopers, and many a hot chase they had when the Russians, annoyed at seeing British officers reconnoitring and sketching close up to their advanced posts, sent some of their hardest-riding Cossacks in pursuit. When the French Force fell back, and it became too cold for surveying, Wolseley was appointed Deputy Assistant-Quartermaster-General to the Light Division, then under the command of

---

* This total was composed of fourteen regiments of Cavalry, about five thousand sabres; fifty-two battalions of Infantry, about thirty-three thousand bayonets; and fourteen batteries of Artillery and nine companies of Sappers, about nine thousand men. The remaining ten thousand were made up of non-combatants, as Land Transport, Army Works, and Medical Staff. Besides the Turkish Contingent of twenty thousand men, there were in the United Kingdom only seven regiments of Cavalry, exclusive of the Household Brigade, and eight regiments of Infantry, besides five in the Mediterranean.

Lord William Paulet, its former leader, Sir William Codrington having succeeded to the chief command on the resignation of Sir James Simpson.

Captain Wolseley remained in the Crimea until, on the conclusion of Peace with Russia, the Allied Army was directed to return home. As Deputy Assistant-Quartermaster-General he assisted Colonel Hallowell at Balaklava in despatching homewards the troops of his Division, a great portion of the Army embarking at Kasatch Bay, near Kamiesch, where the Fleet lay. On 5th of July, 1856, Marshal Pelissier, with his staff, sailed from Kamiesch, under a salute of nineteen guns from our ships in port; and, on the 12th of July, Sir William Codrington, having made over the Dockyard of Sebastopol and Port of Balaklava, to the officer in command of the Russian troops, (a Colonel of Gendarmerie at Kamiesch), embarked on board Her Majesty's Ship 'Algiers.' The honour of handing over the town was delegated to a wing of the 50th—the famous "dirty half-hundredth," which had been one of the first Regiments to land in the Crimea,—and, under the usual salutes, they gave place to a Russian Guard, composed of about sixty Cossack cavalry, and an equal number of Cossack infantry. After the departure of all the Regiments, Captain Wolseley embarked for England, being one of the last men to quit the land where he had done and suffered so much in his country's service.

CHAPTER III.

THE INDIAN MUTINY.

Captain Wolseley proceeds on Service to India—Wrecked at Banca—Arrival at Calcutta—Proceeds up-country—In Action near Cawnpore—March to Alumbagh—The Relief of Lucknow—Wolseley storms the Mess-house—Occupies the Motee Mahul, and effects Communication with the Residency of Lucknow—The Defence of Alumbagh—Campaigning in Oude—Actions at Baree and Nawabgunge—Service on the Nepaul Frontier.

ON his return from the Crimea, Captain Wolseley* rejoined the 90th Regiment, then stationed at Aldershot, but was soon after employed in reporting on a new system of visual telegraphy. For this purpose, he came up to London in order that he might acquire a knowledge of the system from the German Professor, who sought, but unsuccessfully, to introduce it into our

---

* For his meritorious services during the Siege of Sebastopol, and notwithstanding that he had been specially mentioned in Despatches by Lord Raglan, and recommended for promotion by Sir Harry Jones, K.C.B., Wolseley did not receive the brevet-majority to which he might have been considered entitled. The French Emperor nominated him a Knight of the Legion of Honour, and the Sultan conferred on him the Fifth Class of the Medjidie.

Army. On his return to Aldershot, he was attached to the staff of Lord William Paulet, then commanding a Brigade at the camp, as "galloper," which, to the unprofessional reader, may be defined as an extra aide-de-camp without, however, the extra pay.

In the beginning of February, 1857, the 90th, being one of the Regiments under orders to proceed to India, was sent for a few months to Portsmouth to enjoy the pleasures and relaxation of a garrison town, to which it had certainly earned a title after its sufferings in the Crimea. The Regiment, however, had only been a few days at that famous seaport, when orders were received for it to proceed to India at a week's notice. But the authorities at the War Office altered their determination, and a reprieve of a week was allowed; finally, the officers, who had all been hastily recalled from leave, were given to understand that *positively* the Regiment would not embark for foreign service until June, the usual period for the despatch of Indian reliefs, so that the troops might land after the monsoons, in the cool season.

But we were too hasty in penning the word "finally" above; a British soldier, who may be called upon at any moment to defend the most distant dependency of an empire "upon which the sun never sets," can never, even for a few months, consider his destination "finally" settled, while the War Office twenty years ago—there is more consideration for officers and men now-a-days —habitually hated finality in making up its mind to anything, and cared little for the expense and inconvenience it caused to officers who drew the munificent pay of a grateful country. The present afforded a notable instance of this lordly disregard of other people's comfort; for about three weeks after all had been settled, the Regiment received orders to hold itself in readiness to proceed forthwith to China.

At this time the 90th was commanded by Colonel Campbell, an officer whose brilliant defence of the Quarries on the night of the 7th of June,—when our troops, acting alone and without the assistance of our Allies, achieved almost the only striking success throughout the siege—gained him the well-merited honours of the Bath. The Regiment now mustered a thousand bayonets, and it was a goodly sight to see the 90th on parade, as smart a corps as any in Her Majesty's service. Captain Wolseley's company, like all the others, numbered a hundred non-commissioned officers and men, and he had three subalterns, Lieutenants Herford and Carter, and Ensign Haig. Of the entire strength of the Regiment, seven hundred men, with head-quarters, embarked in the ' Himalaya,' under command of Colonel Campbell, C.B., and Major Barnston, with the three remaining companies, under Captains Wolseley, Guise, and Irby, sailed in the ' Transit,' whose history from her cradle to her grave, bore a singular resemblance to that of the ill-fated ' Megæra.'*

---

* Lieutenant (now retired Captain) J. S. A. Herford, to whose work, " Stirring Times under Canvas," and information, always readily accorded, I am much indebted, describes the ship in the following

Besides three hundred men of the 90th, the ' Transit'
embarked for Hong Kong a detachment of the 59th
Regiment and two hundred men of the Medical Staff
Corps, a body recently organised for furnishing military
hospitals with attendants; the whole party being under
the command of Lieutenant-Colonel Stephenson, who
had been appointed Assistant Adjutant-General to the
China Expedition, then fitting out under the command
of the late Major-General the Honourable T. Ashburn-
ham, C.B.   The troubles of the ' Transit' commenced
before she had lost sight of land.   Directly after quitting Spithead, a dense fog coming on, Commander
Chambers, her Captain, brought-to in the Solent; and,
on weighing anchor the following day, found the ship
making water so fast that he had to run back to Spithead, flying the ensign " with the Union down," as a
signal of distress.   The ' Transit' managed to creep

terms:—" The ' Transit' had always been an unfortunate ship.
Bought, if not literally on the stocks, yet in an unfinished state, from
a private company, she was completed by the Royal Navy authorities,
by which ingenious plan, whenever anything afterwards went wrong,
the original builders and the finishers were able to shift the blame on
each other.   She was continually breaking down in her various voyages
to and from the Crimea with troops.   Those who were so unfortunate
as to be embarked in her knew well enough that something was certain
to happen in the course of the voyage.   Yet the Authorities had still a
firm belief in her merits; so, putting a new pair of engines in her, they
determined to send troops in her a short way—only to China!   The
new engines were smaller, but more powerful, than the last had been,
and, to steady the ship and keep her together, two large iron beams,
running fore and aft, were added.   To these beams we, probably, at a
later period, owed our lives."

into Portsmouth Harbour, and, discharging the troops into a hulk, hauled off to the dockyard, nearly sinking before she could be pumped out and docked. It was then discovered that she had knocked a hole in her bottom, which was probably occasioned by her settling on her anchor at low water when in a tideway. On the necessary repairs being effected, the 'Transit,' having re-shipped the troops, and the guns and military stores which formed her cargo, once more proceeded on her long voyage. But it was only to encounter further ill-luck. A strong gale came on in the "chops of the Channel," and the rigging having been loosely set up, the masts swayed about to such an extent that the Captain made all preparations to cut them away. The gale moderating, the 'Transit' put into Corunna, where Captain Wolseley and the other officers proceeded ashore, and visited the grave of one of England's bravest and best soldiers, Sir John Moore. The rigging having been set up, the 'Transit' proceeded once more to sea, and, on May-day, anchored at St. Vincent, where they were joined by the 'Himalaya,' which had sailed from Portsmouth a few days after the 'Transit.' On their arrival at the Cape on May the 28th, it was discovered that the ship had sprung a leak near her stern-post, but, on examination by a diver, it was pronounced as of no consequence, and so the 'Transit' proceeded on her long flight across the Indian Ocean, her donkey-engine working the whole time to keep the leak under. When near St. Paul's, the island on which the 'Megæra,' of evil memory, left her bones, the 'Transit' encountered a hurricane, and it seemed as if the ship was to add another to those mysteries of the deep which are every now and then chronicled in the public papers.

Wolseley says :—"For three days and three nights the cyclone lasted. All our sails were carried away, and the mainyard went to pieces. An enormous leak showed itself; some plates were supposed to have burst so that the water poured in like a sluice. We had on board the 'Transit' nearly nine hundred souls, and it was as much as all hands could do, by constant pumping, to keep her afloat."* But Providence destined the gallant hearts on board the 'Transit' to fight their country's battles in a great crisis, and the gale moderated, when matters looked so serious that it only seemed a question of how many hours they could keep afloat the worn-out hull in which " the authorities " had so perversely sent them to the other side of the world. By dint of hard pumping the leak was kept under, and the ship, having passed through the Straits of Sunda, headed north for Singapore, when officers and men began to count the days before they might expect to sight the rich and varied foliage amid which

* Captain Herford, after describing the havoc aloft, writes of the state of affairs :—"The ship strained and groaned like a chained giant in agony. Soon we began to notice the long faces of some of the ship's officers. It turned out that there was a rent, twenty-four feet long, in the ship's side, and that the water was rushing in! The heads of some of the rivets had come off; one might have passed half-a-crown through the opening easily. Five hundred tons of water were pumped out in one day."

that city is embosomed. Soon they were steaming rapidly through the Straits of Banca, whose well-wooded shores and sandy coves excited their admiration, as we remember it did ours when cruising in those seas. But their acquaintance was destined to be not altogether of a pleasurable tinge, for at ten o'clock on the morning of the 10th of July, as the 'Transit' was passing through the Straits, the Island of Banca being on the starboard hand and Sumatra on the port side, and the sea as smooth as a mill-pond, the crazy old ship suddenly crashed on a coral reef, on which she remained immovable. Then it was seen what discipline could effect among men whose lives were not passed, like sailors, amid the perils incidental to a nautical profession, but who suddenly found themselves confronting a novel danger.

" The majority of the troops," says Captain Herford, " were on the main-deck at the mess-tables. On feeling the first shock they naturally rose *en masse*, and were about to rush on deck, when Major Barnston—who was quietly writing in his cabin—appeared before them, and lifting his hand, said in his usual undisturbed voice, ' It's all right, men ; stay where you are !' These few words coming from an officer who inspired confidence and was generally beloved, acted like magic. The men, like so many children, obeyed and sat down."

The ship's company, meanwhile, lowered the boats, and it was found on taking soundings that there was not less than nine fathoms all round. In the meantime the ship began to settle by the stern, and there was great danger of her sliding off the rock and sinking in the deep water alongside, when a lamentable loss of life must have ensued. The engine-room was soon full of water, which rushed in with great velocity. While the soldiers were busy bringing up on deck the provisions and arms, the sailors lowered the remaining boats, and prepared them for the reception of the troops, who were landed on a reef distant about a mile and a-half, as it was considered desirable to remove all hands from the wreck with the utmost dispatch, the Island of Banca being about two miles further away. When this had been completed, the crew first proceeded to the mainland with what provisions they could save, and, having deposited these on the sandy beach, returned to the reef, which was now nearly submerged by the advancing tide, and removed the soldiers to the neighbouring shore. Here large fires had been lit, and, as a fine stream of water was close at hand, the gallant light-hearted fellows of both Services were soon making themselves merry over biscuit and water, thankful that they had escaped with their lives.

Captain Wolseley lost everything he possessed in the world except the clothes on his back, for strict orders had been issued by Captain Chambers that nothing was to be passed into the boats except provisions, so that officers and men saved only their arms, each man taking with him also four rounds of ammunition. This was the first time Wolseley had suffered this misfortune, one of the most trying of the chances of war, but it was not destined to be the last, for, not

many months later, when the rebels defeated General
Windham and burned Cawnpore, he and his brother
officers lost the second kit they had provided themselves with in Calcutta; among his losses at Cawnpore
were his Legion of Honour and Crimean medal, which
were afterwards found on the body of a dead " Pandy."
Again, during his absence from England on his Ashantee Campaign, Wolseley had the misfortune to lose all
his furniture and goods, which he had warehoused in
the Pantechnicon, in the great fire which, in a few
hours, reduced to ashes that vast building and its
costly contents.

On the following morning, when it was found that
the bows of the 'Transit' were still visible above
water, an attempt was made to secure some baggage
and necessaries, but the salvage from the wreck was
inconsiderable and almost valueless.

The spot on which the shipwrecked crew and passengers of the 'Transit' had landed, was not without a
certain historical interest for soldiers and sailors, for,
on examination, there were found among the trees and
brushwood, the remains of ditches and embankments,
indicating that it was at this spot the British constructed a fort during the Expedition to Java in 1811.
The Island of Banca is under the protection of the
Dutch, whose settlement at Minto was some eight
miles distant. To this place Captain Chambers, on
the morning after the disaster, sent the cutter to ask
for assistance ; and the Governor immediately despatched one gunboat to Singapore to advise the autho-

rities there, and another to protect the wreck from the
depredations of the natives, who had commenced seiz-
ing all they could pick up. As all the fresh provisions
and live stock had been lost, the shipwrecked people
had to subsist on salt meat and biscuits, a fare which
was varied by the flesh of baboons which they shot,
and made into a nutritious, if not very palatable, soup..
The natives also drove a good business in the sale of
pine-apples, yams, bread, eggs, and poultry, though the
supply was limited, and the price demanded so great
as to be almost prohibitory. With such eatables, and
sheltered by the sails of the 'Transit,' which were
spread between the trees, officers and men passed a
not unpleasant Robinson Crusoe sort of life for eight
days ; and, just when the sense of novelty had worn
off, and this mode of existence began to pall, Her
Majesty's gunboat 'Dove' arrived from Singapore, and
brought some startling news that altered the destination of the 90th Regiment, and opened a new chapter
in the adventurous career of Captain Wolseley. This
was the announcement that the Bengal Native Army
was in full mutiny, and had inaugurated the movement
by the destruction of Meerut and the seizure of Delhi,
while massacres were perpetrated throughout the land,
coupled with an urgent demand for the aid of every
European soldier to uphold the banner of British
supremacy and withstand the mighty uprising to
"drive the British leopard into the sea," as Napoleon
would have styled it. Already the head-quarters of
the Regiment, which had sailed in the 'Himalaya,' had

been despatched to Calcutta, and, at once proceeding up-country, formed part of the reinforcements brought up by Sir James Outram, when that most distinguished of Indian Generals, fresh from his Persian triumphs, marched to joined Havelock, then battling against tremendous odds ; and thus a portion of the 90th were fortunate enough to participate in the first Relief of Lucknow.

Two days after the arrival of the 'Dove,' Her Majesty's ship 'Actæon,' Captain Bates, steamed up to Banca, and embarked the three companies of the 90th, which, on arriving at Singapore on the 23rd of July, were quartered in some large roomy huts about three miles outside that picturesque-looking town, whose situation on one of the chief highways of commerce, surely marks it out for a great future. On the 29th, Her Majesty's ship 'Shannon,' Captain William Peel, with Lord Elgin on board arrived from Hong Kong, and, on the following day, she and Her Majesty's ship 'Pearl,' Captain Sotheby, embarked the 90th for Calcutta, Captain Wolseley's company sailing in the latter ship.

The arrival of these reinforcements was most opportune. Delhi had not yet been captured, and Lucknow was closely besieged by the enemy, while every day brought fresh news of rebellion, and the air was thick with rumours of disaster. Men's hearts failed them for fear, and Fort William itself presented the aspect of a fortress in an enemy's country.

On the morning after their arrival at Calcutta, the detachment proceeded in a river steamer to Chinsurah, and here they remained for some weeks, during which the soldiers received a new outfit, and exchanged their arms, which had been damaged, for more serviceable weapons. The officers ordered new outfits in Calcutta, and Captain Wolseley expended £100 in restoring his lost kit; but though they sent in their claims for compensation for lost baggage, which, according to the War Office Regulations, would be immediately honoured, three years elapsed before the expenses they had incurred were refunded.

At length, all the arrangements for the transport of the detachment being complete, on the 29th of August Captain Wolseley's company left Chinsurah by rail for the long journey up-country. The first halting-place was Raneegunge, about one hundred and twelve miles from Calcutta, and as the rail went no further, the company started in bullock "gharees" for Benares. The detachment marched by companies, each "bullock-train" accommodating eighty men and each "gharee" either six men, or two officers with their baggage; one-third of the men with an officer, as a guard, proceeded on foot. The average pace was about two miles an hour, and the bullock were changed every ten miles. Thus the company marched until, on the following morning, a halt was made for some hours at the staging bungalow; as time was of importance, and they were occasionally delayed by the rivers, which were swelled by the heavy monsoon rains, forced marches had sometimes to be made during the heat of the day, which, at first, was found to be very trying to unacclimatized soldiers.

After passing Dehree, burnt bungalows and devastated villages afforded signs that they were approaching the scene of operations, and, on the 10th of September, Captain Wolseley and his company crossed the Ganges in a paddle-boat worked by manual, or rather pedal, labour, and proceeded to a palace of the Rajah of Benares, situated about three miles from that city, which had been prepared for their reception. The Holy City of the Hindoos was, at this time, the hot-bed of sedition. Earthworks mounted with guns commanded the town, and it was intimated to the inhabitants that any overt act of rebellion would be the signal for the destruction of their chief temple.

On the following day the company started from Benares, again by bullock-dâk, and, after two days' marching, re-crossed the Ganges, and entered the fort of Allahabad, which, situated at the junction of that sacred river with the Jumna, is a place of the greatest strategical importance, though, like Delhi and other arsenals in Upper India, at the time of the Mutiny it was denuded of white troops by the insane policy that dictated our military dispositions.

Proceeding by forced marches through Futtehpore, Captain Wolseley arrived about the 27th of September at Cawnpore, whose very name arouses sad memories in the minds of every one who was in India in that terrible year, 1857. Formerly one of the largest and finest military stations in India, Cawnpore now pre-

sented a desolate appearance. On every side were
burnt cantonments and bungalows, and the company
passed the entrenchment defended with so much pertinacity by Sir Hugh Wheeler and his handful of
British troops, and the small low-roofed row of houses
in which was consummated the butchery of the helpless
women and children, and the neighbouring well in
which their still palpitating corpses were cast by the
orders of the monster Nana Sahib. All these sights
were viewed by the officers and men of the 90th, and
aroused in them, as in every Regiment, which, on
arriving up-country had visited in succession the
accursed spot, feelings of hate and revenge, which
found ample vent at the Relief and Siege of Lucknow in
the following November and March.

In October Captain Wolseley had his first brush
with the Pandies. A report reached Cawnpore that
the insurgents were mustering in force at Sheo Rajpore,
some miles from Bhitoor, the residence of Nana Sahib.
At midnight on the 17th of October, Brigadier Wilson,*
of the 64th Regiment, taking with him a field battery,
a few Native horse, and six hundred and fifty bayonets,
—made up of detachments of the Madras Fusiliers and
the 64th and 90th Regiments—carrying four days'
provisions, moved off rapidly towards Bhitoor. It was
the time of the Native festival of the Dewalee, or Feast
of Lamps, and hopes were expressed of inflicting a severe
blow on the rebels. The force proceeded all night, the

---

* This gallant officer fell on the 27th of November, when the Gwalior
troops attacked General Windham in his entrenchments at Cawnpore.

infantry being mounted on elephants and camels; at daybreak they dismounted, and, marching briskly, approached Bhitoor early in the morning. On the way they learned that the enemy occupied a grove of trees half a mile in front, with two guns, a 9-pounder and a 24-pounder, in position. The British column was marching along a hard "pucka"* road, when, the enemy beginning to open fire, Brigadier Wilson deployed his force. Wolseley's company—which, with the detachment of Native cavalry, formed the advanced guard—was marching in column of sections, when the round shot and shell began to fly down the road pretty freely. One shell passed through his files, and, bursting in front of the other companies of the 90th, which were in the rear and in the act of deploying, killed and wounded seven men. The cavalry thereupon turned and bolted, charging through Wolseley's company. He now quickly threw his men into skirmishing order, and Major Barnston proposed to the Brigadier that he should advance upon the guns, for like most soldiers who had served at Sebastopol, and had been daily under shell fire, he had not that dread of attacking guns which generally characterizes inexperienced soldiers. But Colonel Wilson, though personally as gallant a soldier as any in Her Majesty's service, feared to incur the responsibility of the act, and, though Wolseley was already advancing on the guns, countermanded the

* "Pucka" is a word of very general use and many significations in Hindostanee; here it denotes "permanent," as opposed to *cutcha*, raw or new.

attack, and, halting his force, brought up his battery and opened fire on the enemy. This occupied some time as the guns were drawn by bullocks, and, before he had fired many rounds, the enemy had limbered up and made off with their guns, leaving behind only two waggons and three country carts with ammunition. During this action, which lasted about an hour, our casualties were two killed and six severely wounded, all, with one exception, belonging to the 90th; while the loss of the enemy was computed at about one hundred.

The 19th of October was occupied in destroying Bithoor, the troops bivouacking that night in Nana Sahib's compound, and the "bawachee" of Wolseley's mess cooked his masters' dinner by means of the legs of the Nana's billiard tables. On the following day the column returned to Cawnpore, having first destroyed Sheo Rajpore, where a party of the 64th bayoneted some rebels they found concealed in straw.

At this time, though Delhi had fallen, and a portion of the Army—which, at the time of the assault, numbered less than ten thousand effectives—was free for ulterior operations, the position of affairs at Lucknow was still most critical. On the 25th of September, General Havelock and Sir James Outram had effected the relief* of the Residency, but little had been accomplished beyond increasing the strength of the garrison, whereby

---

* In this desperate affair the chief sufferers were the 78th who had forty-five killed and eighty-one wounded, and the 90th, which lost thirty-seven killed and forty-nine wounded.

all immediate danger of its being overpowered was averted, and occupying the Furreed Buksh and Chuttur Munzil Palaces, and other buildings. The entire British Force only numbered three thousand effectives, and the rebel hordes were swelled to some seventy thousand fighting men; still had there been no convoys of women and children, and sick and wounded, Outram, who now resumed the command, would have cut his way out, and retired upon Cawnpore, and he was only dissuaded from adopting this desperate course by his sagacious chief of the staff, Colonel Napier (now Lord Napier of Magdala) who expressed his opinion that any attempt to encounter once more the perils of a mile and a half of street fighting, with a convoy of some three thousand non-combatants, would most probably involve the destruction of the entire force.

On the day preceding his entry into Lucknow, Havelock left at Alumbagh ("Garden of the World") all his baggage and some one hundred and thirty sick and wounded, under a guard of four hundred men, with some guns, under the command of Colonel McIntyre, of the 78th Highlanders.

On the 3rd of October a convoy of provisions was thrown into Alumbagh, and, on the 11th, orders were issued that five hundred men, under Major Barnston, including the detachment of the 90th, with four guns, was to march to Alumbagh with supplies; as they were to return in a few days, this force was ordered to leave behind at Cawnpore all their *impedimenta*, which, however, none of the officers were destined to be encumbered with any further.

Accordingly, on the 21st of October, three hundred waggons, laden with stores, and eight camels, were sent across the river; and, early in the ensuing morning, the column crossed over the bridge of boats, and, after a march of a few miles, halted under some trees, no tents being taken for the same reason that the baggage was left behind. At midnight Major Barnston started again, and marched till eight in the morning. On the second day he learnt that the rebels, seven hundred strong, with two guns, intended to dispute the passage of the river Sye, at the Bunnee Bridge, the centre arch of which they had undermined. Having made his dispositions, Major Barnston advanced his small force, Captain Guise's company forming the advanced guard; "but," writes Captain Herford, "Wolseley, who followed, told Guise that he must let him go in and take one of the guns."

However the gallant officers were disappointed of their game this time, for on reaching the Sye it was found that a battery had indeed been built, but the birds were flown! Nothing remained but to cross the river without the excitement of performing the operation under fire, and this was a work of much difficulty, and requiring considerable time. It took eight hours of hard work before the long train, which covered nearly two miles of ground, was transported across the river and pulled up the steep bank on to the road on the opposite side. Proceeding three-quarters of a mile further on, the force halted under a "tope" of trees. Alumbagh was only about eight miles distant, and the small column marched on the following morning, Captain Wolseley's company forming the rear-guard, which was destined to be the post of honour. The force had just cleared two topes and debouched on a large plain, when the enemy opened fire upon the rear-guard. The road along which they marched was a "pucka" road, and extended through the centre of a vast plain forming a dead level, and admirably adapted for the operations of cavalry. The enemy's horse galloped up in a threatening attitude, but Wolseley received them with a volley, and they hung back. Some desultory fighting then ensued, and the Enfield proved its efficiency at long ranges. Major Barnston ordered the centre column to fall back and assist Wolseley's company; this was done, and the enemy, after a show of resistance, retreated, deserting two stockades they had constructed. Soon after the long convoy was passed in safety into Alumbagh.

Alumbagh, which stands almost three miles due south of Lucknow, was formerly a palace standing in a beautiful garden, and had been a favourite residence of one of the Queens of Oude. At this time it consisted of a walled enclosure, five hundred yards square, and having a turreted building at the four corners, in each of which were mounted two guns. Its defences consisted of an abattis of felled trees, a trench of earthworks, and the walls were loop-holed, while a 32-pounder at the principal entrance commanded the road; but the place was incapable of resisting artillery, had the rebels possessed sufficient enterprise to attack it. From the turrets of the building in the centre, were visible the domes and minarets of Lucknow, as well as the Residency, to which the garrison cast many longing eyes as the goal of their aspirations. The maintenance of this post proved of essential benefit to the beleaguered garrison, as it was the means of securing their communications with Cawnpore: one set of "kossids" carried correspondence, worded in French, but written in the Greek character, from the Residency—a work of the greatest difficulty and danger, and which only very large bribes could induce natives to undertake—and another set performed the comparatively safe task of conveying messages thence to Cawnpore.

Major Barnston had received orders to return to Cawnpore three days after his arrival at Alumbagh; but Colonel McIntyre, requiring the aid of the column to defend the post, obtained leave for them to remain with him. This officer, who was deficient in enterprise, considered that he was only justified in conforming to the exact letter of his instructions. It was his duty to defend Alumbagh, and consequently, notwithstanding the representations of his officers, he refused to undertake any offensive operations. Thus the enemy, emboldened by the pusillanimity of the British, planted heavy guns within range of the enclosure, and very greatly annoyed the garrison, who, though anxious to sally out and capture or spike the cannon, were not permitted to quit the walls, except on foraging expeditions for the supply of the half-starved herd of camels and elephants.

So passed a short period of inactivity, until, at length, the hearts of the 90th were cheered by the news that when the army, assembling at Cawnpore under the Commander-in-Chief, Sir Colin Campbell, was ready to make a forward momement on Lucknow, they were to form part of the relieving force. Brigadier-General (the late General Sir) Hope Grant crossed the Ganges on the 30th of October, with some four thousand men, and, on the 4th of November, the road to Cawnpore being open, all the waggons, with the camels, elephants, and other animals, which were in a half-starved state, were sent thither from Alumbagh, while the convoy of provisions escorted by Grant was thrown into the place.

On the 9th of November, a semaphore communication was opened with the Lucknow Residency from the roof of the building in the centre of Alumbagh, and the first use to which it was put was to announce, on the following day, the arrival of Mr. Kavanagh, of the Uncovenanted Civil Service, who, disguised as a Native, carried a message from Outram to Sir Colin Campbell. It was a most gallant deed, and Kavanagh received the Victoria Cross, was admitted into the Covenanted Service, and awarded a grant of £2,000.

On the 12th of November Sir Colin Campbell arrived at Alumbagh with some additional troops, and, on the following afternoon, the detachment of the 90th received the welcome order to march out of Alumbagh, and join the 4th Brigade camping outside, under the command of Brigadier Honourable Adrian Hope, of the 93rd Highlanders. The brigade was composed of the 53rd, 93rd, and a battalion of about six hundred men, made up of companies of the 90th, 84th, and Madras Fusiliers, under the command of Major Barnston.

The Alumbagh garrison was relieved by the 75th Regiment, which had seen much hard fighting and suffered heavily at Delhi. The Commander-in-Chief had under his command, for the proposed operations for the relief of the Residency, only some four thousand five hundred and fifty men and thirty-two guns.

A direct route, known as the Cawnpore Road, by which Havelock advanced on the 25th of September, runs due north from Alumbagh, crosses the canal at right angles at a point called the Charbagh ("four gardens") Bridge, and, leading through the heart of the city, stops at the Residency, which abuts on the River Goomtee. The canal, which runs nearly east and west, falls into the river, where it makes a bend towards the Martinière School. From this there is a route through tortuous streets past the Barracks, Secundrabagh, Shah Nujeef, and 32nd Mess-house, to the Motee Mahul and other palaces. The enemy, expecting that Sir Colin Campbell would adopt the same route as Havelock, and pass through the heart of the city, had not strengthened the south side of the Martinière with any care, and Sir Colin resolved to reduce it with artillery fire from the Dilkhoosha ("heart's delight"), a brick palace composed of two rectangular buildings, forming half a square, situated near the banks of the Goomtee, about two miles from Lucknow.

On the 14th of November, about nine a.m., the British Army started on its momentous mission of effecting the final relief of our countrymen, the Fourth Brigade bringing up the rear of the main column. The Dilkoosha and Martinière were carried with small loss, and the latter was occupied by the 90th. Wolseley, on ascending to the roof, had presented to him for the first time a magnificent view of the superb Eastern city spread at his feet.

A little later, the 90th were directed to encamp in a tope in rear of a mud wall, behind which the rebels had taken up a position, and the men were about to dine, when a heavy musketry fire denoted that the enemy was making an attempt, in great force, to retake the position. The battalion were at once hurried off to support the 93rd Highlanders, who were out skirmishing to their left, and, forming line, advanced to where two heavy guns of the Shannon Brigade, under Captain Peel, were pounding away at the enemy. Wolseley, profiting by the halt, was snatching the luxury of a "tub," when he was summoned to the front. Hastily dressing himself, he turned out with his company, and came up just as Peel began firing. As he passed between the guns the charge in one of them exploded—owing to the vent not being " served "—and carried off the head of a sailor. Bullets began to fly about plentifully, and a brass shell rolled down and exploded quite close to Wolseley; round shot were also fired from some

guns posted over the canal, and the 90th received orders
to advance and take them. On reaching the canal,
however, it was found that the rebels had dammed it
at this point, and, instead of being only ankle deep, the
water came up to a man's shoulders. It was now
getting dark, and as Sir Colin determined to bivouac
on the banks of the canal for the night, Captain Wolseley received orders to " picket" his company on the
spot, the rest of the force retiring. Sentries were
placed on the canal bank, and Wolseley enjoined the
greatest silence as they were so close to the rebel sentries posted on the opposite side, in front of Bank's
house, that every word these latter said could be heard.
So passed the night, which was dark and cold, for
though the sun was overpoweringly hot during the
day, the temperature fell very considerably after night-
fall. All the following day, during which the troops
remained stationary, waiting for a fresh supply of
ammunition, Major Barnston's battalion was on picket,
retiring a few yards into a hollow, while musketry fire
raged over their heads. At length, after being on continuous duty for thirty-six hours, Wolseley was relieved,
and he and his men enjoyed a night's rest.

On the following morning (16th of November) the
Commander-in-Chief, having left all his baggage at
Dilkhoosha, crossed the canal and resumed operations.
At ten o'clock, he rode up to Major Barnston, and,
calling the officers of his battalion together, told them
that when fired at in the streets it was best not to stop
and return the fire, but to fix bayonets and rush on.

It was decided that Barnston's battalion was to have the honour of being the first of the main body, but, subsequently, this was changed, and Brigadier Hope arranged that they were to follow the 93rd, the 53rd forming the advance-guard. At twelve o'clock the battalion started, and, crossing the canal, made a detour to the right; soon they were in the thick of the firing, but Barnston pressed on, and reached some houses on the edge of an open space, across which ran a road, now commanded by the guns of the rebels. Captain Wolseley was directed to double across this open, a run of about three hundred yards, and occupy some ruined houses on the other side. This he did amid a perfect shower of shot and bullets. After keeping up a musketry duel from behind the remains of some walls scarcely breast high, Wolseley advanced with the intention of driving out the enemy.

Marching rapidly along a narrow lane, his company led into the town. The enemy retired, keeping up a hot fusillade, and, as they gave ground, the guns were brought forward, Wolseley, with a party of his men, himself assisting in dragging them to the front through the sand, which lay ankle deep. At this time, he says, the enemy's fire was so hot that "the bullets hopped off the tires of the guns like peas off a drum." How any man of the score or so of his company, who assisted him, escaped with their lives was marvellous. Among those who particularly distinguished themselves, were Sergeant Newman (now Quartermaster of the 90th), and another of Wolseley's sergeants who, though

wounded by a musket ball, which carried away his
upper lip, and passed clean through his face, refused to
leave, and remained till the close of the action.

Wolseley was now ordered to protect the flank of
Captain Blunt's troop of Horse Artillery, which came
into action in brilliant style. While the rest of Major
Barnston's battalion advanced towards the Secundrabagh, he pushed past that enclosure, and, leaving it
untaken in the rear, advanced to a line of huts. Here
he remained for the rest of the day, protecting the flank
of the forces engaged in taking the Shah Nujeef, and
fighting from house to house. That night Wolseley's
company bivouacked outside the Secundrabagh. Thus
he had his share of the hard fighting that rendered this
day the most memorable during the operations connected with the Relief.

When he retired in the evening with his company,
and joined the rest of the battalion, he was grieved to
learn that his friend and brother officer, Major Barnston,
had been severely wounded in the thigh. Like so many
others who were wounded, he ultimately sank under the
effects of climate, and, though he spoke cheerfully of his
recovery to the last, was destined never more to draw
his sword in his country's service.

Meanwhile Sir Colin Campbell had been conducting
the main operations of the Army with signal success.
The enemy had fortified the Secundrabagh, a garden,
one hundred and twenty yards square, surrounded by
a high wall of solid masonry, which had been carefully
loopholed. The artillery having effected a breach, the

93rd Highlanders and 4th Sikhs stormed the enclosure, and the rebels, mostly Sepoys of the regular service, were slaughtered like rats in a barn.

In the evening, when the bayonet had completed its fatal work, the men were employed in burying the dead in two large pits. Captain Wolseley, who was engaged on this unpleasant task, mentions as a singular coin-cidence, that when counting the corpses, as they were flung into the pits, it was found that they numbered one thousand eight hundred and fifty-seven, the date of the year; this number was exclusive of others who were killed outside when seeking to make their escape.

From the Secundrabagh, Sir Colin proceeded against the Shah Nujeef, a tomb of one of the kings of Oude, and here ensued the sternest struggle of the Relief. Lieutenant Wynne and Ensign Powell, of the 90th, were wounded, and it was while bringing up the re-mainder of his battalion, that Major Barnston received his death-wound from a shell. Peel now battered the place with his heavy guns, after which the 93rd stormed it.

On the morning of the 17th operations were resumed, and the services of Captain Wolseley during the day were of so marked a character that he had the coveted honour of seeing his name specially mentioned in the Commander-in-Chief's Despatch. This was in con-nection with the attack on the 32nd Mess-house,*

* The late Mr. Martin Gubbins, at this time Financial Commissioner

formerly known as the Khoor-sheyd Munzil, ("Happy Palace") a building of considerable size, defended by a ditch and loop-holed wall.

During the morning of the 17th, Sir Colin was engaged in pressing back the enemy, and, about noon, Captain Peel brought up his guns, and kept up a heavy fire on the Mess-house. After the building had been battered for about three hours, Sir Colin determined to storm, and sent for Captain Wolseley, whom he had known by repute in the Crimea. The Commander-in-Chief, addressing him, said that he had selected him to command the storming party, and that he would be supported by a company of Sikhs and the detachment of his Regiment, which was led by Captain Guise, the officer next in seniority to Major Barnston. On Wolseley's expressing his extreme gratification at being selected for this honourable task, Sir Colin described the work as being surrounded by a ditch, about twelve feet broad and scarped with masonry, and beyond that a loopholed mud wall; there were also drawbridges, but he did not know whether they were down. His instructions were that, in the event of the drawbridges being up, and his not being able to effect

---

of Lucknow, in his "Mutinies in Oude," describes the Mess-house in the following terms :—"Its structure is massive; all the windows on the ground-floor are furnished with strong iron gratings, and it is surrounded by a moat all round, passable only at the two entrances, of which the principal immediately faces us. All those windows are bricked-up inside the iron grating for three parts of their height, and the masonry is most carefully loopholed."

an entrance, he was to leave his men under cover and return and report to him.*

Wolseley left the Chief, and proceeded to carry out his instructions. Captain Peel, who was battering the Mess-house with his heavy guns, was requested to cease firing, but just as Wolseley gave the order, "Double," to his men, Peel, characteristically turned to Sir Colin Campbell, and asked leave just to give "one more broadside." The favour granted, Wolseley, amid a hot fire from the neighbouring buildings, out-stripping his men with the fierce energy that distinguished him in the assault of Myat-toon's position, ran over the intervening space; arrived under the garden wall, he halted to get breath, and then clambered over it. Inside the garden he found many matchlockmen, who fired at him, but, though the bullets flew about him, he ran on unscathed and entered the Mess-house without opposition. As he gained the drawbridge, which was down, he called to the bugler to sound the advance to show that he had done the work entrusted to him, and then bounded up the steps to the roof of the building, on which he planted the British flag. The enemy opened fire from every

---

* We have been assured by an officer of the 90th, who accompanied Wolseley on this occasion, that the Commander-in-Chief promised him the Victoria Cross before he dismissed him from his presence.

While on this subject of the Victoria Cross, we may mention that, during the Crimean War, the late Sir W. Gordon, of "Gordon's Battery," recommended Captain Wolseley for the distinction, for his conspicuous gallantry on the 7th of June, and on the occasion of his receiving his wound, on the 30th of August.

gun they could bring to bear on the Mess-house, and so heavy was the fire that twice the flag was struck down, only to be replaced, and, finally, he had to retire with his men under cover.*

At this time Captain Irby came up with his company of the 90th, and Wolseley directed him to take some houses to the left, while he proceeded to attack those to the right, the fire being heavy from both directions.

* Mr. Gubbins, who, in company with General Havelock, witnessed this exploit from their post of observation, the roof of the Chuttur Munzil Palace, thus graphically describes it :—" It is now three o'clock, and if the enemy have any men concealed in that massive pile, the Mess-house, we shall soon see, for the red-coats are approaching ; they are moving down in regular order along the road leading from the Shah Nujeef, and now are lost to view. Presently a part of them are seen advancing in skirmishing order. They have reached the enclosing wall ; they are over it, through the shrubbery, and now the leading officer enters at the door which we have been watching ; and while a larger body follow, rushing at a double up the building, he reappears upon the roof, and presently a British ensign floats on the right-hand tower of the Khoorsheyd Munzil. It is Captain Wolseley, of the 90th, who has placed it there.

" The building was indeed, as we supposed, abandoned, but the fire is so heavy from the Tara Kotee and adjacent buildings that it is no easy work that our noble fellows have to do. See! the ensign is struck down, and now it is again raised and fixed more firmly than before. But again a shot strikes it down, and probably the staff is damaged, for they have taken it down through the garden to that group of officers—probably Sir Colin himself and staff, whose caps are visible inside the enclosing compound wall. To the right, this wall is lined by the captors of the Mess-house, and a heavy fire of musketry, with occasional shot and shell, is directed from the Kaiser Bagh upon them ; and now they cross the wall, enter the Tara Kotee enclosure, charge up its main avenue, and are hid from us by the trees."

Irby succeeded in occupying the Tara Kothie,* or con-
servatory, without meeting with any opposition, though
during the latter part of the day he had hard work in
holding the position.

And now one more task remained—the occupation of
the Motee Mahul,† situated on the banks of the Goomtee, the last post which separated the besieged and their
deliverers. While Irby held the Tara Kothie, Wolseley
proceeded to the attack of the Motee Mahul, and the
success he achieved with only his company, forms one
of the extraordinary episodes of the War. Quitting the
garden of the Mess-house, he ran the gauntlet across
the road under a heavy fire, but, on arriving at the
Motee Mahul, found that the gateway was built up and
loopholed. He was met by a volley, but proceeded
with his company to subdue the enemy's fire, and, at

---

* Tara means " stars," and Kothie, " pucka," or permanent building.

† This Motee Mahul (" Pearl of Palaces "), which, like all similar
edifices, is enclosed within a high wall, is one of the most spacious and
graceful buildings of its kind in Lucknow. Here the king was wont
to regale his European guests; and it was within a walled passage, on
the south side of this enclosure, that, on the 25th of September, during
Havelock's advance, our wounded, under escort of the 90th, were left;
and here fell many gallant officers and men, including Major Cooper
and Captain Crump, of the Artillery, killed; also Colonel Campbell,
of the 90th, who received a severe wound in the leg, which necessitated
amputation, from the effects of which he expired on the 13th of
November. Close to the Motee Mahul stood a building, called
Martin's House, the enclosure of which was separated from the
advanced garden post of the Lucknow garrison by a small open space,
swept by the fire of the Kaiser Bagh, distant about four hundred and
fifty yards.

length by dint of hard fighting, won the loopholes, though with the loss of many of his brave fellows. He now sent back an officer with a few men, to bring up crowbars and pickaxes to force the newly-made brickwork of the gateway. This was a service of some danger, as the road was still swept by musketry and canister. In the meantime, Wolseley kept his company as much under cover as possible. Soon the men were seen returning with the tools, and private Andrews, a gallant fellow who had been Wolseley's servant in the Crimea, ran out from under shelter to show his comrades the way across. No sooner, however, had he darted into the street, than he was shot through the body from one of the loopholes. Wolseley had a particular regard for this fine fellow, and, though he was lying out in the street within five or six yards of the loophole from whence he had been shot, sprang out and bore him back in his arms. As he was carrying Andrews, a Pandy took deliberate aim at the officer, but the bullet passed through the body of the soldier.*

At this time, while Wolseley was busy with his men in knocking a hole in the wall of the Motee Mahul, Mr. Kavanagh arrived on the scene and offered to guide him to a place where an entrance could be effected.

---

* Andrews, we may observe, still lives, and, for his services and wounds, enjoys the magnificent pension of eightpence per diem. Like the greater portion of the 90th, of Crimean and Indian Mutiny days, he was a cockney, as the regiment recruited largely in the metropolis; and, in the opinion of Wolseley, your Londoner is peculiarly adapted for light infantry work, by reason of his superior intelligence and general smartness.

Wolseley gladly closed with the proposal, and, leaving injunctions with his subalterns to get on as fast as they could with the work in hand, accompanied Kavanagh on their perilous mission. Proceeding down the street about one hundred yards with the " whish" of a rifle-bullet occasionally ringing in their ears, they passed through broken walls, and gardens, and deserted courts, but their endeavours to find an entrance into the palace were unsuccessful. After an absence of about ten minutes, during which Kavanagh found that all the entrances he knew of were built up, they returned, and arrived just as Ensign Haig was wriggling through an aperture knocked in the wall.

Soon the hole was sufficiently enlarged for Wolseley and all his men to make their way into a courtyard of the Motee Mahul, whence, proceeding into the Palace, they drove the enemy from room to room, and from yard to yard, firing and receiving their fire as the fight progressed towards the river, on the banks of which the Palace was built. At length they drove them all out of this great agglomeration of buildings, and, closely following the fugitives, forced them into the Goomtee, where a number of them were shot as they tried to swim across.*

Having cleared the Motee Mahul, Wolseley proceeded with his company, which nobly responded to the calls

---

* Kavanagh says of Wolseley, in his work " How I Won the Victoria Cross :"—" Captain Wolseley, who delighted in dash and danger, fell upon the enemy as they tried to escape, and in half an hour he was seen on the top of the inner buildings, waving the British banner."

made upon them by their chief, to force his way into the Residency itself. Now it so happened that the 90th, which, under the command of Colonel Purnell, the successor of the lamented Colonel Campbell, formed a portion of the Lucknow garrison, held the most advanced post in the Residency; and, just at this time, a company of the Regiment made a sortie, so that, strange to relate, the first of the relieved and their deliverers to join hands, were the officers and men of the gallant 90th Light Infantry! It was a singular coincidence, and "terque, quaterque, beatus," to borrow a Virgilian phrase, was Captain Wolseley, in being the undoubted claimant to the distinction of first effecting a junction with the heroic garrison of the Lucknow Residency.

And now the three noble chiefs, Campbell, Outram, and Havelock, at length met, and there was presented the group delineated by the artist, Mr. Barker, in his great painting of the Relief of Lucknow.*

Fortune had certainly smiled on Wolseley. It was so at the Quarries, when he participated in almost the only successful assault of the English Army, and now on this memorable occasion, the "fickle jade" again favoured her favourite child; on his part, this young

---

* The engraving of this painting, with the heads of Hope Grant, Mansfield, Napier, Inglis, Greathed, Peel, Adrian Hope, Alison, Little, David Russell, Hope Johnstone, Norman, Anson, Hodson, Probyn, Watson, Kavanagh, and other gallant soldiers, is well known to old Indians. The painting itself fetched, on the 24th of April, 1875, at the Manley Hall Sale, £1,018.

soldier eagerly seized each opportunity for winning her favours as it was presented to him, and, by his judgment and impetuous valour, justified the choice.

All was now gratulation and hand-shaking ; and the British soldiers and sailors of the relieving force eagerly greeted their comrades and the women and children they had dared so many perils to rescue from the clutches of the rebellious Sepoys surrounding them. The detachment of the 90th, which lately had Major Barnston for its leader, welcomed their comrades, who, embarking in the 'Himalaya,' had marched up-country with Sir James Outram, and earned for the old Regiment immortal renown by their bearing throughout those trying days in September, when Havelock forced his way through the heart of Lucknow with only two thousand six hundred men. Wolseley now learnt, with sincere regret, of the death of Colonel Campbell, who had expired only four days before, and also of other friends and gallant soldiers of humbler rank. The loss sustained by the Relieving Army, which only numbered four thousand five hundred and fifty men, between the 14th and 25th of November, was ten officers and one hundred and twelve men killed, and thirty-five officers (of whom three died) and three hundred and seventy-nine rank and file wounded.

It will be allowed that Wolseley had good reason to anticipate the congratulations and thanks of the Commander-in-Chief for his conduct, but what was his astonishment on learning from his Brigadier, the Hon. Adrian Hope, that Sir Colin was furious with him for having exceeded the letter of instructions, in that when he was only ordered to take the Mess-house, he actually, of his own motion, had driven the enemy out of the Motee Mahul. The Brigadier advised him to keep out of the way as the Chief was asking for him, and he never saw a man more enraged in his life.

Captain Wolseley's company passed the night of the 17th of November in the Shah Nujeef, where the Commander-in-Chief and his Staff had taken up their quarters; the building was commanded by the enemy, who still occupied the Kaiser Bagh, from which they kept up a cannonade, but the British soldiers slept the sleep of the weary, having learned to disregard such interruptions provided they were not too personal.

* Wolseley's adventures on this 17th November did not end when he effected a junction with Captain Tinling's company of his regiment. Being desirous of showing in a practical form his regard for his old comrades, he had brought with him some tobacco, which he distributed among the officers and men of this company, to whom it was a real godsend. But there was still one desideratum which was requisite to make the gallant fellows happy, and that was—rum. This also their thoughtful comrade had not forgotten, but the liquor, being bulky, had been left behind at the place from which he had started in the morning, when proceeding to storm the Mess-house. It was now between six and eight in the evening, and getting dark, but Wolseley, though his exertions had been of a sufficiently arduous character to tire most men, started off on his charitable errand, with four or five men, who volunteered to accompany him. At length, having secured the rum, he slung it on a pole between two men, and commenced his return march. It was pitch-dark as he passed through the Mess-house gardens, and suddenly, as he was proceeding along, himself leading the way, he heard a scream. Turning round, he found that one of the pole-bearers had been run through the body by a Pandy, who was prowling about

After the warning he had received from his Brigadier, Wolseley, on the following morning, kept out of the way of the " Lord Sahib," but Sir Colin espied him, and calling to him, began to administer a severe 'wigging.' He commenced by asking him what he meant by exceeding his instructions; that he had ordered him to take the Mess-house, and how dared he attack the Motee Mahul ? He then told him that he was very angry with him on the previous night; indeed he did not think he was ever so much incensed against any man in his life, and it was lucky for him that he

the grounds, and whom he had himself just passed. In the dark Wolseley lost his way, and it was some hours before he gained the garden of the Furreed Buksh, where he was told his brother officers were assembled, in a summer-house in the centre of the grounds. Proceeding there, he put his head in and glanced round the room, where he saw a number of men sitting at a table in the centre, but he did not recognise any of them. As he was going away, one of the number, Captain (now Sir Harry) Goodricke, called out : " Why, that's Wolseley." He turned, and then recognised his old mess-mates, who were so altered by privation and constant duty that, at first, he actually did not know them.

An amusing circumstance happened during the night. Wolseley heard Lieutenant Carter raging and swearing at some one, and, on inquiring the exciting cause of his subaltern's wrath, learned that, in the dark, some "beastly nigger" had attempted to place one of the legs of a charpoy, or light wooden bedstead, on his stomach. Lieutenant Carter naturally resented this indignity, but the language in which he couched his protest was far from parliamentary, or complimentary to the native in question. After a laugh at this slight *contretemps*, the officers went to sleep. On awaking in the morning, Carter's consternation may be imagined when he discovered that the "beastly nigger" of the previous night was none other than His Excellency the Commander-in-Chief, the lord of many legions.

could not be found. The ire of the old Chief now began to cool, and his tone became half jocular. He invited Wolseley by a gesticulation to pace up and down with him, and, after warning him against the heinousness of exceeding instructions, the veteran, who could not but admire gallantry, such as he himself had displayed throughout his fifty years' service, ended by congratulating him on the courage and ability he had displayed, and expressed his intention to recommend him for promotion.

Sir Colin Campbell having resolved to withdraw from Lucknow, contrary to the advice of both Outram and Havelock, the 90th and other Regiments were engaged in making a direct road from that portion of the Residency where the ladies and children had been confined, to the ground occupied by the Relieving Force. In order to effect this, walls and houses were broken down, and all open spaces between Martin's House and the Motee Mahul and Secundrabagh, were screened from fire by means of shutters, doors, and anything that came to hand. In the evening, after being thus engaged all day, Wolseley's company and the remainder of the detachment were sent back, and placed on picket on the side of the road close to the Shah Nujeef. On the 19th commenced the withdrawal to Dilkhoosha of the ladies and children, who numbered about five hundred, and some of the sick and wounded, one thousand five hundred more.

The 90th pickets had received orders to wait till the garrison had passed out, and cover the retreat as far as

Secundrabagh, a duty which the detachment performed with perfect order and regularity. At midnight of the 22nd, leaving all lights still burning, Outram's soldiers marched silently out of the post they had so long defended, being followed by Hope's Brigade, which had been quartered in the Motee Mohul, the 90th bringing up the rear, while the sullen boom of the cannon told that the enemy, unaware of what had happened, were still firing into the position which was now unoccupied. On arriving at Secundrabagh, the Force continued its movement of retreat in the same order towards Dilkhoosha, which was reached at half-past three in the morning. At noon of the 23rd of November, the detachment drew up in line opposite the Martinière, and the non-effectives, baggage, and ammunition, forming an immense convoy, were passed through it.*

Early in the morning of the 24th of November, the detachment paraded, and Sir Colin's General Order of the previous day, complimenting the Relieving Army, was read to the men; and then, as they were about to rejoin the head-quarters of the Regiment, under the command of Colonel Purnell, Brigadier Hope rode up,

---

* Captain Wolseley was witness to a curious and suggestive scene that happened on this night. Captain Magennis, of the 90th, was in charge of some State prisoners of high rank, including the King of Oude's brother. As they passed, Wolseley, whose company was the last picket in the direction of Lucknow, heard Magennis ask a sergeant where was his prisoner. "Oh, Sir, he wouldn't come on, and so I just shot him," replied the non-commissioned officer, who seemed to think it the most natural, as it was the easiest, way of curing a fit of obstinacy.

and addressed the officers and men on leaving his brigade. This the gallant brigadier did in a graceful, manly speech, which was responded to by three hearty cheers. The 90th was attached to Outram's Division, which it was decided should remain at Alumbagh. The object of this occupation was three-fold, viz., to avoid the appearance of having abandoned Oude; to keep the insurgents around Lucknow in check; and to secure a point on which our advance for the re-conquest of Oude might be made.

The entire Army halted at Alumbagh on the 26th of November, and, on the following day, the Commander-in-Chief commenced his march for Cawnpore with General Grant's Division, and the whole of the sick and wounded, and Lucknow refugees.

Sir James Outram took up a position about one thousand five hundred yards from Alumbagh on the vast plain which, smooth as a billiard table, extends without a break to the Bunnee Bridge. The Alumbagh enclosure was one of his outposts, as were also the neighbouring villages, which were all fortified; and, at these posts, strongly occupied by our troops, desultory fighting took place almost daily. The Division—which numbered only four thousand four hundred of all arms, inclusive of those at Bunnee—consisted of Her Majesty's 5th, 78th, 84th, and 90th Regiments, and Captain Brasyer's Ferozepore Regiment of Sikhs, eight hundred strong, the whole being organized into two brigades, under Colonels Hamilton (78th), and Stisted (64th). The Artillery, under the command of Major

Vincent Eyre, included the batteries of Captain Maude (Royal Artillery), and Captain Olpherts (Bengal Artillery), and many guns of position, forming a total of about forty pieces. The cavalry consisted of Major Robertson's battalion of Military Train, which now acted as light horse, and some of the 12th Native Irregulars, the whole numbering not more than two hundred and fifty sabres. But any deficiency of numbers was made up by the gallantry of these veteran soldiers, the remarkable capacity of the staff and other officers, and, more than aught else, by the *prestige* attaching to the name of the Commander, to which doubtless, was due the fact that a force of little more than four thousand men, was able successfully to defend an open position against the attacks of one hundred thousand rebels, of whom half were trained soldiers, for this was the number of armed men Outram, on one occasion, assured Wolseley were assembled in Lucknow and its neighbourhood according to reliable information he had received.

Outram did not think it beneath his dignity to seek to make his soldiers regard him with personal affection, as well as with that respect which he inspired in the minds of every one who came within his influence; rarely indeed has any character afforded such an admixture of dignity and amiability, of heroism and gentleness, of a high and noble ambition and a yet loftier and purer self-sacrifice, of which his whole life afforded many memorable instances.* Every officer

* Such high authorities as Lord Napier of Magdala, Sir Garnet

and man of the 90th loved the General, who, in return, showed his appreciation of their regard by numerous acts of kindness and thoughtfulness. Among such traits, Wolseley mentions that he would, when visiting the Alumbagh or other outposts, read out to the officer in command any intelligence he had received from Cawnpore or Calcutta in a sufficiently loud tone of voice for the men about to hear the news. His concern also for the honour and interests of the officers under his command was remarkable, and he would never desist pushing the claims of such as he considered had been overlooked or insufficiently rewarded. Outram possessed one of the attributes of genius in the discernment he displayed in the choice of his staff and other officers,* while a notable instance of his far-seeing

Wolseley, and Sir Vincent Eyre are agreed as to Outram's distinction as a General. Lord Napier once said of him :—" Of all those whose names are borne in the annals of the history of India, or enshrined in the hearts of its people, there is none more noble, none more worthy of love, admiration, and gratitude than Sir James Outram." Sir Garnet Wolseley has declared that Outram was "the finest soldier he ever served under ;" and Sir V. Eyre says, " As a commander in the field, he possessed a rare and most valuable combination of pluck and caution, and he knew exactly the time for bringing each quality into play."

* His brigadiers, Hamilton and Stisted, were fighting men like their gallant chief, and Vincent Eyre had already earned a great reputation as the man who had achieved the relief of the garrison of Arrah at a time when a larger force had been almost annihilated. Maude was a fine artillery officer, and Olpherts was distinguished for his reckless personal valour, which had earned him the *soubriquet* of " Hell-fire Jack." No eulogy is needed of Outram's Chief Engineer, Colonel Robert Napier, who had given evidence of his military capacity

and statesmanlike judgment, was displayed in the just view he took of the amalgamation of the Royal and Indian armies, and the masterly Minute in which he enforced his opinions.

Almost daily there was fighting at the outposts near Alumbagh, but the enemy shrank from continuous and determined attacks in full force on the standing camp, and there was no rebel leader of sufficient enterprise to attempt to repeat the tactics of Cawnpore. The camp had Alumbagh in front, the small fort of Jellalabad to the right front, some villages to the left front, and outposts at villages on the right and left rear; a strong detachment also was at Bunnee Bridge, about eight miles on the road to Cawnpore, under command of Colonel Fisher.

Wolseley had not been long at Alumbagh when he was ordered to do outpost duty at the fort of Jellalabad, which was decidedly the pleasantest post in the position, some ten miles in circumference, which Sir James Outram undertook to defend with his small Division. Jellalabad was an old mud fort of some extent, and was formerly used as a depository for the powder of the Oude Force, but had fallen into decay and disrepair. The wall which surrounded the enclosure, was of great thickness, and studded at unequal intervals with bastions and towers, which commanded an uninterrupted

during the Sutlej and Punjaub Campaigns, and especially at Mooltan; while during the advance on Lucknow and in the defence of the Residency, he established his fame as a scientific engineer and able leader.

view of the surrounding country. After the recent hard service before Lucknow, the week's tour of duty in the Jellalabad fort, with its well-wooded and picturesque enclosure, was regarded in the light of a pleasant interlude. On the north side of the fort was a jheel, or large piece of water, the favourite resort of wild fowl, to which the officers would occasionally resort with their guns, and agreeably vary the regimental fare. To place the fort in a state capable of resisting a sudden attack, Brigadier Napier, who was busily employed putting the outposts in the extended position in a proper condition of defence, erected a battery at the principal entrance, and repaired the breach made by our gunners during the advance on Lucknow.

In the middle of December, a convoy arrived from Cawnpore, and then Wolseley and his brother-officers who sailed in the ' Transit,' learned that the kit which they had deposited there, had all been burnt by the Gwalior mutineers who first defeated General Windham —" Redan Windham," as his admirers called him—and then besieged him in his entrenchments. Thus for the second time, Wolesley was a heavy loser by the chances of war.

On the 20th of December, information was brought to Sir James Outram by his spies, that the rebels intended surrounding his position, with the object of cutting off his supplies and intercepting his communications with Bunnee ; and that with this view they had taken up a position at Budroop. He also learned on the following day, that they had been reinforced to a strength of four thousand infantry, four hundred cavalry, and four guns. Outram determined to anticipate them and strike a blow, and, at half-past two, a.m., of the 22nd of December, a column of a thousand men, including cavalry, and two guns, marched out under his personal command to attack the enemy, who, having left a space of about half a mile intervening between their position and the gardens skirting the canal and the Dilkhoosha, Outram, seeing his advantage, resolved to take them by surprise, and cut off their retreat from Lucknow.

It was very cold and rather dark when Captain Wolseley proceeded with his Regiment, which formed the right column of the attacking force. Favoured by a heavy mist, Outram was enabled to approach quite close to the left flank of the enemy, whose cavalry vedettes challenged, and then, firing their carbines, galloped off to the main body. Outram gave the order to deploy, and with a loud hurrah, the right column, under the command of Colonel Purnell, of the 90th, charged the enemy in line, and, in spite of a heavy fire of grape and musketry, carried the position with a rush. The left column, under Colonel Guy, of the 5th Fusiliers, was equally successful, and soon the rebels were in full retreat across the plain, pursued by the cavalry, until they found refuge in a village, from which they opened a heavy fire of grape and musketry. Olpherts now came into action with his guns, and speedily dislodged the enemy, who, changing their line of retreat, endeavoured to reach the city by the Dilkhoosha. The

Military Train, detached to make a flank movement, followed them up so rapidly that they dispersed their cavalry, and drove their guns into a ravine, where they were captured. The British loss was only three killed and seven wounded, that of the enemy being fifty or sixty killed, besides four guns and ten ammunition waggons, with elephants and baggage, which fell into our hands. Outram's arrangements were rewarded with the success they merited; the surprise had been complete, and in the village were found the children and women cooking their *chupatties*, or oat-cakes. The houses were fired after the non-combatants were driven away, and the column returned, the men carrying vegetables and dragging or leading away all the live stock they could lay their hands on, such as goats, sheep, and bullocks. As they were moving off, a large body of the enemy advanced towards the burning village, but finding that they were too late to be of assistance, halted and retraced their steps to Lucknow. Before noon Outram had returned to his camp, having taught the Natives a severe lesson regarding the danger of attempting to interfere with his communications.

On the following day, Captain Wolseley proceeded to Cawnpore, with his company, to escort supplies. The journey occupied three days, the force marching about fifteen miles a-day. The first night the escort halted at Bunnee, up to which point there was desultory fighting with the enemy, The second night they halted at Busserutgunge, a walled village with a high road running through the centre. On arriving at Cawnpore,

Wolseley learnt with deep sorrow the death of Major Barnston,* who had been wounded five weeks before.

The escort returned immediately to Alumbagh with the convoy, and, on New Year's Day, there was a great exhibition of athletic sports on the open space to the left of the camp, Sir James Outram and the officers having subscribed liberally for prizes for the men.

On the 12th of January, 1858, the rebels made a most determined assault on Sir James Outram's position.   On the previous evening he had received information from his spies that the enemy would attack at sunrise on the following morning. He, therefore, made the necessary dispositions, and, at daybreak, the troops breakfasted, and were held in readiness for immediate service.

About sunrise, large masses of the enemy, calculated by Outram to amount " at the lowest estimate to thirty thousand men," were seen on the left front, and they

---

* Though young in years, Major Barnston had displayed during his service in the Crimea and India, many of the qualities we recognize as peculiarly the attributes of those who are leaders of men. Calm and composed in the presence of imminent danger, he possessed a thorough mastery of his profession, and inspired complete confidence in all those placed under his command. In peace time he had gained the love of his men by his kindly manner and thoughtful consideration for their comfort and well-being ; and, in the stern ordeal of battle, recognizing in him a superior genius, they would, at his bidding, have followed him anywhere. Among his brother officers Major Barnston was beloved as an amiable and accomplished companion, and respected as a high-bred gentleman and first-rate officer. Wolseley sincerely mourned his death, and felt that in him he had lost his dearest and most intimate friend.

gradually surrounded the whole front and flanks of the position, extending from opposite the left rear outpost, to the right near Jellalabad, a distance of at least six miles. As soon as their movements were sufficiently developed, Outram marshalled his small array, which was decreased by the absence, on convoy duty, of five hundred and thirty men and four guns, in front of their lines—two brigades, the right mustering seven hundred and thirteen Europeans, and the left, with which was Wolseley's company, seven hundred and thirty-three bayonets, with one hundred of Brasyer's Sikhs. Fighting commenced all along the line about half-past eight a.m., and it was not until four p.m. that the enemy, who suffered very considerably from the fire of the guns, finally withdrew, and returned to Lucknow or to their original positions in the gardens and villages in front of the British camp.

Again, only four days later, the rebels made a determined attempt to overwhelm the small band of Englishmen whom it must have been most galling to them to see entrenched within a few miles of the great stronghold of rebeldom.

Captain Wolseley was on picket at the left-front village, on the morning of the 16th of January, when the enemy were seen advancing in great numbers. They made repeated attempts throughout the day to carry the village, but were driven back with severe loss by the small force under the command of Major Gordon, 75th Regiment. After dark they assembled in great strength n front of the village, and, about eight o'clock, "screwing their courage to the sticking-place," advanced to the attack to the inspiriting calls of many bugles, sounding the "assembly," the "advance," and the "double." They were distinctly heard encouraging one another with "Chelow-bhye," (go on quick, brother,) and other exclamations by which the "mild Hindoo" is wont to prompt his neighbour to deeds of gallantry, and keep up his own failing heart. They occupied a "tope" of trees, to the left of the village, and advanced into the open as if to carry the battery of three guns, which as yet made no sign. On they came in dense array, but the guns and the infantry reserved their fire; at length, when they had approached to within seventy yards of the position, they were met by discharges of grape and shell from the battery, and a volley from one hundred rifles delivered with fatal precision. Still they hesitated, thus giving time to reload to their opponents, whom they might have annihilated, had they mustered only sufficient pluck to charge at this critical moment, when only one hundred British bayonets intervened between them and the revenge they thirsted for. That hesitancy of a moment was fatal. A second volley of grape and rifle bullets swept through their ranks, when they broke and fled in the utmost confusion, carrying away, according to custom, most of their killed and wounded. "After they had retired," says Lieutenant Herford, "we wandered over the ground near the topes, and found a few dead bodies, some pools of blood, and heaps of shoes, which had been kicked off, lying about everywhere."

On the same morning the enemy also made a sudden attack on the Jellalabad picket, led by a Hindoo devotee, who was attired as Hunoomân, the " monkey god," but were repulsed.

An attack was expected on the 22nd, but the day passed without a shot being fired on either side ; and so the month of January "dragged its slow length along," and February was ushered in. The two enemies from whose attacks the gallant Alumbagh garrison most suffered at this time were *ennui* and dust. The former was irksome, after the excitement of long marches and hard campaigning ; but the latter was unbearable, and caused the greatest discomfort, almost amounting to positive misery. The dust, which lay some six inches deep, was blown in great clouds and eddies, which swept over the plain, searching out every chink and crevice of the flimsy tents, and filled the mouth and eyes and entered into the composition of every dish.

Nothing of importance occurred until the 21st of February, when the enemy made the long threatened " grand attack," which was not only carefully designed, but was so well matured that had they evinced determination the Alumbagh garrison would have been hard pressed. The Moulvie, Mansoob Ali, and the Begum, Huzrut Mahul, wife of the ex-King of Oude, agreed to set aside their differences for that day ; and the Oude local troops, and the regulars, entered heart and soul into the matter. The plan was to surround the British Force by making a detour to the rear of Alumbagh.

When the circle was completed, which their great numerical superiority would enable them to accomplish, they were to close upon their prey, and desperate assaults were to be made simultaneously at five or six different points, while demonstrations against the intermediate portions of the wide-extended *enceinte* were to prevent a concentration of Outram's troops, and, at the same time, distract his attention and embarrass his defensive operations. But Outram was not the man to wait quietly on the defensive and allow the enemy to develop their plans. He had received intelligence the night before of the intended attack; and, though he could not learn their detailed plan of operation, he intuitively guessed what it would be, and took steps to baffle the designs of the rebel leaders.

He moved out with cavalry and guns to meet both their right and left advances, taking care to let them complete their intended circle till it formed a horseshoe, when he attacked with spirit, and a rout ensued. Meantime some sharp fighting took place at Alumbagh, where Wolseley was stationed. Trenches and zigzags connected the centre building with the front gateway and the corner towers, and the enclosure had now become a strong position. The first intimation the garrison received of the advance of the enemy, was the firing of heavy guns at three in the morning. A few shots struck the centre building, and soon the whole camp turned out, and every man was at his post.

At seven o'clock the enemy came on at all points, liuing every shrub and tree where they could get cover.

But they were deficient in spirit and dispersed under the musketry fire and discharges of grape.

Towards evening the enemy withdrew, and the rebel commanders confessed to the Durbar that their losses were between four hundred and five hundred; but their intentions were praiseworthy and their preparations complete, for Outram's spies reported that they had scaling ladders all ready for storming Alumbagh.

Sir James Outram went out with some cavalry and guns on the 24th of February, and, again, on the following day, proceeded beyond Jellalabad, when he encountered and defeated the enemy, who had come out under the leadership of the Begum. During the night the rebels attacked all along the British front and left flank, where Wolseley's company was posted, and were bold enough to fire grape from the "tope" on the left front picket where the fighting took place on the 16th of January. They, however, soon retreated, and this was the last time the Alumbagh Force, as such, received molestation from the enemy.

In the meantime, Sir Colin Campbell had been organizing his "grand army"* for the reconquest of

* On the 2nd of March the effective force consisted of: Artillery, one thousand six hundred and thirteen officers and men; Engineers, two thousand and two; Cavalry, three thousand six hundred and thirteen; Infantry, eleven thousand nine hundred and forty; Total— nineteen thousand seven hundred and seventy-one. On the 5th of March it was joined by General Franks' Division, numbering five thousand eight hundred and ninety-three effectives, the Goorka por-

Lucknow and Oude, and on learning that Rose's and Whitlock's columns were well on their march towards Jhansi, he pushed his troops across the Ganges, and arrived at Buntara, about four miles from Alumbagh, on the 1st of March. During the latter part of February, Generals Grant and Franks had been operating in Oude, and, on the morning of the 2nd of March, Sir Colin, who had visited Sir James Outram on the previous day, moved up from Buntara to Dilkhoosha with the Second Division of his Army under General Lugard, and the cavalry commanded by General Grant, who had joined him on the previous day. In the meantime, Jellalabad had been formed into a commissariat depôt on the largest scale, there being attached to the advancing army no less than sixteen thousand camels, a siege train park covering a square of four hundred or five hundred yards, with twelve thousand oxen, and a following of sixty thousand non-combatants.

Since the Commander-in-Chief had evacuated Lucknow, taking with him the women and children of the Residency, the rebels had fortified the city with no little care and skill. Behind the canal they had thrown up earthworks, while the Martinière, Secundrabagh, Shah Nujeef, Mess-house, and Motee Mahul, were fortified; the Kaiser Bagh also was a perfect citadel, and the streets and houses had been loop-holed.

tion of which, three thousand bayonets, joined the Nepaul Maharajah when he arrived before Lucknow with his division, nine thousand strong.

Between the 3rd and 4th of March, the Third Division, under General Walpole, came up to Alumbagh, and, at the same time, Sir James Outram was directed to take command of the *corps d'armée*, which the Commander-in-Chief had determined to detach across the Goomtee to operate on Lucknow from that side. And so the 90th was parted from the General with whom they had associated, to their mutual satisfaction, during many months, and whose name will ever be held in affectionate reverence by every officer and man of the Regiment, who were engaged in the defence of Alumbagh.* Even after thus was severed the connection that had been cemented on the battle-field and the bivouac, the good General showed that he did not forget the gallant fellows who had fought and bled under him, for he used regularly to send the 90th a liberal supply of newspapers and periodicals for the use of the men.

* The garrison of Jellalabad in Afghanistan, gained the title of "illustrious" from Lord Ellenborough for their gallant defence of a position protected by walls and bastions. Though the Afghans are a fiercer race than the natives of India, yet the 37th Bengal Native Infantry—which mutinied in 1857—repeatedly encountered and defeated them; and Akbar Khan, in his great effort against the Jellalabad garrison, on the 7th of April, 1842, only mustered six thousand warriors to his standard, while Outram's force was assailed by thirty thousand, including some of the finest regiments of the Sepoy army. Again, the Afghans were unprovided with artillery, while the Lucknow rebels had among them guns and experienced artillerymen. Sir Vincent Eyre, in a letter addressed some years ago to the author, then employed on a biographical article on Sir James Outram, says:— "Outram's prolonged occupation of Alumbagh plain, comprising a

On the afternoon of the 6th of March, the 90th left their old camping ground at Alumbagh, and started to join the Commander-in-Chief at Dilkhoosha. The night was very dark, and the road bad, and, being encumbered with baggage and ammunition, it was not until the morning, after a march of nearly twelve hours, that they reached the camping ground marked out for them in rear of the artillery park. Scarcely had they arrived, and were counting upon breakfast and a little rest, than they received fresh orders to move again, as it was decided that the 90th should be brigaded* with the 42nd, 93rd, and 4th Punjaub Rifles,

frontage of two miles, and a circuit of seven, with a small army of occupation never exceeding three thousand five hundred men, within cannon range of Lucknow, to hold in check an enemy mustering one hundred thousand strong within the walls, was a masterpiece of cautious warfare, to which justice has never yet been done, because his precarious position there, in obedience to Sir Colin Campbell's commands, has never up to this moment been properly understood." Again, Lord Napier of Magdala, when unveiling the Outram statue at Calcutta, said in reference to this defence of Alumbagh :—" No achievement in the events of 1857 surpassed in skill and resolution the maintenance of the position of Alumbagh with a mere handful of troops against overwhelming numbers, well supplied with artillery. There were no walls or ramparts, merely an open camp, protected by a few well-selected intrenched out-posts, and a scanty line of bayonets, ever ready, day and night, to repel attack." The Alumbagh Force and its heroic chief have never had justice rendered to them, for their defence of this position.

* This Brigade formed part of the Second Division under Major-General Lugard, which consisted of the above Brigade, and the Third Brigade, composed of the 34th, 38th, and 53rd Regiments.

forming the 4th Brigade, under the command of their old Brigadier, the Hon. Adrian Hope. On the following day, the whole Regiment was sent on picket about five p.m., with orders to line some of the walls surrounding the Dilkhoosha Park.

During the morning of the 9th of March a heavy fire was maintained on the Martinière, by six mortars and ten heavy guns and howitzers, manned by the artillery and sailors ;* and General Lugard received instructions to hold his Division in readiness to carry the position in the afternoon. The Commander-in-Chief's orders specified that "the men employed in the attack will use nothing but the bayonet. They are absolutely forbidden to fire a shot till the position is won." For this duty the 42nd Highlanders and 4th Punjaubees were selected, supported by the 53rd and 90th, which was relieved from the position it had occupied in the Mahomed Bagh, near the Dilkhoosha, by the 97th, from General Franks' Division. The first intimation the 90th received that they were to be specially engaged, was the order to go to dinner at twelve o'clock ; and, after finishing the meal, they were drawn up, with the other Regiments, in rear of the Dilkhoosha. At two o'clock the Highlanders and Sikhs stormed the Martinière, with slight loss, and the 90th, who were supporting the Highlanders and Sikhs, did not fire a

---

* During the day Sir William Peel was wounded in the thigh by a match-lock ball, and soon after caught the small-pox, to which he succumbed.

shot, only losing one man from a discharge of grape. During the afternoon, Hope's Brigade, including the 90th, seized on the enemy's abandoned works, searched by Outram's fire from the opposite bank of the Goomtee, and pickets were established on the canal parapet though the advance towards Banks' House was checked by their fire. The 90th passed the night of the 9th in the Martinière, and, on the following day, was divided into detachments, which were placed on picket in different places.

At sunrise of the 10th, the heavy guns opened fire from a battery outside the Martinière Park, on Banks' House, and, by noon, the enemy evacuated the position, which was occupied by our troops. Thus the rebels were steadily driven back to their second line of defence, the Mess-house, barracks, and other buildings. Captain Wolseley was employed with his company during the day, covering the pontoon bridge which had been thrown across the Goomtee just beyond the enemy's first line of works. While the Commander-in-Chief was pushing on slowly but steadily, Outram kept up a vertical and direct fire on the defences in the interior of the Kaiser Bagh, from ten mortars and ten guns, while two more enfiladed the Mess-house. The engineering operations of the army were under the direction of Brigadier Napier, who displayed his wonted capacity in pushing the approaches through the line of buildings towards the Kaiser Bagh, without exposing the troops to any great loss. During the night of the

10th, the 53rd and 90th, with the exception of Wolseley's and two other companies, were sent in advance to occupy a building near the Secundrabagh; and, on the following morning, the Secundrabagh itself was seized by the 53rd, without any opposition, the rebels, probably, having a lively recollection of the terrible scenes in this Golgotha, when one thousand nine hundred Pandies bit the dust in a *mauvais quart d'heure.*

Early on the morning of the 11th, Wolseley's (the I Company) with two others of his Regiment, was directed to cover some horse-artillery guns engaged in the open. While thus employed a round shot carried away the end of an elephant's trunk, when the poor beast, frantic with rage and pain, came rushing down through the skirmishers. After this service, Wolseley proceeded on picket in the open space in front of the Secundrabagh,* where he remained all night. The Begum Kothie was stormed on the 11th by the 93rd Highlanders, supported by the 4th Sikhs and one thousand Goorkhas. Nothing of great importance occurred during the 12th or 13th. The British were now inside the first line of works, and the Engineers, under Brigadier Napier, proceeded from the Begum

---

* While under the enemy's fire, Wolseley was attracted by a curious-looking projectile which dropped near him. Taking it up, he found that it was a large cut-glass knob, which the native gunners, being hard pushed for round shot, had doubtless broken off from one of the magnificent chandeliers of the Kaiser Bagh. This singular projectile he presented to Sir Hope Grant, by whom it was used as a letter-weight.

Kothie to sap up through the adjacent enclosures, towards the Imaumbarra, or Great Mosque, which was the next stronghold to be assaulted.

During the night of the 13th, a very heavy fire was kept up on the Kaiser Bagh and Imaumbarra, which latter was carried with little opposition by the 10th Foot and Brasyer's Sikhs, who, pressing on, followed the flying enemy through the detached houses and courts, and with them entered the Kaiser Bagh itself; and thus on Sunday morning, the 14th of March, the chief stronghold of Lucknow was won.

The 53rd, and the three detached companies of the 90th, having been relieved by the 97th, were ordered to proceed to the Kaiser Bagh in support. Passing up loopholed streets, round by batteries, the guns of which still threatened them, and over a bridge of loose planks past burning timber, they reached the enclosure of the Kaiser Bagh, where they found that the remainder of the 90th Regiment were already established, they having rushed in by one entry while the Sikhs and 10th Foot effected an entrance by another. The scene that presented itself within the building, or rather collection of palaces, courts, and gardens, which, for magnificence and costliness of fittings, enjoyed a reputation that was not belied by the reality, baffles description.*

---

* Mr. Howard Russell, who entered the Kaiser Bagh soon after Wolseley, says :—" Our men were just crashing through the rooms of the palaces, which were as yet filled with the evidence of barbaric

The Kaiser Bagh was given up to plunder, and there ensued a scene of vandalism and wilful destruction that can only be paralleled by reference to those pages of Gibbon wherein he describes the sack of Ctesiphon, in the year 627, by the Saracenic hordes led by the ruthless Caliph Omar. Sikh and Briton vied with each other, as with clubbed muskets they shivered to fragments the costly glass chandeliers, battered to pieces the statues and gilt furniture, and strewed the floor with the mirrors they could not remove. Filled with the wanton spirit of mischief they broke into atoms on the floor " large boxes of japanned work containing literally thousands of cups and vessels of jade, of crystal, and of china." Entering the library, they tore into fragments the books, and lit their pipes with the beautifully illuminated MSS., and coloured miniatures, while boxes, swords, and pistols, were shattered

magnificence and splendour, and the cries of the dying were not yet stilled when we entered. In every room throughout the endless series there was a profusion of mirrors in ponderous gilt frames. A universal gilding of cornices, furniture, and everything that would bear the process, seemed the prevailing taste in the Royal Court. From every ceiling hung glass chandeliers of every age, form, colour, and design. As to the furniture, in many instances it looked like collections from the lumber-rooms of all the old palaces of Europe— Louis Quatorze clocks and cabinets, Renaissance mirrors and chairs, buhl-worked ebony chests, marqueterie tables, solid lumpy old German state chairs, gilt all over; but these were relieved by the richest carpets, by sumptuous divans, by cushions covered with gold embroidery, by rich screens of cashmere shawls, and by table-cloths ponderous with pearls and gold."

to pieces for the jewels with which they were inlaid. Ludicrous mistakes occurred in many instances, when men refused large sums of money for paste and glass ornaments under the impression that they were diamonds, or sold for a few rupees, priceless jewels, believed to be worthless on account of their size and bad setting.* Officers in many instances were seized with the desire to grow rich, though Wolseley was among the number of those who could contemplate the loot with Platonic indifference, and he did not appropriate a gold mohur, or any article whatever. His men secured their fair share of plunder, and one officer, who had a bundle of thirty Cashmere shawls, gave him, unsolicited, one of great value; however, he did not long retain the gift, for while sleeping on it that night, he hurried out on the occasion of an alarm, and upon his return the shawl had been appropriated. On the following day, the men of his company presented him with two large silver bowls, but he was equally unfortunate with these mementoes, for one night some thieves stole from the head of his bed the box in which they were deposited.

After the capture of the Kaiser Bagh, Captain Wolseley's company rejoined the head-quarters of the Regiment, which was operating in the immediate neighbourhood. During the day, the Mess-house, Tara Kothie, Motee Mahul, and the Chuttur Munzil, were

---

* In one instance, a soldier sold for £10 ready money, some bracelet s and jewels which fetched £7,500 at a jeweller's.

rapidly occupied by our troops, and the 15th was employed by the Engineers in securing the position, which presented a combination of massive palaces and walled courts, every outlet of which had been covered by a work, with barricades and loopholed parapets on every side.

On the 16th of March, the 90th—which had been employed with other troops in extending the area of the portion of the city in our possession, sometimes meeting with no resistance, and then again having struggles in driving the enemy out of the strongly-fortified houses around—were relieved by the 97th, and returned to camp near the Dilkhoosha.*

After the capture of Lucknow, Sir Hope Grant was placed in command of a Division, called the "Lucknow Field Force;" and, on the 1st of April, the 90th, which was to form part of the force, struck their tents at Dilkhoosha, and marched into the city. They were

---

* During the day, Sir James Outram crossed the Goomtee opposite the Secundrabagh, and, moving rapidly forward, captured the Residency, took the Iron Bridge in reverse, and, advancing about a mile beyond it, seized the Muchee Bhawan and Great Imaumbarra. On the morning of the 19th, a combined movement was carried out, by which Outram carried the Moosabagh, held by six thousand men and thirteen guns, the last position of the enemy on the line of the Goomtee. The losses of Sir Colin Campbell's Army between the 2nd and 21st of March inclusive, were as follows: sixteen officers, three Native officers, and one hundred and eight men killed; fifty-one officers, four Native officers, and five hundred and forty men wounded; grand total, including thirteen men missing, seven hundred and thirty-five. The 90th Regiment had thirty-two casualties.

quartered in a palace called Zoor-Buksh, situated near the Kaiser Bagh, which may be described as a collection of seven quadrangles contained within a surrounding wall, each building consisting of corridors and verandahs on the ground-floor, and large rooms upstairs, with a fountain in the centre of the quadrangular space. But Wolseley's good fortune in always sharing in whatever fighting was in progress, again favoured him, and he did not for any length of time occupy his new quarters.

When the arrangements were in progress for forming the Staff of Sir Hope Grant's Division, Colonel the Honourable William Pakenham, (now the Earl of Longford), an excellent officer who succeeded General Estcourt as Adjutant-General in the Crimea, and held the same office for the Royal Troops of the Bengal Army, recommended Captain Wolseley, with whose service he was familiar, for staff employ. Wolseley was, accordingly, appointed to the charge of the Quartermaster-General's Department of the Oude Division; and had not been many days in his new post, when, on the 11th of April, he accompanied Sir Hope Grant in an expedition, or *dour*, to Baree, a village twenty-five miles from Lucknow, on the Seetapore road, where Mansoob Ali—known as "the Fyzabad Moulvie"—who had displayed great ability and energy in the defence of Lucknow, had taken up a position with a strong body of rebels.

On the 13th of April, the column, numbering three

thousand men of all arms, came up with the enemy, who, numbering at least six thousand Infantry and one thousand Cavalry, had taken up a strong position on the banks of a stream, having hills on either side. As the General had received intelligence of the close proximity of the rebels, Captain Wolseley,* as Quartermaster-General of the Force, proceeded to reconnoitre their position, taking with him a guide, and an escort of some Native Cavalry.

It was three o'clock in the morning when he started, the rest of the troops following soon after. About daybreak he suddenly came upon the enemy's Cavalry, which, led by the redoubtable Moulvie in person, was seen charging down the road. Wolseley, who at this time was in advance with only five troopers, galloped back to the advanced guard, consisting of a squadron of the 7th Hussars, a detachment of Wales' Punjaub Horse, two guns, and about one hundred and fifty Infantry, under Colonel Hagart. There was barely time to unlimber the guns, and fire a round of grape into the enemy, before the rebel horsemen were down upon

* On Wolseley devolved the task of learning the roads, marking out the camping ground, and securing the services of guides. The following was the method he adopted for acquiring trustworthy guides. In the evening he would send out a chuprassie, or one of the Native police, to the next village. The first four men he encountered in it were asked if they knew the way to such and such a place; if they answered in the affirmative, they were immediately seized and brought into camp. When the march was over they were dismissed; but woe to them if they misled the column.

them. Wolseley had to draw his sword, and a sharp hand-to-hand affair ensued. The enemy's Cavalry charged the guns, but were repulsed by a well-directed fire, and by the Sikh Cavalry, under Lieutenant Prendergast, who was wounded. Sir Hope Grant soon came up with the Infantry, and the enemy's Cavalry now moved round to the rear, and attacked the baggage, but were again repulsed and driven off by a troop of the 7th Hussars, under Lieutenant Topham, which met the enemy at the charge, that officer and seven men being killed and wounded.

Wolseley was hard at work all day, which was a busy one for all arms of the small force, and very trying, owing to the excessive heat; and he met with an accident which caused him considerable inconvenience and pain. While jumping over banks carrying orders, and seeing to the disposition of the force, his sword tilted up, and struck the elbow-joint, inducing the formation of a large abscess, which caused him much suffering, though he refused to lay up and continued his duties with his arm in a sling.

The column visited various places, and, on the 23rd of April, Sir Hope Grant returned to Lucknow. On his arrival there Wolseley was gratified to learn that he had been gazetted Brevet-Major for his distinguished services during the Mutiny.

Sir Hope now received orders from Lord Clyde to make a *dour* to disperse a large rebel force. Leaving Lucknow on the 27th of April, the column visited

Poorwah, Parthan, Dhoundhea Keira, and other places, and at eleven p.m. on the 11th of May, proceeded on its march to Nuggur, over a broken country. On the following day—after a killing march of seven miles in the blazing sun, over ploughed fields, standing crops, and brushwood, when many men suffered from sun-stroke—Sir Hope arrived about five o'clock at Sirsee, where he was informed the rebel leaders, Bene Madhoo and Shewrutten Singh, had assembled an army of fifteen thousand Infantry, one thousand six hundred Cavalry, and eleven guns.

On his arrival at Sirsee, he found the enemy had taken up a strong position along a nullah with a jungle, containing the village and fort of Towrie, in their rear. The rebels opened fire about five o'clock, but, forming his column with the Cavalry and Horse Artillery cover-ing his right flank, the General attacked them with such boldness and vigour that they gave way, and were driven into the jungle, leaving two guns in the hands of the victors. Owing to their superior numbers, the enemy at one time almost surrounded the small British force, but the Cavalry and Artillery succeeded in clear-ing the right flank, while Brigadier (now General Sir Alfred) Horsford, with the Second Battalion Rifle Brigade and Sikhs, supported by the 90th, drove them away from the left flank, the 38th meanwhile support-ing the guns. In this affair, Shewrutten Singh, the rebel talookdar who held the neighbouring lands, was killed, and the enemy experienced considerable loss.

On the following morning—13th of May—the column returned to Nuggur, and, proceeding by easy marches, encamped near the Martinière on the 21st of May. This *dour* was attended with serious loss to our troops, for out of less than three thousand five hundred men, thirty-two had died outright of sunstroke, and five hundred were sick, being nearly one-sixth of the entire force.*

But Sir Hope, ever active, was not disposed to allow even the hot weather that had set in with unusual intensity, to deter him from resuming active operations, and, learning that the enemy, under Bene Madhoo, were threatening the Cawnpore Road, marched on the 25th of May. He visited Jessenda and Poorwah, but hearing that the enemy were gathering in force at

---

* Of this number the 90th lost four men died, and seventy-five who went into hospital. Since the Regiment left England early in the preceding year, death had wrought havoc in its ranks. Thirteen officers had died, viz.: Killed—Lieutenants Graham, Nunn, and Moultrie. Died of wounds—Colonel Campbell, C.B., Major Barnston, Brevet Major Perrin, Captain Denison, and Lieutenant Preston. Died of sickness—Lieutenant Carleton, Ensigns Knox, Chute, and Gordon, and Assistant-Surgeon Nelson. The losses of this gallant Regiment since Wolseley joined them five years before, had been heavy indeed. During the Crimean War, between the 4th of December, 1854, when it landed at Balaklava, to the fall of Sebastopol, the 90th lost four officers and fifteen men killed; thirty-seven men missing; and seventeen officers and two hundred and sixty-one men wounded, many of whom died. This is exclusive of the large number who died from the effects of disease in hospital.

Nawabgunge Bara Bankee,* a village on the Fyzabad
road, about eighteen miles from Lucknow, Sir Hope, at
eleven o'clock on the night of the 12th of June, formed
up his column on the Fyzabad road, and, having left his
baggage and supplies in charge of Colonel Purnell,
proceeded across country with great rapidity, his intention being to accomplish the distance of twelve miles
while his movements would be shrouded by darkness,
and his men would escape the fearful effects of a
forced march in the hot sun. Major Wolseley had a
busy time making the necessary inquiries regarding
the route, procuring guides, and seeing to the other
arrangements of his department.

The enemy, who numbered sixteen thousand men,
had taken up a strong position on a large plateau, surrounded on three sides by a stream, which was crossed
by a stone bridge at a little distance from the town, on
the fourth side being a jungle. The General's object
was to turn their right, and to interpose between them
and the jungle. The forced march across country
was made with the loss of several men from heat
apoplexy, and the stone bridge was reached about
half-an-hour before daybreak.

After a short rest, the troops fell in at daylight, and
the advance having crossed the stream, the enemy were
soon driven from their first position, upon which Sir
Hope immediately advanced against what appeared to

* The "big" Nawabgunge, so called to distinguish it from the
Nawabgunge on the Cawnpore Road.

be the centre of the position. Though the enemy had been surprised by the celerity of the attack, they opened fire with much determination on the front and both flanks, and tried to surround the force, but they were repulsed by Johnson's guns, supported by the Bays, while their attack on the right rear was met by the third Battalion of the Rifle Brigade and Hodson's Horse, which had just crossed the stream. A severe struggle ensued, and the enemy stood their ground well, but they were driven back, the Rifles attacking with the bayonet, and Hodson's Horse charging over broken ground in gallant style. Meanwhile Mackinnon's troop and the 7th Hussars, were hotly engaged to the front, and, supported by the remainder of the Rifle Brigade, under Colonel Glyn, drove the enemy with serious loss from their position on the left. At this time a body of Ghazees displayed the most desperate courage; after sustaining the fire of Major Carleton's battery, they withstood two charges of two squadrons of the 7th Hussars, led in gallant style by Sir William Russell, and some one hundred and twenty-five corpses were strewed round two guns they defended. During the action Brigadier Horsford attacked the enemy on the extreme left and captured two guns, and Colonel Hill with the second Battalion of the Rifle Brigade, protected the rear.

The action lasted three hours, and the troops were thoroughly exhausted, having been under arms from ten p.m. on the previous night, to nine a.m. on the morning of the 13th, when the enemy finally quitted the field of battle, on which they left six hundred dead and nine guns. The British loss in killed and wounded was sixty-seven; and, in addition, thirty-three men died from sunstroke, and two hundred and fifty were taken into hospital.

In his despatch, the General, who had before specially mentioned the services of Major Wolseley during the action at Baree, speaks of him as having again afforded him great assistance. After the battle, Major Wolseley surveyed the ground, and drew a plan which was sent to the Commander-in-Chief. Indeed, at Baree, and after every action throughout the campaign in Oude, of which province there were no maps in existence, Wolseley executed plans, which were forwarded to head-quarters, and were of essential use to Lord Clyde when he went over the same ground.*

After gaining this important success, which had a

---

* Wolseley was in the habit of keeping a journal of all the marches and movements, which were posted up daily, the book being stowed away in a large pocket on his person. In this journal he entered the hours of marching and halting, and minute details of the towns and villages, their inhabitants and capabilities. These particulars were transferred to a weekly report, which was sent to the Quartermaster-General of the Army; but it was so injured by damp while kept in store, that some years after, upon his applying to the Quartermaster-General in Oude, portions of the writing were found to be obliterated; what could be deciphered was copied out, at his request, and sent to England, but unfortunately it was destroyed, with the rest of his papers and effects, at the fire at the Pantechnicon. Wolseley also kept a private journal of his Indian experiences, but this he unluckily lost in China.

marked moral effect upon the rebels, greatly dispiriting them and their leaders, the column emcamped on the large sandy plain in rear of the village of Nawabgunge, where they erected huts with straw-thatched roofs.

But Sir Hope's energy was untiring, and, thanks to a strong constitution and a spare habit of body, he appeared to be exempt from the evil effects of campaigning during the four monsoon months. While his forces melted away under the fervent heat, and the members of his personal and divisional staff, one after another, suffered from its effects—the gallant Anson, his aide-de-camp, being ill with dysentery, and Hamilton, his Assistant-Adjutant-General, dying while proceeding to Calcutta on his way to England—the veteran General knew not what it was to have a day's illness, an immunity also enjoyed by Wolseley, whom wounds and exposure to Arctic cold and torrid heat appeared to have hardened to the point necessary for a soldier whose fortune it was to fight his country's battles in the four quarters of the globe.

On the 21st of July, Sir Hope Grant marched to Fyzabad to the assistance of Maun Singh, a powerful chief, who, after being one of the main-springs of the rebellion, had deserted a failing cause, and was besieged by a large body of the enemy at Shahgunge. But before the arrival of the British column at Fyzabad on the 29th of July, the rebels had dispersed, and Sir Hope pushed on to Ajudia, four miles lower down on the Gogra, where his guns opened fire on a portion of the fugitives as they were crossing the river. On the 9th of August, the General despatched Brigadier Horsford towards Sultanpore to follow up the rebels, who had been besieging Maun Singh. The Brigadier drove the enemy across the Goomtee, and occupied that town, but as the rebel force, which was increased to a strength of twenty thousand men and fifteen guns, opposed his passage to the right bank of the river, Sir Hope marched from Fyzabad, to which he had returned, with the main body of his troops, and after an irksome march across cultivated fields and through marshes, in which the guns sunk to the axle, joined Brigadier Horsford at Sultanpore on the 22nd inst.

The Engineers having constructed a raft from some small boats and canoes, the General crossed the greater part of his force over the Goomtee, between the 25th and 27th of August, an operation which was skilfully performed in the face of the enemy, who, led by Bene Madhoo, opened fire with their guns posted on high ground on the opposite bank. At three a.m. on the 29th of August, Sir Hope, after repulsing an attack on the previous night, moved on the enemy, who, however, evacuated the position they had taken up.

Sir Hope entrusted all the arrangements for the passage of the river, which, owing to the heavy rains, was greatly swollen, to Major Wolseley, who had no rest for two nights and one day, while superintending the transport of the little army. The manner in which was accomplished the difficult operation of crossing a swiftly-flowing and broad stream (the Goomtee at Sultanpore being four hundred feet wide), in the face of a strong rebel army, with a powerful artillery, and with only three rafts made from dinghies, was creditable to the General, his two Engineer officers, Lieutenants Scott and Raynsford, and particularly to Major Wolesley, "who," says Sir Hope Grant, "as Deputy Assistant-Quartermaster-General, had the superintendence of the arrangements for crossing the river, and who performed them to my perfect satisfaction."

The country was now tolerably clear, and the force remained at Sultanpore, further operations against the rebels being deferred until the cold weather in October. The interval was employed in throwing a bridge across the Goomtee, in which Wolesley gave his advice and assistance to the Engineer officers. Sir Hope Grant marched on the 11th of October with a small column towards Tanda, but returned to Sultanpore on the 23rd, proceeding thence again to Kandoo Nuddee, were four thousand of the enemy were posted with several guns. But the rebels fled on the approach of the British force; and, a few days later, the column returned to Sultanpore.

The Lucknow Field Force was not allowed a lengthy period of repose, and, on the 3rd of November, Sir Hope marched to Amethie to operate against the rebel Rajah, in conjunction with Lord Clyde, and, accompanied by Major Wolseley and his staff, reconnoitred the fort, which he found to be of great strength and extent. However, the Rajah surrendered on the following day, and Sir Hope proceeded to Purseedapore on the 11th of November, and, on the following morning, took possession of the strong fort of Shunkerpore, belonging to Bene Madhoo, whom he had defeated at Nawabgunge. Under instructions from Lord Clyde, Sir Hope proceeded to Fyzabad, on the Gogra, which he crossed before daylight on the 27th of November, and, under fire of his heavy guns, carried the enemy's position. The cavalry and field-artillery went in pursuit, and six guns were captured and brought into camp.

On the 3rd of December, the column, which had returned to Nawabgunge, marched in the direction of Bunkussia, and, whilst proceeding to reconnoitre, suddenly came upon the main body of the Gondah Rajah's troops, about four thousand men. The enemy opened fire from three guns, upon which Sir Hope advanced and drove them through the jungle, a distance of two miles, capturing two guns. On the 7th, the column reached Bunkussia, the principal fort of the Gondah Rajah, which was destroyed, after which Sir Hope crossed the Raptee, and visited Bulrampore and Toolsepore. As his great object was to prevent the enemy escaping to the Goruckpore district, he marched to Dulhurree, close to the Nepaul frontier, where he awaited Brigadier Rowcroft's column, which had been employed preventing the rebels from passing between the hills and the north of the Goruckpore district. Sir

Hope then proceeded to Pushuroa, and, after disposing two small columns under Brigadiers Rowcroft and Taylor, to cut off the escape of Bala Rao, who, with a force of six thousand men and fifteen guns, had retreated to near Kundakote, moved forward to attack the rebel chief on the 4th of January, 1859. While a small column advanced through the jungle in a westerly direction towards Kundakote, the General, shortly after, followed in the same direction with the main body, until he came to where the principal force of the rebels was posted in thick cover. The enemy were, however, so thoroughly disheartened by the continuous defeats they had sustained, that neither Bene Madhoo, Bala Rao, nor any other of their leaders (the Fyzabad Moulvie, the most able of them, having fallen) could succeed in bringing them to face our troops, and they once more adopted their usual tactics, and fled, leaving fifteen guns in the hands of the victors. Thoroughly discouraged at the loss of their guns, the force, led by Bala Rao, now dispersed, most of them making their way into Nepaul.

As, notwithstanding Jung Bahadoor's proclamation to them to lay down their arms and submit themselves to the British, the rebels continued to occupy a menacing position near the Sitka Ghat beyond the first pass, Sir Hope Grant, accompanied by Major Wolseley, marched to Fyzabad, whence he proceeded by boat to Amorha, on the opposite side of the Gogra. Here he received information that four thousand of the enemy had taken up a position near Bunkussia, and another party of one thousand eight hundred had made for the Gogra. The General, determined to give the rebels, who were moving from Nepaul into the Terai, "no rest for the sole of their feet," continued to chase and harry them, laying plans, in conjunction with his staff, to head them off a ford or a village with one or more columns, while he made a dash on them with his main body. Now dividing his forces, he sent one portion by Rampore Thana to scour the jungles, himself following in their track along the banks of the Gogra, while a third column was despatched into the jungle about Bunkussia. At midnight of the 20th of May, the General marched from Burgudwa, and arrived soon after sunrise at the jungle covering the entrance to the Jerwah Pass, with Colonel Beauchamp Walker's Field Force. Here he received information that the Nana and Bala Rao, with two guns and two thousand men, were at the mouth of the Pass, and Mummoo Khan, with five hundred followers, a little to the west, on the same ground where he had inflicted a severe defeat on Bala Rao on the 4th of January. Sir Hope, having ordered the cavalry and artillery to encamp, sent Colonel Brasyer with his Sikhs against Mummoo Khan, who, however, dispersed on his approach, and himself moved with the 7th Punjaubees into the Pass. The enemy occupied the spurs of the mountain stretching into the jungle on either side of the Pass, from the gorge of which their two guns opened fire. One company of the Punjaubees climbed the hill to the left and drove the enemy before them, and the remainder of the Regiment cleared the ridge on the right and captured the guns, but owing to the troops having marched twenty miles, they were not able to overtake the retreating enemy. Sir Hope writes in his Journal:—"I sent a company up the hill to turn the enemy's right; but finding they were not clever in their ascent, I directed Biddulph, together with Wolseley and Wilmot, both on my staff, to lead them up. These three officers did their work well."

Thus ended almost the last conflict of this great and memorable struggle, which had lasted two years, as it was on Sunday, the 10th of May, 1857, that the 3rd Bengal Cavalry mutinied at Meerut. As the last band of the rebels, deprived of their only remaining guns, was now driven into the Nepaul frontier, the General, leaving some small columns to meet any attempt on their part to break through, proceeded to Lucknow on the 4th of June, and, with his staff, took up his residence in the Dilkhoosha.

In the distribution of honours on the conclusion of the Mutiny, Wolseley received the brevet of Lieutenant-Colonel. He was young to have attained so high a rank, for it was on the twenty-sixth anniversary of his birth, that, in company with his chief, he entered Lucknow, and, for a brief period, enjoyed the " blessings of peace." He was now employed in laying out the new cantonments, those formerly in use by our troops having been utterly destroyed by the rebels. Henceforth it was decided that Europeans should form a large proportion of the garrison of this important city, and his experience in quartering troops was of essential service when this question of the new cantonments came up for consideration.

Wolseley had only been established some five months in his comfortable quarters in the fine old palace near Lucknow, when he was once more offered a position on the staff of an army about to take the field, and, action being to him as the breath of life, he gladly accepted the proposal.

Early in October, Sir Hope Grant was informed by Lord Clyde, then at Cawnpore, that the Duke of Cambridge had nominated him to the command of the troops about to proceed, in conjunction with a French army, to the north of China, to bring to terms the Imperial Government. Sir Hope Grant was desirous of appointing Colonel Wolseley to the head of the Quartermaster-General's Department, but Lord Clyde nominated the late Colonel Kenneth McKenzie, a most able and distinguished officer, and Wolseley went as Deputy Assistant-Quartermaster-General in charge of the topographical department.

Had it not been for the sudden outbreak of the Indian Mutiny, Wolseley would have been serving during the past two years in China, to which country, by a singular coincidence, he found himself once more under orders. And what an eventful period in the

history of this country, and of her great Asiatic dependency, as well as in his own life, had been those
two years just concluded !

India has ever afforded the grandest field for the
display of those talents and qualities which have rendered this country the Rome of modern history. In
India, whether in war or statesmanship, the Anglo-
Saxon race has appeared to the greatest advantage ;
this may in part be due to the superiority over natives,
which we share with all European nations, but we do
not think we should be guilty of self-laudation, if we
chiefly attribute it to that peculiarity of the Anglo-
Saxon family, by which resistance and difficulties only
increase the determination to succeed. It is morally
certain that no other Power save England could have
retained her hold of India during the year 1857, with
a military force which, at the time of the outbreak,
only numbered thirty-eight thousand soldiers in the
three Presidencies. To use Canning's phrase, " India
is fertile in heroes," and probably at no previous period
of our history have the attributes which peculiarly distinguish our countrymen and countrywomen received a
more striking illustration. Our women were heroines,
and our incomparable rank and file nobly did their
duty ; while as for the officers throughout the long-
drawn hardships, the dramatic episodes, and the glorious triumphs of the Indian Mutiny, we cannot do better
than repeat the saying of that great leader who may be
regarded as the type, as he was the greatest representa-

tive, of the class. "Brave," would the great Duke of
Wellington impatiently say, when any one spoke in
commendatory terms of the courage of British officers,
"of course they are; all Englishmen are brave; but
it is the spirit of the gentleman that makes a British
officer."

Those who were privileged to take part in those
glorious feats of arms, the Siege and Storm of Delhi
and the Defence and Relief of Lucknow, may be con-
gratulated in having been actors in one of those his-
toric scenes, the record of which—like the deeds of
"the three hundred" at Thermopylæ, and the "Retreat of the Ten Thousand" under Xenophon—will
never fade from the page of history.

CHAPTER IV.

THE CHINA WAR.

The Occupation of Chusan—The Disembarkation at Peh-tang—The Action at Sinho—The Capture of the Taku Forts—The Advance on Pekin—Narrow Escape of Colonel Wolseley from Capture—The Looting of the Summer Palace, and Surrender of Pekin—Wolseley's Visit to Japan and Mission to Nankin—Return to England.

COLONEL WOLSELEY accompanied Sir Hope Grant to Calcutta, and, with the other members of his staff, sailed on the 26th of February, 1860, in the 'Fiery Cross,' one of Jardine's steamers, which cast anchor at Hong-Kong on the 13th of March. As the transports arrived from England, India, and the Cape of Good Hope, the troops were disembarked and encamped at Kowloon, opposite Hong-Kong, which Colonel Wolseley surveyed, the other officers of the Department, under Colonel Kenneth Mackenzie, being engaged in clearing out and preparing the ground for the reception of the British troops. In a very short time, with the assistance of the Engineers, the required space was converted from a rocky waste, having a few patches of garden cultivation, into a neat camp, with tents and lines for the horses and batteries. There was some uncertainty at first as to whether an ultimatum, couched in very mild terms, and addressed by our Minister, Mr. Frederick Bruce, to the Imperial Government at Pekin, would have the effect of averting a war, but all doubts were soon set at rest by the receipt of an insolent despatch, rejecting the British demands.

The first step was the joint occupation, by the British and French Forces, of the island of Chusan, which was accordingly undertaken under instructions from the Home Government, who, in this, followed the precedent of the war of 1840-42, though Colonel Wolseley has expressed his opinion that the step was of little use, either from a military or political point of view.* The expedition rendezvoused off King-tang, opposite the town of Chin-hai, at the mouth of the Ning-po, and, on the 21st of April, dropped anchor in the noble harbour of Ting-hai, the capital of Chusan, which immediately capitulated.

On the following day, the naval and military commanders, with their staffs and a small guard, landed and made an inspection of the town and its vicinity, at which Wolseley, being the only officer of the Quartermaster-General's department, was present with the General.

* See Colonel Wolseley's valuable and trustworthy "Narrative of the War with China, in 1860," written daily while the operations were in progress.

One thousand soldiers only were landed, there being great difficulty in finding accommodation in the various yamuns, or official residences, and three hundred Marines were placed in the Custom-house and adjoining buildings. Wolseley took over the requisite buildings from the native officials, and made the necessary arrangements, in conjunction with the French staff-officer, for the quartering of the garrison. He returned with Sir Hope Grant to the 'Grenada,' on the evening of the 23rd of April, and, on the following morning, the steamer proceeded to Poo-too, an island lying to the eastward of the Chusan group, and which, it was considered, might be suitable for a military sanatarium. Wolseley proceeded on shore with the General, and visited the temples and monasteries, of which this sacred city alone consists. In the evening the party returned to the 'Grenada,' which then proceeded to Hong-Kong.

One of the chief difficulties that had to be encountered in the organization of the Army destined to proceed to the north of China, was that of transport, but at length, in May, every preparation being completed, some sailing transports left Hong-Kong for the seat of war, with a portion of the Infantry, and the main body followed on the 8th of June.

The British Army, of which the Divisional Commanders were Sir Robert Napier and Sir John Michel, Brigadier Pattle, being in command of the Cavalry, numbered about fourteen thousand men, and that of the French, under General Montauban, which was mustering at Shanghai, about seven thousand. The fleet, under Admiral Sir James Hope, consisted of seventy ships of war, including gunboats, and the hired transports numbered one hundred and twenty sail.

On the 16th June, the ' Grenada,' in which Colonel Wolseley had embarked with the Commander-in-Chief, and some troop-ships, proceeded to sea, and put in at Shanghai, where, at the earnest entreaty of the European residents and Chinese authorities, some troops were landed to protect the town against the rebels, better known as Taipings, who, for the past eight years, had desolated the country.

Three days after quitting Shanghai, the ' Grenada ' cast anchor off the town of Wei-hei-wei, on the western shore of the Gulf of Pechili, the transports, with the greater portion of the troops, having already arrived at Talien-wan, on the eastern side. Wolseley and other officers landed at Wei-hei-wei, and visited the town, which is of considerable extent. On the following morning he explored the neighbouring country, but its capabilities for supplying water were unpromising in the extreme.

According to the plan of operations agreed upon between the allied commanders, the French were to rendezvous at Chefoo,* in the province of Shantung, and the British at Talien-wan.

* Che-foo and Talienwan were fixed upon as the respective bases of operations of the French and English armies, because it was known that along the coast near Takoo the ice in winter prevented all approach

Sir Hope Grant, with his staff, remained on board the 'Grenada,' in Victoria Bay, whence a small steamer daily went the round of the great bay or harbour, carrying orders to the various encampments.

Lord Elgin arrived at Talien-wan on the 9th of July, in the Indian Navy steam-frigate 'Feroze,' and, after many conferences, it was decided by Sir Hope Grant and General Montauban that both Armies should sail for Peh-tang on the 26th July.

Accordingly, on that day, the vast Armada weighed anchor, and started with a fair wind for the general rendezvous, twenty miles south of the Peiho, affording a grand and soul-inspiring sight; and in the evening of the same day, the French fleet of thirty-three sail hove in sight, passing round the Mcatow Islands. On Saturday, the 28th of July, the entire Expedition was assembled at the appointed rendezvous, and, on Monday, weighed and stood in for the mouth of the Peiho river.

A Memorandum was issued by the Quartermaster-General for the guidance of the officers superintending the disembarkation of the troops, and, on the 1st of August, the Honorable Company's ship 'Coromandel,' having on board Sir James Hope and Sir Hope Grant, with his staff, including Colonel Wolseley, led the way, followed by the gunboats, with their decks crowded with men, each towing six launches, full of troops.

for several months; but there was deep water at these places, which were free from ice all the year round. Colonel Wolseley visited Che-foo, and speaks in the highest terms of the order and regularity that existed in the French Camp near that town.

VOL. I.   O

The French flotilla also put off at the same time.

Soon after two o'clock, the gunboats anchored about two thousand yards from the famous Taku forts, all the embrasures of which were masked, and no troops visible. These forts are about three miles from the mouth of the river, the passage of which they command, the town standing immediately in their rear.

It was decided by Generals Grant and Montauban that a reconnaissance should be made in the direction of a causeway running towards Taku, and four hundred men, drawn equally from the English and French armies, were landed on a soft, sticky, mud flat, through which, for nearly a mile, the men floundered and struggled before reaching a hard patch of ground. "Nearly every man," says the *Times* correspondent, " was disembarrassed of his lower integuments, and one gallant brigadier led on his men with no other garment than his shirt." The Tartars now retreated along the causeway, and the rest of the force was disembarked by five o'clock.

"Never," says Mr. Bowlby, " did more hopeless prospect greet an army. Mud and water everywhere, and 'not a drop to drink.' Pools of brackish water were scattered about here and there, but perfectly undrinkable, and not a well or spring could be found.

" The English Army then advanced, the Rifles to the right, the 15th Punjaubees in the centre, and the 2nd Queen's on the left. They were on an island cut off from the causeway by a deep ditch forty feet wide, through which the tide flowed. In plunged the brigades, and sank middle deep in the vilest and most stinking slush; but the men struggled gallantly on, and in a few seconds the whole force was on the road." The bridge and gate of the town were occupied, but the greater portion of the troops rested for the night on the causeway, and Colonel Wolseley and a large party halted on the hard ground cut off from it by a deep ditch. They were all in a plight calculated to try the temper of Mark Tapley himself, for not only were they destitute of water, every man having long before consumed the pint he carried in his water bottle, but they were cold and wet, and had to lie on the damp ground. It is under such circumstances that the real nature of a man reveals itself. As Wolseley says:— " The noble-hearted come to the front, at once ready to help others, and being themselves generous and jolly, make the best of untoward events; whilst the selfish man stands out in his true colours, whining and pining like an ill-tempered child, a picture of misery himself, and likely to make others so, by his captious ill-humour. We were a large party of people, odds and ends, of all sorts, including some who, in the dark, could not make their way any further to the front. All were horribly thirsty. To go back to the boats for water, through the slush, was really a fatiguing journey; but the task had to be accomplished, and never did the weary traveller in an arid desert hail a spring with greater joy than we all did our Judge-Advocate-General's return with a small barrel of water, after his trip there. Subsequently the invaluable

Coolie corps* made their appearance with breakers of a like nature, which supplied every one."

But Wolseley in his published work omits to mention that he accompanied Major Wilmot on his errand of mercy—for such it really was, as many of the men were so fatigued and overcome by thirst, that their tongues were hanging out of their mouths—and on their return from their long tramp through the mud, laden with the precious liquid, the gallant officers were cheered heartily by their comrades.

The night was as unpleasant a one as Colonel Wolseley ever spent, even bearing in mind his Crimean and Indian bivouacs. He had, of course, no bedding, and it was impossible to lie down on the wet mud with any hope of obtaining rest. So he walked about and shivered through the night without closing his eyes. In the morning the town was occupied, but "looting" was strictly prohibited, and any men found indulging in the unlawful pursuit, were instantly tied up and flogged on the spot.

Our men landed with three days' provisions, but after the fourth day, supplies of food and water were regularly issued to them. The French arrangements not being so complete or successful, our gallant Allies had exciting sport in chasing and killing all the pigs they could lay hands on, not even disdaining to regale themselves on such deceased porkers as they found in

* The Coolie corps, which was organised and led by Major Temple, of the Indian Army, consisted of two thousand five hundred Chinamen, recruited at Canton and Hong-Kong.

ditches; indeed, for the first week, they seemed to subsist on little else. Our military system also appeared in favourable contrast to that of our Allies, as regards strictness of discipline and employment of the troops, for while their officers and men were sauntering about the town with their hands in their pockets, our men, of all ranks and arms of the service, were busily employed constructing wooden wharves and piers, and improving the principal thoroughfares for the passage of guns.

The Allied Generals having decided on a reconnaissance in force of the enemy's position, on the 3rd of August, a strong column, consisting of one thousand French and as many English, under the command of General Collineau, moved out along the raised causeway leading towards the Taku Forts. Colonel Wolseley was selected by Sir Hope Grant to accompany the force, and indeed throughout this war, so highly did the General estimate his services, that whenever he decided to undertake some duty requiring tact or capacity, he would always inquire, " Where's Wolseley ? Send him." And Wolseley, ever ready to undertake any charge entailing responsibility, would respond to the call with cheerful alacrity. His duties as the officer in charge of the topographical survey of a country totally unknown, naturally required his presence in the van of the Army, and whether there, or sweeping round the flanks with a handful of Native Cavalry for an escort, he carried his life in his hand and narrowly escaped capture, which would have involved torture or death at the hands of the barbarous enemy; on one occasion, the fate that befel another lamented officer of his Department, Captain Brabazon, would have been his, but for an accidental circumstance, or rather should we say, having regard to the services he was spared to render to his country, by the interposition of that Divinity which, says Hamlet,

" shapes our ends, rough-hew them how we may."

The Allied force started at four a.m., and, after a march of about four miles, came upon the main body of the enemy, who were waiting just beyond a bridge, about half a mile further on. As soon as the French, who led the advance, had passed the bridge, the enemy opened fire, and a large body of Tartar Cavalry threatened the flanks of the Allies, when General Collineau opened fire with two guns, and, having forced them back, advanced, the French on the right, and the English on the left, towards a large entrenchment about a mile distant. The force now halted, and Brigadier Sutton sent Colonel Wolseley to Sir Hope Grant to apprise him of the state of affairs, and request reinforcements if the enemy's position was to be forced. Wolseley galloped back, and, having given the necessary information, returned with two guns, and the Allied Generals immediately followed with a reinforcement, but the reconnoitring party was already on the return march to Pehtang, and the day's proceedings ended somewhat abortively, the Tartars, in their ignorance of the object sought to be attained, claiming a victory, and sending flaming reports to Pekin of their having forced the white soldiers to retreat.

On the 9th of August,* Colonel Wolseley was selected to command a second reconnoitring party, consisting of two hundred Cavalry and one hundred Infantry, and Sir Hope gave him positive instructions, before starting, on no account to bring on an engagement. Proceeding along the causeway for two miles, he placed his infantry in position in a ruined farmhouse, usually held by a cavalry picket of the enemy, while he moved off to reconnoitre with the cavalry, whose exposed flank was thus protected. Leaving the causeway to his left, Wolseley made a long circuit, until he approached within a mile of the enemy's works on the Peiho, and, having surveyed the whole of the enemy's position, and the line on their flank by which the advance was to be made, and having further ascertained that the country in that direction was practicable for all arms, and abounded in pools of fresh water, he returned without having exchanged a shot with the enemy. Immediately on his arrival in camp, Wolseley made a report of the survey he had completed, and having that night executed a plan, he had copies struck off from a steel plate of the size of a sheet of foolscap, and by an early hour on the follow-

* On the 4th of August, Sir Robert Napier landed, and took up his residence in a temple in the town ; General Michel, who had come ashore with the landing party of his Division, occupying another. Sir Hope Grant, with his staff, resided in the fort, under canvas, and General Montauban in the town.

ing morning, these copies were in the hands of every staff officer of both armies.

On Sunday, the 12th of August, the Allied Army began its march towards the Taku Forts, and everyone was in high spirits at leaving that detestable place with its inodorous smells. It was arranged that the 2nd, or Sir Robert Napier's, Division, should move out along the track reconnoitred on the 9th, guided by Wolseley, who had laid down the route by which the Division, when attacking in flank, should march so as to avoid the swamps and quicksands which abounded on both sides of the causeway, and yet at the same time keep intact the communications with the main body. Sir Robert Napier was directed to turn the left of the enemy's position, whilst the 1st Division and French, advancing along the causeway, should attack the enemy's works in front. As the ground on the right was admirably adapted for the operations of Cavalry, the whole of that arm were attached to Napier's Division. At four a.m. the march began through slush and mud which was terribly heavy for the Artillery horses. After advancing for three miles from the causeway, Napier opened fire on the enemy with fifteen guns, and he expressed his admiration of the unflinching fortitude with which the Tartar Cavalry stood the iron hail at four hundred and fifty yards' range. A portion of them charged our Cavalry, but were met half way, and utterly routed by the Sikh horse, led by those gallant *sabreurs* Fane and Probyn, supported by a squadron of Dragoon Guards.

In the meantime, the 1st Division and the French, moving along the causeway leading from Pehtang towards the enemy's entrenched camp before the village of Sinho, deployed within one thousand four hundred yards of these works, and, after a brief artillery fire, the whole army advanced and occupied the place.

Throughout this China War, our Allies, notwithstanding their gallantry, did not show to advantage, which was chiefly due to the incapacity of General Cousin de Montauban, who was a gasconading, self-opiniated man, without a particle of military talent. At no time throughout the campaign did the French Division muster more than four thousand effectives, while we had in China a well-appointed Army numbering nineteen thousand men, of whom fourteen thousand were at the seat of war. Thus the co-operation of the French was quite unnecessary, but Lord Palmerston, sacrificing military considerations to the political requirements involved in the maintenance of the *entente cordiale*, accepted the proffered assistance of the Emperor Napoleon. The campaign had not been inaugurated many hours before Montauban gave evidence of his military incompetence, which went so far in assisting to wreck his country in the memorable days preceding the catastrophe of Sedan.*

* Wolseley was in the heart of the American Continent, conducting his Red River Expedition, in the Autumn of the memorable year, 1870, when he received intelligence that the Count de Palikao had been

From the Allied position, distant about two miles and a half, was visible the large entrenchment around the village of Tangku, having a long, narrow causeway, with ditches, leading from Sinho towards it; the country to the north of this causeway was very swampy, and quite impassable for all arms, but, on the south side, the ground appeared sufficiently firm to bear guns. Round the village of Tangku, which is situated in a bend of the Peiho, was a crenellated mud wall, about ten feet in height.

General Montauban was very desirous of advancing at once upon the enemy's position; but Sir Hope met the proposal with a decided negative, and expressed his intention of moving on the morrow, after bridges had been thrown across the canals which separated the roadway and village from the open, firm, ground to the south of the causeway. But though it was evident to the merest tyro in the art of war, that, without these bridges, an advance could only be effected along this narrow causeway, which was commanded by the enemy's guns, Montauban resolved to attempt the task alone. Accordingly he sallied out with his Division, but after two hours spent in a purposeless cannonading, returned to Sinho, *re infectâ*.

On the following day, bridges were thrown across the several canals, and roadways made over the marshy places in the line of advance, while Colonel Wolseley,

nominated Minister-at-War, thus receiving charge of the destinies of his country at a most momentous crisis. Turning to his officers, he exclaimed: "Then it is all over for poor France!"

and other officers of his Department, made a reconnaissance up the banks of the Peiho, which resulted in
showing that the enemy had retired to the southern
bank of the river, with the exception of the troops gar-
risoning the forts.

On the morning of the 14th, the First Division, with
all the Artillery, having their right flank resting on the
Peiho, advanced to attack the enemy's entrenchments.
Our Allies, having taken up a position on our left,
their left flank resting upon the Tangku causeway, the
whole line of Artillery, consisting of twelve French and
twenty-four British guns, opened fire, under which the
Infantry advanced, and soon a party of the 60th Rifles,
under Lieutenant Shaw, entered the enemy's entrenchments and hoisted the Union Jack. Although the
French guns were at this time still pounding away,
they had the effrontery to claim the merit of being the
first within the hostile works, and General Montauban
promoted the soldier who hoisted the tricolour.

About forty-five guns, of various calibre, between
four and 24-pounders, of which sixteen were brass, and
the remainder iron, fell into the hands of the victors.

Colonel Wolseley accompanied the Commander-in-
Chief in his reconnaissance towards the Taku Forts,
but not much information was gained, as the enemy
opened fire on the escort.

Sir Hope Grant now busied himself in perfecting his
arrangements for the attack on these formidable works;
heavy guns and ammunition were brought to the front,
and ten days' provisions collected at Sinho. The British

and French Ministers were also busy negotiating with the enemy, who sent a flag of truce; but as was foreseen by all but the diplomatists, the Chinese Government, represented by Ho, the Governor-General of Pechili, only wanted to delay, and had no real intention of acceding to our terms, or of executing any treaty not extorted and enforced at the cannon's mouth.

And now came up for consideration the knotty point of the attack on the Taku forts, and it was one upon which the British and French Commanders-in-Chief were divided. Sir Hope Grant, who was strongly supported in his views by Sir Robert Napier, proposed to operate against the northern fort, which enfiladed the southern forts, and was the key to the position, but General Montauban was loud in favour of crossing the river and assaulting the southern forts.*

Finding his colleague determined to abide by his own judgment, Montauban made a formal protest, and then,

---

* Wolseley treats of this vexed question in his book in detail, and concludes by saying: "If we had operated by the southern bank of the Peiho, as our Allies wished, and supposing that everything had turned out in the very happiest manner, we could not possibly have been by the 1st of September as far advanced in the work of the campaign as we actually were upon the evening of the 21st of August, when, in pursuance of Sir Hope Grant's plan of attack, we had stormed and taken the northern forts. I need scarcely remark that time was everything to us. We had opened the campaign later than was expected at home, having been delayed a month at Talien-wan, so that every day was of the greatest value to us. The cold weather was reported by all to commence towards the middle of October, and the climate in November was said to be most intolerable, the rivers being then frozen, and ice for some two or three miles out to sea along the coast."

with a proper soldierly feeling, acted in loyal concert with the British General. During the halt at Tangku, the Engineers had been busy constructing a road towards the forts, also bridges or causeways over the canals, and batteries, which were armed, during the night of the 20th, with sixteen guns and three mortars. At daybreak, on the following morning, twenty-three pieces of ordnance, including four of the French, opened fire on the forts, which replied with spirit.

The British Force detailed for the assault, was drawn from Sir Robert Napier's Division, and numbered two thousand five hundred men.* The French assaulting column, numbering one thousand men, was under the command of General Collineau.

About six o'clock, a tremendous explosion took place in the nearest fort; half an hour later, a second explosion occurred in the larger northern fort, and, by seven o'clock, most of the enemy's guns had been dismounted. The field-guns were advanced to within five hundred yards of the fort, and the fire of the works having been silenced, a breach was commenced near the gate, and the storming party advanced to within thirty yards, keeping up a hot fire, the French Infantry being on the right, and the English on the left. Under

* The assaulting column consisted of a wing of the 44th, under Lieutenant-Colonel McMahon, a wing of the 67th, under Lieutenant-Colonel Thomas, the other wings of these regiments acting as supports; the Royal Marines, under Lieutenant-Colonel Gascoigne, and a detachment of the same corps carrying a pontoon bridge for crossing the wet ditches, under Lieutenant-Colonel Travers; and Major Graham with his company of Royal Engineers.

a heavy musketry fire from the enemy, who quitted their cover on the troops forming up for the assault, our men advanced straight to their front towards the gate of the fort, the French advancing by the right, and approaching the angle of the work resting on the river's bank. It very soon became apparent that our engineering arrangements had been faulty, for, instead of using a number of light ladders, or a small plank bridge resting on wheels, on which to cross the wet ditch, a pontoon bridge had been taken, and a round shot, passing through one of the metal pontoons of which it was constructed, rendered it unserviceable.

The French, with great dash, succeeded in crossing the wet ditches and dragging over three or four ladders, which they placed against the walls, and after many attempts at escalading, at length planted the tricolour on the summit, and entered the works. Almost simultaneously the British flag waved over the main gate, the men having forced their way through the breach in single file, the foremost being Ensign Chaplin, of the 67th, who planted the colours on the top of the parapet, and Lieutenants Rogers (44th), Lenon and Burslem (67th).

In seeking to lay down the pontoon bridge, no less than fifteen Sappers were almost instantaneously placed *hors de combat,* and, by an unlucky round shot, the bridge was rendered useless. Wolseley was with the advance party at the time, and used his utmost endeavours to withdraw the bolt by which the damaged portion was fastened to the superstructure; this, however, was a work of extreme difficulty, as owing to a portion of the bridge being in the water, a great strain was brought to bear on the bolt, which could not be withdrawn. Wolseley recounts some instances of gallantry that attracted his attention, which was always interested in observing the exhibition of that greatest of military virtues in others. While our men were endeavouring to cross the ditches, he was standing by Major Graham, V.C.—an old comrade in the dreary days in the trenches before Sebastopol—who, on the present occasion, being almost the only mounted officer, offered an easy mark to the Chinese matchlockmen; so deafening was the uproar of great guns and small arms at this time, that Wolseley, having some remark to communicate to Graham, placed his hand on that officer's thigh to draw his attention. "Don't put your hand there," exclaimed Major Graham, wincing under the torture, "there is a gingall ball lodged in my leg." It was the first notice he had taken of his wound. Colonel Mann, commanding the Royal Engineers, was one of the first to cross the two ditches, and Major (the late Colonel) Honourable A. Anson, aide-de-camp, on reaching the other side, which was covered with pointed bamboo stakes, proceeded to swarm up a pole, to the summit of which the rope drawing up the drawbridge was made fast. The daring act attracted the fire of the enemy's marksmen, but the gallant officer, nothing daunted, hacked away with his sword, until he cut the rope, when down fell the drawbridge with a great clang. It was so shattered by shot that it seemed scarcely capable of sustaining any weight, but our men managed to cross a few at a time.

The scene presented by the interior of the captured work, evinced the determination with which the garrison had held the place, and among the dead, who were estimated to number about two thousand, was a General and the officer commanding all the northern forts.

The losses incurred by the Allies in achieving this really brilliant triumph, were moderate, considering the strength of the defences they had stormed. Our loss was seventeen killed and one hundred and sixty-one wounded, of whom twenty-two were officers. The French had about one hundred and thirty casualties.

Without loss of time, preparations were commenced to attack the large northern fort, distant exactly one thousand yards, which had a raised causeway running towards it, with wet ditches on either side.

Colonel Wolseley proceeded, with a small escort, under a heavy fire, to reconnoitre the ground to the north of the causeway, and slowly advancing his party in skirmishing order towards the space, ascertained its fitness for the purposes required. But the Chinese had no heart for further resistance, and as the Allied troops advanced towards the north fort, the garrison, numbering two thousand men, threw away their arms and surrendered at discretion. A little later the enemy evacuated the southern works, and in the evening, Mr. (now Sir Harry) Parkes received the unconditional surrender of the whole country on the banks of the Peiho as far as Tientsin. The day closed with a tremendous storm of wind and rain, and soon the roads by which the troops had advanced, were quite submerged. The camp was flooded, and, under such depressing influences, Wolseley rode back a distance of five miles, to find the interior of his tent a pond, with every article therein floating about as if another flood had covered the face of the earth. Thus, without light or fire to dry the wet clothes on his back, and after a frugal supper of biscuit and brandy-and-water, he turned in, ruminating, doubtless, on the changes and chances of this mortal life when it happens to be that of a soldier.

The first phase of the War was completed by the capture of the famed Taku forts, which, though taken by our sailors in 1858, had, in the following year, successfully resisted a naval force, under Admiral Sir James Hope, when conveying the British Minister to Pekin, for the purpose of exchanging the ratification of the Treaty concluded at Tientsin in June, 1858. Our Government now determined that the violated treaty should be ratified at Pekin, as this would imply a sense of defeat and humiliation which the Imperial Government, skilled as it was in sophisms, could not argue away in the lying proclamations it was in the habit of addressing to its many millions of subjects.

Sir James Hope pushed on to Tientsin on the 23rd of August, and, so demoralised were the enemy, that the forts at that place were occupied without a shot being fired. Two days later Lord Elgin and Sir Hope

Grant followed with the troops, leaving a garrison at Taku and Sinho. Eight days were wasted at Tientsin in negotiations with unaccredited envoys, and, at length, it was decided to commence the march towards Tung-chow. But there were difficulties to be overcome; the road between Tientsin and Pekin was little known, as also the capabilities of the country to furnish supplies for the large number of soldiers, non-combatants, and animals. It was Colonel Wolseley's duty to collect information on these points, and the topographical department, of which he had been in charge from the outset of the campaign, was, at this time, reorganised. It now consisted, besides himself, of Lieutenant Harrison, R.E.—who had served at Alumbagh and Lucknow —and Mr. Robert Swinhoe, Interpreter in the British Consular Service, who had hitherto been acting in that capacity on Sir Robert Napier's staff.

Owing to the difficulty as to supplies, it was arranged that the two Armies should advance by detachments. Brigadier Reeves started on the 8th of September, with his Brigade, and, on the following day, Lord Elgin and Sir Hope Grant, and Wolseley with his assistants, quitted Tientsin.

The French troops, about three thousand, quitted Tientsin on the 10th of September, and Sir J. Michel marched with the remainder of the First Division on the 12th, Sir Robert Napier remaining behind with the Second Division to garrison the place. On their arrival at Yangtsun, the head-quarters camp remained immovable, owing to the flight of the drivers with the mules and ponies.* Parties were sent out into the country to try and recover the lost animals, or procure others, but without success, and, at length, as no other means of transport were available, several junks were seized, into which the greater portion of the stores and luggage was stowed.

Colonel Wolseley commenced his surveying duties immediately upon quitting Tientsin; he himself, accompanied by the interpreter, proceeded along the road, Lieutenant Harrison taking the course of the Peiho for his part of the survey. The country on either side of

---

* During the night of the 10th, all the Chinese drivers of the carts of Lord Elgin's and Sir Hope Grant's establishments had decamped, taking with them the whole of their mules and ponies. Wolseley alone retained his drivers, and that he did so was owing to an amusing circumstance. While riding out of Tientsin, he was conversing with the Ressaldar, or native commissioned officer, in command of his escort, and told him to impress upon his men that unless he and they looked sharply after the native drivers and prevented them from deserting, they would be left behind, and could not participate in the capture of Pekin. The native officer and his sowars took the hint, and, on the following morning, there was not a driver in the camp, except his own, who had all been tied together by their tails, and then made fast to the tent pole! Thereafter, this was done every night, and Wolseley arrived at Pekin with the carts and drivers and ponies he had started with, the only officer who did so. "The small camp of our Department," says Mr. Swinhoe, "consisted of one Indian tent and two bell-tents. The Chinese servants and carters generally built huts of mats and millet stalks, and the two native servants were accommodated with a *tente d'abri*. Besides our three horses, picketed in a row, there were six luggage ponies belonging to the carts, and the carts themselves, and in the group hard by, the eleven Sikh troopers detailed to us as guard, with their tents and horses. The whole made quite a conspicuous little group to the observation of passers by."

the Peiho, which is fenced in with artificial dykes, is one vast level plain, covered as far as the eye could reach, with crops of maize and millet; and were it not for occasional brick-kilns and watch-towers, an accurate survey of the road would have been most arduous. As it was, Colonel Wolseley, in order to insure accuracy, paced the road, and afterwards compared the distances so noted with the revolutions of the perambulator. On their first day's march to Pookow, about twelve and a-half miles from Tientsin, several distant large villages were passed, the names of which may be found in the survey maps of the road to Pekin executed by Colonel Wolseley and Lieutenant Harrison. On the 11th he proceeded on to Yangtsun, on the 12th to Nantsai, and on the 13th to Ho-se-woo, where he was engaged upon the survey of the river, and his assistant worked on the road. As this town appeared to be a good half-way station between Tientsin and Pekin, being about forty miles distant from each, a hospital and a depôt were established here.

At a meeting held at Tungchow between Messrs. Wade and Parkes and some Imperial Commissioners, it was decided that the Allied Army should march to within one and a-half miles of Chang-kia-wan, whence Lord Elgin, with an escort of one thousand men, was to proceed to Tungchow, and, after signing the Convention, to the capital for the purpose of ratifying the 1858 Treaty. On the 17th of September, the British Force, with one thousand French, marched to

Matow, a distance of twelve miles, and Wolseley resumed his survey of the road, but encountered great difficulty in procuring information, as the native villagers fled on the approach of their invaders, and had to be chased and run down by the Sikh escort. The following day, the 18th of September, was destined to be a memorable one in the history of the campaign, and, before the sun went down, convincing proofs were afforded—though, indeed, none were required save to enlighten the understanding and open the eyes of the diplomatists—that the Chinese Government and its Commissioners were acting with their wonted duplicity and treachery. Speaking of the simplicity displayed by the representatives of our Foreign Office, Wolseley observes:—" Military men are far less confiding than civilians in dealing with uncivilised nations. The little experience that I have had, goes to prove that the latter are far more rash and less liable to take the precautions which ordinary military knowledge would indicate as necessary. How often have I known civilians, accompanying an army, scoff at the caution of general officers, forgetting altogether that any commander who fails to provide against every possible mistake, or probable contingency, is deeply culpable. By the strange contrariety of human nature, it is generally these irresponsible gentlemen who are first loudest in their abuse of officers who fail in anything through rashness, or want of caution."

The Army marched at daylight on the 18th of September; but Wolseley remained behind during the forenoon, having obtained permission from Sir Hope Grant, on the previous night, to halt at Matow, and continue the survey of the road, promising, on its completion, to join him at Chang-kia-wan. After being busy for some hours, he was sitting in his tent, when Captain Gunter, of the King's Dragoon Guards, galloped up, calling out to him to be on his guard. "The General," he said, " had sent him with orders to move up the rear-guard, which had charge of the baggage, with all despatch, as there was a large body of cavalry ahead." Soon after Wolseley, who had betaken himself to the raised road, saw puffs of smoke in the air, denoting the firing of shells, and clouds of dust, such as are caused by cavalry charges. The thought flashed across him of the precarious position in which he and his party were placed, as in that open plain their white tents were visible a long way, and would, doubtless, draw upon them the observation of some of the Tartar cavalry, which was even now clearly carrying out the tactics of surrounding the Allied Army, which Sang-ko-lin-sin was always able to adopt, by reason of his numerical superiority. With the utmost dispatch, he caused the tents to be pulled down and packed, himself and his officers assisting, and, in a few minutes, the party was on its way to join the Army. Wolseley says that he never spent a more anxious time in his life than while making that march of four miles. It was not that he feared for himself and his mounted followers, but his soldier-servant and the corporal of Engineers were on foot, and he could not desert them in the event of an attack by the Tartar horse. He had made up his mind to throw himself and his men into the first house they passed on the road, and defend themselves to the last extremity with the guns and pistols they could muster. But, at length, he began to breathe more freely as he approached a village in which was the baggage in charge of a strong rear-guard ; and, in a few minutes, he had the satisfaction of seeing in safety, not only the *personnel* of his detachment, but also all the results of his surveys which had cost him so much labour, and were almost equally precious to him. To show how critical was the position of the party, and how near they were sharing the sad fate that overtook some of our countrymen, who were tortured to death by the savage foe, it may be mentioned that a large force of Tartar cavalry had actually passed between them and the rear-guard, and crossed the river less than half an hour before their arrival. Leaving his baggage along with the rest, Colonel Wolseley's party galloped along the road, turned off to the left along the bank of the Seau-ho ("little river"), and proceeded to the spot where Sir Hope Grant was resting under the shade of some trees.

They now learnt that the Allies had encountered and driven from their positions, a Chinese Army of about twenty thousand men, which barred their progress towards Tungchow, and captured seventy-four guns, with but slight loss. But the elation consequent upon this great success, was dimmed by the consideration that the enemy had in their hands many of our countrymen, and fears were entertained for their safety, which proved but too well founded. Captain Brabazon, Lieutenant Anderson, Messrs. Bowlby and De Norman, and many of the sowars and Frenchmen, died a cruel death, which Wolseley was near sharing, as Sir Hope Grant had sent for him to accompany Mr. Loch, of the Embassy, to proceed to Tungchow, to bring back the party there, and it was in consequence of his absence in the rear, completing the survey of the road, that Captain Brabazon was directed to proceed in his place.

On the 20th September, Colonel Wolseley rode back to Matow, and having completed the survey of the road between that village and Chang-kia-wan, returned in time to move out with the Allied Army, which, at daybreak on the following morning, marched to engage the enemy, who were drawn up about two miles distant from the town.

Colonel Wolseley attended Sir Hope Grant during the day, and, with the rest of the staff, had a narrow escape of falling into the hands of the enemy. He says:—" When we had marched a mile, we found ourselves in presence of a large army, their cavalry stretching away to the right as far as we could see, and endeavouring to turn our left flank; their infantry strongly posted in the numerous clumps of trees and enclosures which lay between us and the canal. As soon as we came within range, they opened fire upon us from hundreds of jingalls and small field-pieces, to which our Allies replied with their rifled cannon. Sir

Hope Grant rode forward towards the French for the purpose of examining the position, and having advanced beyond our line of skirmishers, rode almost in amongst the Tartars, mistaking them for the French. Upon turning back to rejoin our troops, the Tartar cavalry, seeing him and his numerous staff cantering away from them, evidently thought it was some of our cavalry running away, and at once gave pursuit with loud yells. Stirling's guns, however, opened heavily upon them when they were about two hundred and fifty yards from our line, saluting them well with canister, which sent them to the right-about as briskly as they had advanced." Soon after the Tartar cavalry tried to outflank the Allies, upon which our Cavalry charged them; and, says Wolseley, "riding over ponies and men, knocked both down like so many ninepins."

Sir Hope Grant now moved in pursuit to the left, and captured several camps, with tents standing, which were all burnt. The enemy having disappeared from the front and flank, he retired towards the wooden bridge over the Yuliang-ho canal.

The French had meanwhile captured all the camps which lay near the Pa-le-cheaou* Bridge, over which they drove the enemy at the point of the bayonet, with great slaughter. Here General Paou, commanding the Tartar cavalry, received his mortal wound, in revenge for which he caused the execution of our unfortunate

---

* General Montauban took his title of Count de Palikao, from this bridge, which means "8 le bridge," so called because it is 8 le, or 2¾ miles, along the paved road from Tung-chow.

countryman, Captain Brabazon, though according to other accounts, his fate was never ascertained. Towards the evening, the French encamped close to the canal upon the British right.

Sir Hope Grant, though within sight of Pekin, was unable to push his advantages and compel the surrender of the capital, as, relying upon the assurances of the diplomatists, he had left his siege guns at Tientsin. However, Sir Robert Napier, to whom he had sent word after the action of the 18th, advanced by forced marches, and arrived on the 24th of September. Five days later the siege guns came into camp, and, by the 3rd of October, all the available troops from the rear had arrived.

During the halt, Colonel Wolseley was very busy surveying the country between Chang-kia-wan and Pekin, and also reconnoitring about the capital and obtaining information from the villagers as to the movements of Sang-ko-lin-sin's Army, which was reported to be in position to the north of the city. Proceeding almost daily with a small party of cavalry as an escort, he, and other staff officers, advanced occasionally within a few hundred yards of the walls of Pekin.

On the 3rd of October, the camp at Pa-le-cheaou was broken up, and the British Force, six thousand strong, crossed the canal by the bridge of boats prepared for the purpose, and encamped on the paved road leading to Pekin; and two days later, the French having received the reinforcements for which they had been waiting, the combined Army, numbering about ten thousand combatants, carrying three day's cooked rations, and without tents, advanced in lines of contiguous columns. After a march of between four and five miles, our Army halted at a strong position to the north-east of Pekin, and, at the request of General Montauban, whose troops had made a longer march, Sir Hope Grant prepared to bivouac.

Colonel Wolseley located himself and Department in an old broken-down homestead, the sole occupant of which was a deaf and imbecile old woman ; and, ere " the early village cock had twice done salutation to the morn," was only too glad to be astir and quit his squalid quarters. The enemy's vedettes retreated as the Allied troops advanced ; and, a halt being called for breakfast, the Commanders-in-Chief conferred and arranged their plans. From some high brick-kilns they could command a good view of the surrounding country, also of the gates of Pekin, and the towers and minarets of the Imperial Palaces. After breakfasting, the Allied Armies advanced ; the English moving on the right, and making a slight *détour* so as to attack the line of ruined earthen ramparts upon their northern face, whilst the French, advancing direct to the left, entered them at the salient angle. Our cavalry, at the same time, moved away to the extreme right, with orders to cut off the retreat of the enemy from the Teh-sing 'gate, north-wards towards Zehol.

The British column advanced about three miles, and gained the earthen embankment, which was found to be deserted. Sir Hope now sent a message to General Montauban, informing him of the retreat of the enemy, and of his intention to push on for Yuen-ming-yuen, whither the Tartar Army was said to have gone. The British continued to advance and soon came upon the main road leading to the Anting gate of the city. As nothing could be seen of the French, who, without knowing it, had passed in rear of his troops, and as evening was approaching, Sir Hope Grant halted for the night close by the ground upon which Sang-ko-lin-sin's Army had been encamped.

Meanwhile, the British Cavalry, commanded by Brigadier Pattle, arrived at the large Peh-ting Temple, some three miles from the Tey-shun, or second gate of the north face of the city, close to which they found the French had halted; and the French General intimating his intention to advance on the Summer Palace, the Brigadier offered his co-operation, which was accepted.

The French arrived about sunset at the central gate of the Summer Palace, which is distant about six miles in a north-westerly direction from Pekin, and having posted a guard at the main gate, bivouacked under the trees; the British Cavalry also passed the night in an open spot in the fields beyond the large village of Hai-teen.

At daybreak on the following morning (the 7th of October), Sir Hope Grant, in order to apprise our Cavalry and the French of the position he had taken up, fired two guns from the high earthen rampart

close to his encampment, and directed Colonel Wolseley
to proceed with an escort of two squadrons of Cavalry,
and ascertain their position. Wolseley took the road
towards the Summer Palace, and, passing through an
opening in the western face of the high earthen entrenchment, proceeded nearly due west for about a
mile. He adopted the course familiar to fox-hunters
at home, and took "casts" in order to come on the
track of the French. At length he sighted, in the distance, a sowar, who was on duty as a Cavalry vedette.
Wolseley rode towards him, but the man, mistaking
the escort for the enemy, put spurs to his horse, and,
notwithstanding that Wolseley shouted to him to stop,
the fellow rode at full speed, and so the chase continued
for a distance of two miles. Following the fugitive,
Wolseley entered the parks and gardens of the Summer
Palace—known as Yuen-ming-yuen, or, "Round and
Brilliant Garden"—which are enclosed on all sides by
high granite walls, having within the area the guard-
houses of the Tartar watchmen, and the residences
of the Government officials and Emperor's relatives,
each with walled-in enclosures and high embankments
thickly planted with pine and cedar trees. General
Montauban had fixed his camp in a fine grove of trees
near the grand entrance, and Wolseley, after commu-
nicating with him and Brigadier Pattle, rode back to
head-quarters to report, escorted by two sowars.

About noon, Lord Elgin and Sir Hope Grant, guided
by Colonel Wolseley, who had just time before starting
to snatch a hasty breakfast, rode over to Yuen-ming-

yuen, for the purpose of conferring with General Montauban. On arrival, the Generals with their staffs, proceeded into the Palace.

It was a curious sight that met Wolseley's eyes as he entered the Palace, which, for two hundred years, had been the most cherished abode of the dynasty of the Emperor Hien-fung, who, among other titles, arrogated to himself those of "the Sacred Son of Heaven," and "the Governor and Tranquilliser of the Universe." The grand entrance opened into a paved courtyard, crossing which, the party of "barbarians" entered the Hall of Audience, at the upper end of which, opposite the door, was the Imperial throne. The chamber was highly coloured and gilt, and the floor was of polished marble; an immense picture, representing the surrounding palaces and gardens, covered the upper portion of one wall, and the rosewood throne, surrounded by an open-work balustrade, was a fine piece of workmanship. Around the apartment were handsomely-carved sideboards and tables, on which were arranged enamel and china vases, porcelain bowls, and large French clocks. Passing through the gardens, the party of British and French officers entered the suite of private rooms occupied by the Emperor, which were filled with the rarest and choicest articles of *vertu* of Native and European manufacture. When Wolseley entered, everything was *in statu quo* as when the Emperor fled. "His small cap, decorated with the character of longevity embroidered upon it, lay upon his bed; his pipe and tobacco pouch were upon a small table close by. In all the adjoining rooms were immense wardrobes filled with silks, satins, and fur coats. Cloaks covered with the richest golden needle-work, mandarin dresses edged with ermine and sable, and marked with the representations of the five-clawed dragons, showing that they were intended for royalty, were stored in presses. The cushions upon the chairs and sofas were covered with the finest yellow satin, embroidered over with figures of dragons and flowers. Yellow is the Imperial colour, and none but those of royal birth are permitted to wear clothes made of it. Jade stone is of all precious articles the most highly prized in China, some of it fetching immense prices. For centuries past the finest pieces have been purchased by the Emperors, and stored up in Yuen-ming-yuen. In some rooms large chests were filled with cups, vases, plates, &c., made of Jade stone." The private apart-ments of the Emperor were surrounded by those of his wives, retainers, eunuchs, and servants; these, in addition to the buildings, each stored with different articles of use or luxury, made up a vast group of some fifteen or twenty pavilions. One was full of furs, another of silks, another of drawings, a series of four thousand, illustrating the whole history of China, which, during the sack, the soldiers, ignorant of their value, trod underfoot, and used as firing, so that scarce two hundred were saved. Then there was the Carriage Palace, in which were found two howitzers, and two magnificent coaches, presented by Lord Amherst to the Emperor Taou-Kwang in 1818, but which had never been used; also Lord Macartney's presents to the "Brother of the Sun and Moon," during his embassy in 1793; and, lastly, in his Majesty's private room, was found Lord Elgin's Treaty of 1858, in its envelope.

Passing to the rear of the buildings, Wolseley took a brief survey of the park, enclosed by a wall some twelve miles in circumference. The walks and paths seemed endless, and led over marble bridges, canals, and fish ponds, upon some of which were mimic fleets of war-junks armed with brass cannon, which afforded amusement to the Emperor.

A Mixed Commission was nominated to divide the booty between the soldiers of the two Armies; but the French managed to secure more than their rightful share by looting.*

On the 11th of October, a sale was held of the booty which realized 123,000 dollars (about £24,000 sterling), a sum which enabled each soldier to receive seventeen dollars, (£3 10s.), and the officers, who were divided into three classes, and received one-third of the whole, were paid in like proportion. With characteristic generosity,

---

* " If the reader will imagine," says Wolseley, "some three thousand men let loose into a city composed only of Museums and Wardour Streets, he may have some faint idea of what Yuen-ming-yuen looked like after it had been about twenty hours in the possession of the French. Officers and men seemed to have been seized with a temporary insanity; in body and soul they were absorbed in one pursuit, which was plunder, plunder. I stood by while one of the regiments was supposed to be parading; but although their fall-in was sounded over and over again, I do not believe there was an average of ten men a company present."

Sir Hope Grant declined to take his share, throwing it into the common fund, an example which was followed by Sir Robert Napier and Sir John Michel, the Generals of Division.

Wolseley returned with Sir Hope Grant to the British camp before the Teh-shun gate, and, on the 9th, the French, having burnt the Emperor's private residence to the ground, quitted Yuen-ming-yuen and encamped to the British left, opposite the An-ting gate of Pekin.

On the following day the Allied Commanders drew up and forwarded a summons to the Prince of Kung, demanding the surrender of the An-ting gate by noon of the 13th of October, failing which the city should be bombarded; and proclamations, signed by Sir Hope Grant, were posted up in the suburbs, warning the inhabitants of his ultimatum, and advising them to clear out of the city. A reconnaissance was made of the northern face of the city defences, during which Wolseley, and other officers of the staff, rode up to the edge of the ditch, and a position was settled for the breaching batteries, about six hundred yards to the east of the An-ting gate.

On the night of the 12th all arrangements for opening fire at noon of the following day, were completed, and the batteries were unmasked; when at the last moment the resolution of Prince Kung gave way. At five minutes to twelve, Colonel Stephenson, who, with Mr. Parkes, had taken up his station close to the An-ting gate to receive any overtures, was seen galloping up to Sir

Robert Napier, who stood watch in hand, and announced that it would be surrendered. A party of the 67th Regiment and 8th Punjaubees, immediately advanced, and, driving before them the dense crowd of natives, took possession of the gate. The French then marched in, and soon the Union Jack and Tricolour were flying side by side on the walls of the chief city of the most populous kingdom of the world.

A few days after the occupation of Pekin, Colonel Wolseley, while engaged on a survey of the west wall, accompanied by his interpreter, Mr. Swinhoe, and an escort of cavalry, encountered a party of Chinamen with five carts, and, on examination, found that each contained a coffin with the body of one of our countrymen who had been captured on the 18th of September, and died of the cruel treatment to which they had been subjected. On the head of each coffin was pasted a piece of paper, inscribed with the name, in Chinese, of the deceased person it contained, and one marked " Po-ne-pe, died of disease on the 25th of September," was supposed to refer to Mr. Bowlby. The persons in charge of the bodies said that they had been brought from a town some forty miles north of Pekin. By the 16th of October the remains of our ill-fated countrymen, except those of Captain Brabazon and the French Abbé de Luc, of whom the Chinese authorities said they knew nothing, had been returned, and Sir Hope Grant, in order to impress the population with a sense of the estimation in which they were held, resolved to give them the honour of a military funeral. General

Ignatieff, the Russian Ambassador, having of his own accord offered the Russian cemetery, near the An-ting gate, as a place for interment, the funeral took place on the following evening. All the officers of our Army, a large number of French officers, and the attachés of the Russian mission, joined the procession, which consisted of a troop of the King's Dragoon Guards, a troop of Fane's Horse, an officer and twenty men from each infantry Regiment, and the band of the 60th Rifles. Lord Elgin and Sir Hope Grant attended as chief mourners, and three volleys having been fired over the coffins, which were laid side by side, the earth closed over the remains of a band of gallant and accomplished gentlemen, whose sad fate formed the most melancholy episode of the China War.*

Lord Elgin demanded as compensation the payment of 300,000 taels, about £100,000, which was paid on the 22nd instant, and in expiation of the foul crime, his Lordship directed the destruction of the Palace of Yuen-ming-yuen, which was accordingly carried into effect by Sir John Michel's Division.

Colonel Wolseley was present during the 18th and 19th of October, while the work of destruction was in progress, and took the opportunity of inspecting the

---

* Of the party of twenty-six Englishmen and sowars, thirteen, including Messrs. Parkes and Loch, were surrendered on the 8th and 12th of October, and six out of the thirteen Frenchmen. The bodies of the deceased Frenchmen were interred in an old Jesuit burial-ground, with military honours, Sir Hope Grant, with his staff and numerous officers, attending; and the Sikhs performed the last offices for their countrymen, by reducing their bodies to ashes.

country around the palaces, and that lying between them and the neighbouring hills. He was among the last to quit the heap of smouldering ashes that alone remained to mark the site of the palace, in which, for centuries, the Emperors of the Mantchoo, or Ta-tsing, dynasty received the embassies of some of the most powerful nations on earth.

The ratification and signature of the Treaty of Tientsin took place on the 24th of October, Colonel Wolseley, in consequence of rumours of treachery, having, on the preceding evening, proceeded into the city and made a careful inspection of the Hall of Ceremonies, one of the six Imperial Boards, the scene of the meeting.

On the 22nd October, Colonel Wolseley proceeded to Tungchow to superintend the transport, by boat, from there to Tientsin, of the sick and heavy stores. During his stay before Pekin, by great diligence he and his assistant, Lieutenant Harrison, had managed to make surveys of the country around Pekin, with the exception of the south side, which was too distant from the camp to enable him to reconnoitre there with a suitable force and return on the same day. In all other directions, however, the localities were closely examined, and the beautifully-executed maps he prepared are, doubtless, to be found in the Quartermaster-General's Department at the Horse Guards. In his history of the campaign, where his own name nowhere appears, he states that the maps were prepared " under the superintendence of Colonel Mackenzie," and merely adds :—

"All the information that could be obtained was collected, so that in the event of any future operations being required in those regions, our work will be much simplified." The good work he had done, did not, however, escape the notice of those most competent to judge, and whose favourable opinion would be, therefore, all the more highly appreciated. The Commanding General bestowed high praise upon him, and frequently mentioned him in despatches.

On the 7th of November the 2nd Division quitted Pekin, Sir Hope Grant and the First Division marching on the following day. Quitting Tungchow, the Army marched to Tientsin, where a garrison was left under Brigadier Staveley. The embarkation was commenced about the middle of November—the cavalry proceeding on to Taku, where they embarked—and completed by the end of the month, and very hard work it was for the officers of the Quartermaster-General's Department and the gunboats, which day and night were busy, amid very severe weather, conveying the troops to the fleet. But the arduous duty was performed with exemplary regularity, and without a hitch or accident of any kind, though not a day too soon, for, on the 25th of November, the mouth of the Peiho was completely frozen over near the city, and Colonel Wolseley and other officers walked across the river.

Wolseley accompanied Sir Hope Grant to Shanghai, where they, and twelve other officers, hired a Peninsular and Oriental steamer, and made a pleasure-trip to Japan, every important port of which interesting country they visited. On their arrival at Yokohama the party rode to Yeddo, a distance of nine miles, and stayed at the British Embassy; and, finally, having obtained the permission of the Japanese Government, proceeded, on their return voyage—this being only the second steamer to make her appearance in those waters —through the famous Inland Sea, the beautiful scenery of which has been described by Oliphant and other writers.

With the departure of Sir Hope Grant for England, the China War of 1860 was " as a tale that was told."* As this campaign was one of the shortest, so it was one of the most ably-conducted, this country had hitherto waged. The more recent Abyssinian and Ashantee Expeditions have accustomed us to short and sharp campaigns, crowned with brilliant success, for which we are indebted to the genius of the commanders who led British soldiers across the mountain passes of Abyssinia, and the fever-laden forests of the Gold Coast; but the Chinese War of 1860 is not without its lessons, and, though not so romantic in its incidents, or watched with such eager expectancy by the British public, as were those two memorable Expeditions, Sir Hope Grant scarcely received adequate praise or reward for the great success he achieved. The storm of the Taku forts was a gallant feat, and the advance

* The Army engaged in this War received a medal, and those present at the storm of the Taku forts and the capture of Pekin, were awarded two clasps. The thanks of both Houses of Parliament were voted to Sir Hope Grant and those who had served under his command.

upon, and occupation of, the populous Chinese capital, —the Kamballi of Marco Polo, around which hung a halo of romance as the place whence Kublai Khan issued his decrees to the ambassadors of dependent nations—was a daring act for so small a force to execute. The distance traversed was limited in comparison with that over which Sir Robert Napier and Sir Garnet Wolseley advanced, and though there were no natural obstacles to overcome, the country might have been made impracticable had Sang-ko-lin-sin adopted the tactics of Napoleon in 1812, while the population was enormous, though happily unwarlike. The loss in all three instances, whether in the field of battle or on the march was very small, and the operations were conducted with extraordinary rapidity and a masterly adaptation of means to ends. Not only is the conduct of these campaigns fraught with weighty lessons to all students of the art of war, but, in each case, the drama is full of interest to all Englishmen, and the *dénouement* was replete with tragic effect and grandeur. The treacherous murder of our countrymen by Hien-fung, the wholesale massacres of Theodore, and the sanguinary orgies of Koffee Kalcalli, received a fitting expiation in the destruction by the purifying agency of fire, of the Summer Palace, of Magdala, left a blackened rock, and of Coomassie, with its Golgotha of decaying corpses.

After the restoration of peace, Admiral Hope proceeded up the Yang-tze-Kiang with a squadron of gunboats, and, in the month of January, 1861, Colonel Wolseley was directed to proceed, accompanied by an interpreter, to Nankin on a semi-diplomatic, semi-military mission, with the object of reporting to the military authorities, upon the position and prospects of the Taipings,* who had now been eleven years in arms ; also of notifying to the rebel King, our Treaty with the Imperial Government, by which the Yang-tze-Kiang was opened to foreign trade, and that our merchants intended to send vessels up to Hankow immediately, and our Government proposed establishing Consulates there and at Hu-Kau and Ching-Kiang-foo. He was accommodated in a palace belonging to the Chung-wan, or "Faithful King," one of the eleven Taiping Chiefs, and received daily a supply of fowl, eggs, and other

* The Taiping cause at that time excited much compassionate fervour among a small clique in England, who appeared to think that, as these people were nominally Christians, they were justified, in their iconoclastic zeal, in committing wholesale murder and rapine. The real facts of the case were misrepresented, from interested motives, by some of the merchants, and from bigoted zeal by certain of the Protestant missionaries, who regarded these rebels with favour because they expressed a determination to extirpate idolatry, whether heathen or Popish, from the face of the land. But their religion was a mixture of blasphemy and barbarity, the chief head, "Tien-wan," being a prophet who lived at Nankin, in seclusion with his three hundred female domestics and sixty-eight wives, in a state of the most grovelling sensuality, until he died by his own hand, some four years later. All who opposed the new religionists were put to the sword, and entire provinces were desolated, the rebel soldiers pillaging the cities they conquered, and recruiting their armies by pressing into their service all males capable of bearing arms. Colonel Wolseley says that, knowing the imbecility and corruption of the Imperial Government, he went to Nankin strongly prejudiced in favour of the Taipings, but he came away enlightened as to the real character of this mock Christianity.

eatables, for which no money was required, it being the avowed intention of the leaders to abolish the use of coin, and reduce society to the patriarchal state; actually, on Wolseley's offering money to the wretched starving coolies who carried his wearing apparel, they refused to accept it if any one was present, from dread of the executioner's sword.

All communications between him and the Taiping authorities were carried on through Tsan-wan, the cousin of Tien-wan (the "Heavenly King") with whom he had great influence. Wolseley used to stroll about the city unquestioned, visiting all that was worth seeing, including the famous "Porcelain Tower," the old tombs of the Ming dynasty, and the extensive field-works surrounding the walls, thrown up by the Imperialists during their siege of the city, extending over several years. The only annoyance he suffered was caused by the crowds of idlers who followed him about, much as a London mob tracks the footsteps of any Eastern visitor, whose peculiarity of dress attracts the eye of the Cockney *gamin*. But in China the "hoi polloi" though, perhaps, not more personal in their remarks, are certainly less complimentary, and the opprobrious epithet of "fan-qui," (foreign devil) was applied to Wolseley more audibly than was at all agreeable.

"Crowds of men and women," he writes, "came daily to see us; all were most good-humoured, and took considerable pleasure in examining our clothes, and watching us eat. One evening a great procession carrying lanthorns visited us."

Wolseley visited a new palace built by Tien-wan, which was levelled to the ground by the Imperialists in 1864, in order to witness the ceremonies attendant upon the promulgation of a royal edict, and one which he saw, was worded in the most blasphemous language, the name of Tien-wan being coupled with the Trinity, as he was declared to be the brother and equal of Christ.

During Wolseley's stay at Nankin, the ' Yang-tse,' a fine steamer belonging to Messrs. Dent & Co., arrived there on its way to Hankow, and Admiral Hope's squadron not having yet appeared, he gladly availed himself of an invitation to proceed thither from a member of the firm who happened to be on board. On the 28th of February, 1861, he quitted the city of Nankin, and, after a pleasant trip up the Yang-tze-Kiang, which he describes in detail in his Journal, arrived at Hankow at four p.m. on the 5th of March.

Wolesley was received with the utmost consideration by the Viceroy, Kwang-wan, and, on the occasion of his making a state visit, was attended by the Commandant and a " three button Mandarin," who escorted him in the state barge, a vessel of one hundred and fifty tons burden. A triumphal arch, covered with flags and coloured cloth, was erected in his honour, and a vast crowd lined the river front of the city along which he was carried in a sedan chair, all anxious to catch a glimpse of the " foreign devil," and only kept in order by the police, who freely used their whips of twisted thongs. Colonel Wolseley quitted Hankow on the 10th of March, and reached Shanghai on the evening of the 16th, when he bade adieu to the hospitable owner of the " Yang-tse," having greatly enjoyed his trip. In quitting Shanghai for his mission to Nankin, Wolseley had been furnished with merely verbal instructions to gain all the information practicable of the position and prospects of the Taipings, considered from a military point of view. The conclusion he arrived at from a close survey of their resources, was most unfavourable to their eventual success. In the opinions he formed he was not, however, supported by British officials, who, it might be thought, from their long residence in the country, and intimacy with the people and their language, would have arrived at juster conclusions. Thus, Consul Meadows, in a Despatch to Lord John Russell, dated 19th of February in this year, took a favourable view of the rebel power, stating: —" I entirely deny that the Taipings have no regular Government, and have no claim to be considered a political power;" and to combat the prejudice excited against them on account of their atrocious custom of carrying fire and sword into every captured city, actually adduced such a military precaution as " the destruction of the suburbs of Shanghai by the British and French garrisons on the approach of the Taipings a few months previously," as equally indefensible! Consul Meadows also expressed an opinion that, to subjugate his interesting *protégés*, it would require on the part of the power which had just humiliated the Imperial Government, and defeated and dispersed its armies, "a large fleet of steamers and some twenty thousand troops operating in three or four armies in the country under their authority, extending eight hundred or nine hundred miles from north to south, and one thousand or one thousand one hundred east and west." Colonel Wolseley, in his Report, took a far different view of the strength of the Taipings, which turned out to be but weakness when, with native troops alone, Colonel Gordon, in his brief campaign of three months, completely shattered this power, which, to the consular mind, appeared so formidable a military organization.

From Shanghai, Colonel Wolseley proceeded to Hong Kong, whence he embarked, the last of the head-quarter staff to leave the country, in one of the steamers of the Peninsular and Oriental Company, and landed in England in May 1861, after an absence of something over four years.

During that brief space in Wolseley's military career, incidents had been crowded sufficient to make a life-time eventful. This country had emerged from one of the most tremendous crises, as regards the integrity of her dominions and the honour of the flag, that she has encountered in her "eventful story;" and she had struck down to the dust the pride and military power of the most populous, and one of the most ancient, empires in the world. By these achievements England had regained her pride of place, for though her position as one of the Great Powers can never be disputed, as long as she wields the sceptre of the seas, her prestige and military status had received a severe shock by the events of the Crimean War.

During those four years, also, Wolseley had frequently found himself face to face with Death in many of the varied forms "the lean abhorred monster" assumes in his battle with life. He had encountered him amid the terrors of the storm and shipwreck, when it seemed as if the sea was to engulph the "twice five hundred iron men," who had embarked in the ill-fated 'Transit.' He had met him in the battle field, and when struggling through the narrow streets of Lucknow with countless matchlockmen aiming at him from "tower and turret and bartizan;" and he had wrestled with him in the form the destroyer assumes, when he is in his fellest mood,—that of the pestilence which, even in the hour of victory, dogs the footsteps of our Armies in the East, and, in the shape of cholera or heat apoplexy, carries off his victims from among our bravest and most vigorous. From all these perils, by land and by sea, by battle, fire, and wreck, he had been preserved to land once more in his country, and we doubt not that on sighting the white cliffs of his native land, he offered up heartfelt thanks to the Providence that had watched over his safety during the four past eventful years.

On his arrival in England, Colonel Wolseley, who was promoted for his services to a substantive majority, got his long leave of eighteen months, and, after visiting his family, proceeded in the Autumn of 1861 to Paris, where he employed his leisure in painting in oils

and water colours, for, like some other officers of the
British Army, he added to his professional acquire-
ments the skill of an accomplished artist. Wolseley
seemed, however,—like the "Stormy Petrel" of the
ocean—to be the harbinger of wars and rumours of
wars, for, as on his return from Burmah, he had
scarcely set foot on the soil of his native land, than he
found her embroiled in a stupendous conflict with one
of the most powerful empires of the world, in the
vortex of which he was himself quickly drawn, so
again, hardly had he landed from service in the East,
than there was every indication that this country would
be soon grappling in a life-and-death struggle with the
greatest Republic of modern times.

CHAPTER V.

CANADIAN SERVICES.

The Trent Affair—Wolseley Embarks for Canada, and is employed on Transport Duty—His Visit to the Head-quarters of Generals Lee and Longstreet, and Impressions of the Confederate Armies—Wolseley's Services during the Fenian Invasion in 1866.

IN this politically hard-living age—when, within a decade, empires are founded and subverted, ancient despotisms humbled to the dust, and new republics given to the European system; when wars of the first magnitude are waged, resulting in battles and sieges, wherein hundreds of thousands of combatants are engaged, only, however, to lay down their arms—it has, perhaps, escaped the memory of many among us that, in 1861, this country was on the verge of hostilities with the United States, then not long entered upon that "War of Secession" which demonstrated the vast resources of the Great Republic, and the warlike spirit which only slumbered within the breasts of her citizens, who, whether as Confederates or Federals showed, themselves no unworthy scions of the Anglo-Saxon stock.

In the winter of 1861, nothing looked more certain on the political horizon, than the embroilment of this country in that momentous struggle, the issues of which would, in that event, have been far different from what history records. At that time the destinies of England were still wielded by the aged statesman, Lord Palmerston, who exhibited in this crisis all the warlike spirit and energy for which his name was almost a synonym, until the Danish business, when what Lord Derby called the "meddle and muddle" policy of the Foreign Secretary, caused it to be associated with something like pusillanimity. *Stat magni nominis umbra* might have been written of his Lordship after that *fiasco*.

The incident which nearly precipitated this country into war, was that known as the " Trent Affair," when, on the 8th of November, Commodore Wilkes, commanding the United States' ship-of-war, 'San Jacinto,' boarded the British Mail Company's steamship 'Trent,' on the high seas, and seized Messrs. Mason and Slidell, the Confederate Agents accredited to the Courts of London and Paris. Though the act was a clear violation of national rights and international law, Commodore Wilkes was raised to the height of popularity among the rowdy writers of the American press, who indulged in that species of "tall" talk expressively known as "spread eagleism;" and even an eminent statesman like Everett, who had been Secretary of State to President Fillmore, and previously Minister in England, gave Wilkes' conduct the sanction of his approval. The Commodore had, however, by his rash deed, landed the Federal Government on the horns of a dilemma. Either it was a belligerent power or it was not. If it was engaged in merely putting down a rebellion of its own subjects, as President Lincoln maintained, it was not belligerent, and therefore had not even the right of search to ascertain whether the neutral vessel carried contraband of war or not.

England was seized with a patriotic mania, and the most pacific were fired with a determination to uphold the honour of the flag and avenge this outrage, if reparation were not promptly made by the surrender of the Confederate Envoys. But the American press and public were equally outspoken against the possibility of concession, and for some weeks a war seemed inevitable. Our Government displayed the utmost energy in the preparations they made to meet the contingency, and—while the country waited with feverish anxiety the reply to Lord Russell's ultimatum of the 30th of November, addressed to Lord Lyons, requiring " the liberation of the four gentlemen and their delivery to your Lordship in order that they may again be placed under British protection, and a suitable apology for the aggression which has been committed,"—the dockyards resounded with the din of workmen fitting vessels for sea, troops were despatched to Canada with all possible despatch, and that colony, with the loyalty for which it has ever been remarkable, called out its militia and volunteers, so as to be ready to defend its borders from aggression. Happily, however, wise counsels prevailed in the Lincoln Cabinet; it was seen by the American Government and people, that John Bull was really in earnest this time and meant to fight; all the Governments of Europe were as one upon the merits of the question, and the cabinets of Paris, Berlin, and Vienna, addressed weighty remonstrances to the Washington Government, recommending them to make the *amende* and release the prisoners; and, finally, after an irritating delay, a despatch was received through Lord Lyons, from Mr. Seward, dated 26th of December, who, after arguing the case at most immoderate length, stated that "the four persons in question are now held in military custody at Fort Warren, in the State of Masachusetts. They will be cheerfully liberated. Your Lordship will please indicate a time and place for receiving them." This was done by placing them on board Her Majesty's ship 'Rinaldo,' Commander (now Admiral Sir William) Hewett, who was specially sent out to receive them; and they arrived at Southampton, on the 29th of January, 1862, in the 'La Plata.'

On the 17th of November, the day the news of the 'Trent' outrage reached London, a Cabinet Council was held, and, on the following day, the War Office ordered the despatch to Canada of a battery of Armstrong guns, a large supply of arms and accoutrements for the Colonial Militia, and a vast quantity of shot, shell, powder, ammunition, and other warlike stores.

The Controller of Transports chartered the steamer 'Melbourne,' but he could scarcely have made a more unfortunate selection, as she was old and worn out, and incapable of resisting the ice, which is sometimes met in the St. Lawrence after the month of October. However, she was readily available, being in the Port of London, and, on the 7th of December, sailed with a Battery of Artillery, thirty thousand stand of arms, and between eight and nine hundred tons of stores.

The War Department having determined to send out Special Service officers to prepare for the reception of the troops, which were to be despatched in large swift steamers, Colonel McKenzie was appointed Quartermaster-General, and he immediately asked for the services of Colonel Wolseley.

At this time Wolseley, who was on leave, was hunting in the County Cork. He had just bought two horses, and had enjoyed one day's sport on each animal, when a telegram came from Colonel McKenzie offering him employment on active service as Assistant Quartermaster-General. Not many hours were suffered to elapse before the hunters were given away, and Wolseley was in London. Colonel McKenzie proposed to the War Office that he, and the other selected officers, should proceed to Canada by the next mail steamer, but, with singular obtuseness, it was directed that they should embark in the 'Melbourne,' which was notorious during the China War, where it was employed as a transport, for its slowness and a habit it had of breaking down. In vain Colonel McKenzie, who knew from experience the steamer's unseaworthy qualities, pointed out that the object for which the Special Service officers were proceeding to Canada, namely, to prepare for the reception of the troops under orders for that country, would be best attained by their embarking in a swift mail steamer. It was all to no purpose, and the influences which were paramount when the question of embarking valuable lives in the 'Transit,' and, more lately, in the 'Megæra,' was under consideration, again prevailed.

The 'Melbourne' had on board, besides Colonels McKenzie and Wolseley, Colonel Lysons,* (selected to organize the Canadian Militia.) Captain Stoddart, R.E., and the late lamented Sir William Gordon, R.E., of "Gordon's Battery," a man of the true heroic mould, who proceeded in command of the troops. No sooner

* The ground to be traversed by the troops proceeding to Quebec was familiar to Colonel Lysons, who, in 1843, when a young officer in the Royal Scots, on the occasion of the wreck at Cape Chat, near the mouth of the St. Lawrence, of the 'Premier,' sailing transport, conveying his Regiment from Canada, volunteered to proceed on snow-shoes to Quebec, a distance of three hundred miles. This distance he actually accomplished by walking and travelling in carts, within six days. A ship was started off to the rescue immediately on his arrival, and was just in time to embark the troops before the river was frozen over. On the occasion of the wreck it was mainly by his gallantry and devotion that the lives of some hundreds of men, women, and children were saved.

had the 'Melbourne' sailed than she showed her un-seaworthy qualities.

After a weary passage, the ship, according to orders, tried to get through the ice to Bic, on the St. Lawrence, but this being found wholly impracticable, she bore up, under stress of weather and want of coal, for Sydney, Cape Breton Island. The miseries of that passage had been paralleled before by Wolseley in his ' Transit ' experiences, but still it was a peculiarly hard fate that forced him and his shipmates to pass the Christmas Day of 1861, coiled up on tables and benches in the cuddy, while the "green seas" washed at their sweet will through that apartment, and the ship laboured heavily against the wintry gale. The 'Melbourne' was thirty days performing a voyage which the 'Persia,' carrying a portion of the reinforcements, for whose reception they had been despatched to prepare, made in nearly one-third of that time. While at Sydney, a telegram arrived from Halifax, announcing the surrender of Messrs. Mason and Slidell, and that all chance of war was at an end. The 'Melbourne' then proceeded to Halifax, where she found three transports which had disembarked their troops, the War Office having determined to send to Canada ten thousand men and four batteries of Artillery.

From Halifax Colonel Wolseley and other officers proceeded, by a Cunard mail steamer, to Boston, on their voyage to Montreal. It was feared that the Boston people would be uncivil, and the officers were warned that the lower classes, in the excited state of public feeling, might even offer violence were they to display the British red coat in the streets. On their arrival, however, they found it was far otherwise; they were treated most respectfully while walking about during their afternoon's stay, looking at the lions of the city, and were regaled sumptuously by a private citizen. The same night they started for Canada, and, after a cold journey during the depth of an inclement winter, arrived at Montreal on a Sunday. On the following morning Colonel Wolseley started off on a journey of three hundred miles, down the river to Rivière du Loup, situated on the terminus of the Grand Trunk Railway, where the troops coming from St. John's, New Brunswick, including a battalion of the Scots Fusilier Guards and two batteries of Artillery, which arrived out in the ' Hibernian,' were transhipped from sleighs, or sleds, in which they had travelled, *viâ* Fredericton, to the railway by which they proceeded to their destinations at Quebec, Montreal, Hamilton, Kingston, or Toronto. Colonel Wolseley was the only staff officer at Rivière du Loup, and had to make all the arrangements for the accommodation and passage of the troops, who, after sleeping one night at the village, continued their journey on the following morning.

During his stay at this cheerless little place, the troops passed through at the rate of nearly two hundred men a day. It was his task to lodge, feed, and clothe them from the stores placed under his charge; and then to start them off on their long journey by rail.

These duties were fulfilled without a hitch or a single accident, and of the large force that passed through his hands, only one man deserted, although during the transit they passed close to the American frontier, at one place only a frozen river forming the boundary, and inducements were held out to them to forsake the flag of their country. In the middle of March, on the completion of his duties at Rivière du Loup, Wolseley returned to Montreal, the head-quarters of the Army in the Dominion, then under the command of Sir W. F. Williams (of Kars).

Soon after these events Colonel McKenzie proceeded to England, and Wolseley acted for some months as Deputy Quartermaster - General, until relieved by Colonel Lysons, who, soon after his first arrival in Canada for the purpose of organising the Militia, had returned to England, upon the rejection by the Opposition, led by the late Sir George Cartier, of the Government Militia Bill, a measure founded upon the scheme elaborated by Colonel Lysons at Quebec, and brought forward by the Ministry of that able and patriotic statesman, Sir John Macdonald, who resigned upon failing to pass his bill.

Colonel Wolseley went on leave in the latter part of August, 1862, but like many great actors, who, they say, on taking a holiday, may generally be found in the stalls of a theatre scrutinizing the performance of a brother artist, his strong professional proclivities induced him, instead of enjoying a little well-earned relaxation, to repair to the seat of war then raging in its fiercest intensity between the Federal and Confederate States. While living at Montreal with his friend, Inspector-General (now Sir William) Muir, Chief Medical Officer in Canada, they decided the question as to which of them should join the head-quarters of the Northern, and which those of the Southern, Army, with the view of comparing notes afterwards, by the familiar method of "tossing up." Wolseley "won the toss," and elected to proceed South, in order to seek instruction under that unequalled master of the art of war, General Robert Lee—"unequalled," we say advisedly, for it is Wolseley's opinion that in military genius Lee has had no superior since the great Napoleon, and he even places him above the great German Generals of the War of 1870. But to join a Confederate Army in the field, or even to enter Richmond, was not only a most difficult, but an extremely hazardous, adventure, for, even if he escaped the toils of the Northerners, and avoided being seized as a spy, the British Government highly reprobated such proceedings on the part of their officers, and the experiment was one that entailed the risk of his commission. However, such considerations were not likely to deter Wolseley from carrying out any scheme on which he had set his heart, so he proceeded to lay his plans, and procure letters of introduction to leading Southerners from sympathisers and correspondents. Having first proceeded to New York, he left that city for Baltimore on the 11th of September, and there made arrangements, in conjunction with his friends, for crossing the frontier by "underground railway," as the method by which communication was kept up between the North and Secessia, was called.

Armed with letters of introduction, he prepared to follow in the footsteps of the adventurous messengers, who were wont to " run the blockade of the Potomac," when conveying information between Richmond and the Northern States. There was, however, a difficulty in his case, for his " patois English," as the Yankees called it, would inevitably betray his nationality, and all our countrymen were under a ban in the North, as " rebel sympathisers ;" then there was the inevitable portmanteau of civilised life, without which an English gentleman, who has a regard for personal cleanliness and a change of linen, would not care to travel in country places where hotels are unknown, but which was not considered a necessity in a land where your " free-born American " thinks himself amply provided with a few paper collars and a pocket-comb.

When preparing to leave Baltimore he met the Honourable Frank Lawley, a brother of Lord Wenlock's, at that time one of *The Times* correspondents in America, a clever and adventurous gentleman, and they soon agreed to run the blockade together. But in the first instance, it was a matter of difficulty to reach the banks of the Potomac, whose broad stream, again, patrolled by numerous Federal gunboats, offered an almost impassable barrier to any seeking to cross over into Dixie's Land. Though the Federal gunboats patrolling the river, were not as numerous as between

July, 1863, when the battle of Gettysburgh was fought,
and April, 1865, at the close of the War, on the other
hand, at this time, as Mr. Lawley observes, " there was
no such organization for running the blockade between
Baltimore and Richmond as was established during
1863, and as was available for those rightly initiated
into its mysteries until the spring of 1865."

The Potomac at the point of crossing, is rather an
arm of the sea than a river, and varies between ten and
thirteen miles in breadth, so that during the prevalence
of south-east winds, its broad bosom is scarcely less
agitated than the Atlantic outside the Capes of the
Chesapeake.   Mr. Lawley says :—" It was necessary
for the boatmen connected with the Signal Service of
the Confederate Government to be well acquainted with
the moods of the mighty and dangerous river, in order to
understand the seasons when it was safe for a row-boat
with muffled oars to cross. In addition, the phase of the
moon had to be closely watched, in order that a dark
night might be selected.   But even during the blackest
night there were the Federal gunboats, which were at
last no less thick upon the stream than policemen in
the Strand between midnight and sunrise.   Each of
these boats was armed with a calcium or lime-light,
and, if the slightest sound was heard at night upon the
surface of the stream, a broad luminous ray of light
was shot forth from the sentinel vessel, which illu-
mined the river for a quarter of a mile, so that the head
of a swimming otter was discernible."

But before the Potomac could be crossed, the two

Englishmen had to smuggle themselves from Baltimore to the northern bank, every road and path leading to which was patrolled by bodies of Federal troops. The start was made in a waggon and pair, driven by a trusty agent, who had been well paid for the trouble and risk. In this conveyance they contrived to slip from the country-house of one Secession sympathiser to another, and as bodies of patrolling Cavalry and Infantry had at that time regular beats and fixed hours for traversing them, which were well known to the farmers in that part of Maryland, who were nearly all Secessionists, they managed to eluded the patrols while proceeding from house to house. " I travelled," says Colonel Wolseley,* " about thirty miles a-day, until I reached the village from which I had arranged that my final start should be made, and where I was informed certain people, with whose names I had been furnished, would arrange all matters for me.

" For the first few nights of our journeyings we stopped at different gentlemen's houses, where we were entertained with patriarchal hospitality. It was interesting in some instances to hear the history of these homesteads; many of them had been built before the Declaration of Independence, and more than one was of brick imported from England. All the proprietors boasted of their English descent from good families,

---

* See an article in " Blackwood's Magazine " for January, 1863, entitled " A Month's Visit to the Confederate Head-quarters, by an English Officer." This is not the only article Colonel Wolseley has written in " Old Ebony."

and seemed to attach far greater importance to blood and ancient pedigree than even we do."

At length they arrived at a farm-house on the river, but had great difficulty in procuring a boat; and after many disappointments they were directed to a smuggler on the river, who had a craft of his own, in which he consented to take them over. "We remained," says Wolseley, "for a night at his abode, sleeping in a garret destitute of windows, but abounding with rats which sadly disturbed my friend's rest, though I slept soundly being accustomed to rough it in every part of the globe."

. They were astir early, and embarked in the smuggler's boat. "The creek," says Wolseley, "into which we had hoped to run on the Virginian shore, was about a couple of miles higher up than the point from which we started, but, unfortunately, a gunboat lay off the entrance to it, and there were two others at no very great distance. After due deliberation, it was determined that we should make for a spot about five miles higher up, and endeavour to get there by running close along the left bank of the river, so as not to attract attention, and, when clear of all gunboats, to push out into the centre of the stream, and then watch a favourable opportunity for steering into the desired haven. The tide being in our favour, we dropped slowly up on it, until about mid-day, when it turned, and, the wind dying away, we were obliged to make close in for shore and anchor. My friend and I had landed, and spent the day in an old ruined shed surrounded by reeds and rushes. Large steamers and gun-vessels of various sizes kept passing and re-passing all day; but none of them seemed to notice our little craft. On one occasion we saw a boat put off from one of the gunboats and come in our direction; but instead of visiting us, its crew boarded a small cutter which lay becalmed in the centre of the river, and then returned to their own vessel. At sunset a slight breeze arose, before which we glided directly up the river. When we passed the mid-stream and approached near the Virginian shore, the owner of the boat became quite nervous, and began lamenting his fate in having to turn smuggler; but the hard times, he said, had left him no alternative, his farm having been destroyed by the Northern troops. He seemed to have a superstitious awe of gunboats, too; and told us he had heard that the officers on board of them possessed telescopes through which they could see distinctly for *miles* at night. Several steamers passed us when we were about two-thirds of the way over, but although the moon every now and then emerged brightly from behind the drifting clouds, we had got under the shade of the land, and managed so that she always shone upon our sails on the side away from the 'enemy.' We could hear the steamers for about twenty minutes before we caught sight of their light, and during that time the anxious face of the smuggler would have made a glorious study for an artist of the Rembrandt school. The cargo consisted of coffee and sugar, and, if safely landed, would be in itself a small fortune to the owner of the boat; that he should feel alarmed for its safety, therefore, was not surprising. As we approached the shore, the wind died away, so we were obliged to punt the little craft along; the men thus employed taking off their boots, lest they should make any noise in moving upon the deck. Now and then one of the gunboats, anchored off the neighbouring creek, would throw a light along the waters in all directions; once we all fancied that it was approaching nearer to us, and on another occasion we thought we heard the sound of oars, and as there was not a breath of wind to help us along, and punting is a slow process, we felt far from comfortable. Half-past ten found us safe in a little creek almost land-locked, so there was no danger of discovery there; and a run of about a mile and a half up it took us to the point of landing. After a dreary walk of about five miles over a forest road, we reached a small village, and, having spent a considerable time in knocking at the door of the house to which we had been directed, we at last succeeded in gaining admittance. The landlord was absent, being in concealment at a farm-house in the neighbourhood; but his niece, a very nice girl, did the honours in his stead. She told us that the Yankees had made a descent upon the village, and carried off several of the inhabitants as prisoners to Washington. The place was suspected of containing smugglers, consequently the Federal troops frequently visited it in search of contraband goods."

Mr. Lawley thus describes the passage across the Potomac, and an interview in the smuggler's cottage with a Federal officer commanding a patrol, which, but for the presence of mind they both displayed, must have proved fatal to the success of their undertaking, if not to their liberty:—"We succeeded, one evening at night-fall, in making our way to a cottage which looked down upon the broad and tranquil river. Its owner was a fisherman, who told us that his house was usually visited during the night by a patrol, and that it would be unsafe for us to sleep there; but he promised that, if we would return on the morrow at noon, he would have a friend named Hunt to meet us, with whom we might probably make a bargain. Mean-time, we adjourned to a village some two or three miles distant, where, what between heat and insects, we passed an awful night. At noon, we were again at our friend's house, and covenanted with a son of Hunt, the fisherman, for twenty dollars a piece in gold, that his father's boat would take us on board that night at ten o'clock in an adjoining creek, and would land us before daybreak on the Virginian shore. But the intervening afternoon brought with it fresh adventures. We were forbidden by our host to leave the house, because the telescopes of the Federals in the neighbouring gunboat were said to be constantly sweeping the shore, and would infallibly detect the presence of strangers in the little hut. Shortly after two o'clock, we were horrified by the sight of a Federal officer, in the well-known blue uniform of the United States' Army, who was ascend-ing on foot by a little path which led to the house from the river. In his hand he carried a revolver, and behind him followed seven soldiers, who, with their leader, had just got out of a boat. The consternation of our host during the few seconds of suspense before the Federals reached the house, was pitiable in the extreme. There was scant time for consultation, and when the officer looked into the hut and descried Colonel Wolseley and myself, he seemed scarcely less disquieted than our host. Having in previous years shot canvas-backs and blue-wings on the Potomac, I stepped forward as spokesman, and asked the officer whether it would be possible for us to hire a boat, as I had often before done, with a view to doing some 'gunning' on the river. The officer answered that no 'gunning' was now permitted on the river. I then asked him how it would be possible for my companion and me to get back to Washington. Just as he was hesitating about his answer, Colonel Wolseley adroitly advanced, cigar-case in hand, and offered him a 'regalia.' That judiciously proffered cigar turned the balance in our favour. The officer answered that a steamboat would call the following morning about four o'clock at the neighbouring wharf, by which we might take passage to Washington. We parted the best friends, in spite of the whispered remonstrances of a sergeant, who probably thought our appearance suspicious, and remarked that we had no guns with us. Long before four o'clock of the following morning, Hunt and his two sons had landed us in Virginia. Colonel Wolseley and I had to lie down and conceal ourselves below the gunwale, and I remember how long the *trajet* seemed to us, as the fishing-boat tacked hither and thither while casting its nets, and approached uncomfortably near the Federal gunboat. After I had passed two or three months at Richmond, and become intimate with the officers of the Signal Service, I heard that poor Hunt had been subsequently caught in carrying passengers across the Potomac—that his boat had been seized, and himself sent to prison. But I have often thought how severely the Federal authorities, and especially Mr. Seward, would have blamed the young gentleman who thus allowed so distinguished a British officer as Colonel Wolseley to slip through his fingers."

On landing in Virginia, Colonel Wolseley and his friend walked to the village of Dumfries; it was dark and the roads were bad, but they were light-hearted and contented at having crossed the dreaded Potomac and eluded the Federal cruisers. At Dumfries they procured a farmer's cart without springs, drawn by two mules, and in this comfortless conveyance, which jolted along over "the very worst road" Wolseley had seen even in all his Indian and China experiences, they drove into Fredericksburg, crossing the Rappahannock river. Early on the following morning they again started, and, taking the road leading under Mary's Heights, which, three months later, was the scene of one of the most sanguinary struggles of the War, reached Beaverdam station, on the Virginia Central Railroad, in time for the afternoon train, which took them to Richmond.

Colonel Wolseley says :—" All the carriages were crowded with passengers, of whom a large proportion were the sick and wounded coming from General Lee's Army at Winchester. They had been all day on the railroad, and some of the poor fellows seemed quite worn out with fatigue. My friend and I stood on what is called the platform of the car, during the journey of two hours and a-half, as the regular passenger-cars were full, and those containing the sick and wounded were anything but inviting, as men with legs and arms amputated, and whose pale, haggard faces assumed an expression of anguish at even the slightest jolting of the railway carriages, lay stretched across the seats. At every station where we stopped, a rush for water was made by the crowds of men carrying the canteens and calabashes of those whose disabled condition prevented them from assisting themselves. The filth and stench within those moving hospitals were intolerable, and, though well inured to the sight of human suffering, I never remember feeling so moved by it as during that short railway journey.

" Upon reaching Richmond we found a dense crowd on the platform, men and women searching for brothers, fathers, husbands, and lovers. A military guard, with fixed bayonets, was endeavouring to keep order and a clear passage for those on crutches, or limping along with the aid of a stick or the arm of some less severely wounded comrade. We drove off to the Spottiswood Hotel, but were informed that there was not even one room vacant. The same answer was given at the

American ; but at the Exchange we obtained a little double-bedded apartment up four flights of stairs. Congress was sitting, so the best rooms at most houses were engaged by the Members of the Legislature, and wounded men occupied almost all the other available bedrooms. When black tea is selling at sixteen dollars a-pound, and everything else, except bread and meat, is proportionately expensive, it may be readily imagined that the fare is far from good. Four dollars a-day, however, for board and lodging, is not very exorbitant ; but no wine or spirits is to be procured at any hotel, the manufacture and sale of all intoxicating liquors having been prohibited by Government."

On this question of spirits as it concerns the health of soldiers on active service, Colonel Wolseley has always entertained opinions in consonance with those of Sir Wilfred Lawson, and, though no teetotaller, has ever been averse from serving out spirits to troops in the field.*   This view he has studiously

* He remarks : "When the Confederate Army was first enrolled, each man received a daily ration of spirits ; but this practice has been long since discontinued, and, strange to say, without causing any discontent amongst the men—a practical refutation of the assertion that a certain amount of stimulants is absolutely necessary for soldiers, and that without it they cannot endure the fatigues of active service. For what army in modern times has made the long marches, day after day, that Jackson's corps of 'foot cavalry,' as they are facetiously called, have accomplished ? Doubtless there are circumstances when an allowance of grog is very beneficial to health—such as bivouacking in swampy places, and during heavy rains ; but in ordinary cases, and in fine weather, I am convinced that men will go through as much continuous hard work without any stimulants whatever as with them."

carried out in the two campaigns which he himself has conducted, and he attributes the health enjoyed by the troops in the Red River and Ashantee Expeditions, in no small degree, to the fact of their abstention from spirituous liquors.

Wolseley and his friends were received with open arms by the Southern leaders, and such letters of introduction as they had managed to retain, having previously sewn them up in their clothes, proved an "open Sesame" in society. They were received and hospitably entertained by the members of the Government, including Mr. Benjamin, Secretary of State for Foreign Affairs, and General Randolph, the Secretary at War, who was most obliging in furnishing them with passes to go wherever they pleased, and with letters to the various military authorities. The first Confederate officer who called upon them at their hotel, was the late General John B. Magruder, who, when in Canada, had made many friends among the British officers.

One can scarcely realise the intensity of the passionate fervour with which the gallant Southerners maintained the unequal conflict with their gigantic opponent. Whatever had been the original cause the War, it was now, as Lord Russell stated, "a contest for dominion on the part of the North, and for independence on the part of the South," a conclusion which the *Times* endorsed on the 19th of January, 1862, when it declared that the War was "a purely political quarrel," adding, "that as the cause of Italy against Austria is

the cause of freedom, so also the cause of the South
gallantly defending itself against the cruel and deso-
lating invasion of the North, is the cause of freedom."*

* Early in the struggle it was manifest that the Northern statesmen
and Congress would sacrifice principle to retain the seceding States, for
on the 3rd of March, 1861, after the formation into a Confederacy of
the six States and the inauguration of Jefferson Davis, and on the day
preceding the installation of Abraham Lincoln, President Buchanan
and the Congress amended the Constitution in these terms :—"That
no amendment shall be made to the Constitution which shall authorise
or give Congress power to abolish or interfere within any State with
the institutions thereof, including that of persons held to labour or
servitude by the laws of the said State." Also in March, 1862, President Lincoln presented to Congress a " proposition," which was "sub-
stantially to end the Rebellion " by purchasing the slaves of those States
that would return to the Union ; but, wisely conceiving that th ecountry
—unlike England, which, in 1834, paid twenty millions sterling to buy
up the slaves of the West India Islands—would prefer the cheaper
expedient of coercing the South, and freeing the slaves, to the enormous
expense of purchasing four millions of negroes at £100 per head—
which was the sum the little State of Delaware, with its one thousand
eight hundred slaves, magnanimously asked for washing its hands of
the " accursed thing "—President Lincoln observed that if his proposal
" does not meet with the approval of Congress and the country, it is at
an end." Cordially hating slavery as we do, whether in its worst form,
as we have seen it on the east coast of Africa, or as a " domestic insti-
tution," as it appeared in the Southern States, we cannot but rejoice
that it was crushed out once and for ever from the American Continent. Englishmen should remember, with humility and shame,
that all the misery and bloodshed of this great Civil War was the
damnosa hereditas bequeathed by our ancestors to our American colo-
nies. Though slaves were first imported into America by the Spanish
missionary, Las Casas (who was horrified by the cruelty with which
the Aborigines were treated by the European settlers), it was in 1562,
l ng before the settlement of Virginia, that Queen Elizabeth founded

At the time of Wolseley's arrival at Richmond, the
Confederate Army had just returned from the Expedition into Maryland, after having fought, on the 17th
of September, the sanguinary but indecisive battle of
Antietam, or Sharpsburg ; and he mentions, as an
interesting fact, that during a conversation with
General Lee, he assured him that throughout the
day he never had more than thirty-five thousand men
engaged, and with these he fought a drawn battle
with McClellan's host of ninety thousand men, General
Stonewall Jackson being engaged in reducing Harper's
Ferry with the remainder of the Confederate Army
which had crossed the Potomac.   While at Richmond,
Wolseley visited the scene of the seven days' desperate
fighting which took place in its vicinity in the previous
June, when, in his opinion, General Lee showed himself as consummate a master of the art of war as
Napoleon himself.   He says of these battle-fields :—
" In some places the numerous graves and pits filled
with dead bodies but slightly covered over, testified to
the severity of the fighting there.   The *débris* of all
things pertaining to an army, which lay strewn about
on the ground camped on by McClellan's troops, was
immense.   In many places the blackened embers of
flour-barrels, clothing-cases, and commissariat stores
covered large spaces, showing the haste with which the

a company for its promotion, while Charles II. made grants of lands
to the colonists in proportion to the number of their slaves.   William
III. gave further encouragement to slavery, and finally, in the reign of
George II., free trade in slaves was declared.

general retreat was commenced, and the great quantity of stores which it had been found necessary to destroy. In some parts the very trunks of the trees were riddled through, huge pines being cut down by round shot, and great branches torn off by bursting shells." His comments of the strategy of the rival Commanders, as coming from a master of the art, and one who had studied the ground, are of great interest and no little value.

Before leaving Richmond, Colonel Wolseley and Mr. Lawley spent a day at Drury's Bluff (or Fort Darling, as it was called in the North), which was attacked by the 'Monitor,' 'Galena,' and some other Federal iron-clad gunboats, when McClellan's Army was on the peninsula. Captain Lee, formerly of the United States Navy (brother to General R. Lee, and father to General Fitzhugh Lee), was in command of the troops and position, and was most obliging in showing them round the works, and pointing out all the new improvements in guns, carriages, and projectiles.

Wolseley also inspected the 'Richmond' (or Merrimac No. 2), and was astonished at the success of the efforts of the Southerners in the art of shipbuilding and the manufacture of gunpowder and other munitions of war.

Having been furnished by General Randolph, the War Minister, with letters of introduction to General Lee, and the necessary passes, they left Richmond by the Virginia Central Railroad, and reached Staunton in the evening. This place, owing to the War, was in a forlorn condition; no business was doing, and Wolseley searched in vain through a number of shops for so common a domestic utensil as a teapot or kettle of any description. Being the railway terminus, and the commencement of the turnpike-road line of communication with the Army, Staunton had become an *entrepôt* for stores, waggons, and ambulances, and most of the best houses had been converted into hospitals.

No other means of transport being available, they succeeded, with some difficulty, in getting permission to proceed in an ambulance cart, one of a large number going up to carry back sick and wounded men. It was four-wheeled, fitted with a tarpaulin hood, and drawn by two horses, the body of the cart being made to carry two men on stretchers, with room for another man beside the driver. The cart was mounted on very tolerable springs, but being one of a batch lately made in Richmond after the Yankee pattern, and having been hastily put together by unskilled workmen, its construction was so bad, and the wheels so weak, that it must have tumbled to pieces in one day's march over the ordinary country roads of Virginia, though, fortunately, the road down the Shenandoah Valley was Macadamised, being the only regularly metalled road in the State. There were thirteen ambulance carts in the train with which they travelled, but they had not proceeded more than about six miles when two or three of them had to halt at a smith's shop for the purpose of having the wheel-tires cut and reduced in size, the dry weather having so affected the new wood, that the spokes were rattling loosely about. Owing to this delay not more than five and twenty miles were made the first day, and a halt was called for the night in a field a few miles short of Harrisonburg.

The night was cold, with a very heavy dew, but they soon lighted good fires, and, squatting around them, made themselves tolerably comfortable. The waggon would only admit of two sleeping in it, so one of their party of three had to lie on the ground with his feet to the fire in correct bivouac fashion.

The following night the ambulance train halted between Mount Jackson and Woodstock, and, on the third night, at Middletown, about thirteen miles from Winchester. It had been raining all day, and the prospect of a bivouac was far from agreeable, so Wolseley and his two companies shouldered their baggage and marched for the inn at the village. As usual the place was crowded to excess, men even sleeping in the hall; but, being tired, wet, and hungry, they were prepared to pay any sum that might be asked, provided they could only get a room to themselves. "It was a very dark night," says Colonel Wolseley, "and the street almost ankle-deep with mud, when my two companions, one carrying a candle, sallied forth in search of a lodging for the night, I remaining sentry over our traps the while. They were sent from house to house for some time, no one caring to take in three strangers, but at last a good old woman's heart was touched by our forlorn condition, and she consented to give us shelter. She proved to be most kind and hospitable, giving us a good breakfast the next morning, and seemed quite disinclined to accept any remuneration for the inconvenience we had caused her."

On the fourth day after leaving Winchester* they arrived at Staunton, and, having procured passes from the Provost-Marshal, without which no one could have passed the guards posted on all the roads, proceeded to General Lee's head-quarters, which were close to the Martinsburg road, about six miles from Winchester. Colonel Wolseley and his friend presented their letter

---

* Wolseley remarks in his Journal : " Every day during our journey to Winchester we passed batches of convalescents marching to join the Army, many of whom were totally unfit for any work, which, of course, spoke very highly for the men. Each day we also passed batches of sick and wounded going to the rear ; those totally unable to march being conveyed in ambulances, or the empty waggons returning to Staunton for more supplies. It was an extremely painful sight to see such numbers of weakly men struggling slowly home, many of them without boots or shoes, and all indifferently clad ; but posts were established every seventeen miles along the road, containing commissariat supplies for provisioning them. Into whatever camp you go, you are sure to see tents, carts, horses, and guns all marked with the " U.S." Officers have declared to me that they have seen whole regiments go into action with smooth-bore muskets and without great-coats, and known them in the evening to be well provided with everything—having changed their old muskets for rifles ! The Northern prisoners we passed on the road were well clothed in the regular blue frock coat and light-blue trousers, whilst their mounted guard wore every variety—jackets or coats, it seemed to matter little to them ; and, indeed, many rode along in their shirt-sleeves, as gay and happy as if they were decked with gold and the richest trappings." As General Lee said to Wolseley, when alluding to the ragged uniforms of his soldiers : " There is one attitude in which I should never be ashamed for you to see my men—that is to say, when they fight."

to the Adjutant-General, by whom they were intro-
duced to the famous Commander-in-Chief of the Confederate Forces, who received them with kindness and
the stately courtesy for which he was remarkable. Of
General Lee, and the impression he created in his
mind, Wolseley says:—" He is a strongly built man,
about five feet eleven in height, and apparently not
more than fifty years of age. His hair and beard are
nearly white; but his dark brown eyes still shine with
all the brightness of youth, and beam with a most
pleasing expression. Indeed, his whole face is kindly
and benevolent in the highest degree. In manner,
though sufficiently conversible, he is slightly reserved;
but he is a person that, wherever seen, whether in a
castle or a hovel, alone or in a crowd, must at once
attract attention as being a splendid specimen of an
English gentleman, with one of the most rarely hand-
some faces I ever saw. He had had a fall during the
Maryland Expedition, from which he was not yet recovered, and which still crippled his right hand considerably. We sat with him for a long time in his
tent conversing upon a variety of topics, the state of
public affairs being of course the leading one. You
have only to be in his society for a very brief period
to be convinced that whatever he says may be implicitly
relied upon, and that he is quite incapable of departing
from the truth under any circumstances."

Wolseley, who had seen so many French and British
Armies in the field, was greatly struck with the marked
absence of all the " pomp and circumstance of glorious

war" at General Lee's head-quarters. "They consisted," he says "of about seven or eight pole tents,
pitched with their backs to a stake fence, upon a piece
of ground so rocky that it was unpleasant to ride over
it—its only recommendation being a little stream of
good water which flowed close by the General's tent.
In front of the tents were some three or four wheeled
waggons, drawn up without any regularity. No guard
or sentries were to be seen in the vicinity, and no
crowd of aides-de-camp loitering about. A large farm-
house stands close by, which, in any other army,
would have been the general's residence: but as no
liberties are allowed to be taken with personal property in Lee's Army, he is particular in setting a good
example himself. His staff were crowded together two
or three in a tent: none are allowed to carry more
baggage than a small box each, and his own kit is but
very little larger. Every one who approaches him does
so with marked respect, although there is none of that
bowing and flourishing of forage caps which occurs in
the presence of European Generals; and whilst all
honour him and place implicit faith in his courage and
ability, those with whom he is most intimate feel for
him the affection of sons to a father. Old General
Scott was correct in saying that when Lee joined the
Southern cause, it was worth as much as the accession
of twenty thousand men. Though his house on the
Pamunky river was burnt to the ground, and his residence on the Arlington Heights not only gutted of its
furniture, but even the very relics of George Washing-

ton were stolen from it and paraded in triumph in the saloons of New York and Boston, he neither evinced any bitterness of feeling, nor gave utterance to a single violent expression, but alluded to many of his former friends and companions amongst the Northerners in the kindest terms. He spoke as a man proud of the victories won by his country, and confident of ultimate success under the blessing of the Almighty, whom he glorified for past successes, and whose aid he invoked for all future operations. He regretted that his limited supply of tents and available accommodation would prevent him from putting us up, but he kindly placed at our disposal horses, or a two-horsed waggon, if we preferred it, to drive about in."

Upon leaving General Lee, they drove to Bunker's Hill, six miles nearer Martinsburg, where that extra-ordinary man, General Stonewall Jackson, had his head-quarters. With him they passed a most pleasant hour, and were agreeably surprised to find him very affable, having been led to expect that he was silent and almost morose. Wolseley's description of this noble soldier, whose loss, soon after, dealt an irrepar-able loss to the Confederate cause, is graphic and full of interest :—" Dressed in his grey uniform, he looks the hero that he is ; and his thin compressed lips and calm glance, which meets yours unflinchingly, gave evidence of that firmness and decision of character for which he is so famous. He has a broad open forehead, from which the hair is well brushed back ; a shapely nose, straight and long ; thin colourless cheeks, with only a very small allowance of whisker; a cleanly-shaven upper lip and chin; and a pair of fine greyish-blue eyes, rather sunken, with overhanging brows, which intensify the keenness of his gaze, but without imparting any fierceness to it.   Such are the general characteristics of his face; and I have only to add, that a smile seems always lurking about his mouth when he speaks; and that though his voice partakes slightly of that harshness which Europeans unjustly attribute to *all* Americans, there is much unmistakable cordiality in his manner: and to us he talked most affectionately of England, and of his brief but enjoyable sojourn there.   The religious element seems strongly developed in him; and though his conversation is perfectly free from all puritanical cant, it is evident that he is a man who never loses sight of the fact that there is an omnipresent Deity ever presiding over the minutest occurrences of life, as well as over the most important. Altogether, as one of his soldiers said to me when speaking of him, " he is a glorious fellow!" and, after I left him, I felt that I had at last solved a mystery and discovered why it was that he had accomplished such almost miraculous feats.   With such a leader men would go anywhere, and face any amount of difficulties.   "For myself," adds Wolseley, with the enthusiasm of a soldier, "I believe that, inspired by the presence of such a man, I should be perfectly insensible to fatigue, and reckon on success as a moral certainty."*

* Wolseley thus analyses the different nature of feeling with which

The Army at Winchester was composed of two *corps d'armée* under the command of Generals Jackson and Longstreet, each consisting of four divisions. Wolseley was present whilst the latter officer inspected one of his divisions, and was highly pleased with the appearance of the men, and the manner in which they marched. He says:—"I remarked that, however slovenly the dress of the men of any particular Company might be, their rifles were invariably in good serviceable order. They marched, too, with an elastic tread, the pace being somewhat slower than that of our troops, and seemed vigorous and healthy. I have seen many armies file past in all the pomp of bright clothing and well-polished accoutrements; but I never saw one composed of finer men, or that looked more like *work*, than that portion of General Lee's Army which I was fortunate enough to see inspected."

Wolseley saw but little of the Confederate Cavalry, as General Steuart had left for his raid into Pennsylvania the day he reached head-quarters, and only

these two remarkable soldiers inspired their devoted followers : " Whilst Lee is regarded in the light of the infallible Jove, a man to be reverenced, Jackson is loved and adored with all that childlike and trustful affection which the ancients are said to have lavished upon the particular deity presiding over their affairs. The feeling of the soldiers for General Lee resembles that which Wellington's troops entertained for him—namely, a fixed and unshakable faith in all he did, and a calm confidence of victory when serving under him. But Jackson, like Napoleon, is idolised with that intense fervour which, consisting of mingled personal attachment and devoted loyalty, causes them to meet death for his sake, and bless him when dying."

returned a couple of days before he commenced his homeward journey. He remarked, however, " that though their knowledge of drill is limited, all the men rode well, in which particular they present a striking contrast to the Northern Cavalry, who can scarcely sit their horses, even when trotting."

Colonel Wolseley had quitted New York for his trip " down south " on the 11th of September, and had to report himself at Montreal on the expiration of his six weeks' leave. The short time at his disposal was the great drawback to the enjoyment of this visit to the head-quarters of the Confederate Army, but he made the most of it, and altogether he never passed a pleasanter time than when "running the blockade," with its attendant excitement, while as an enthusiastic soldier he considered himself amply repaid for any discomfort by his conversations with Robert Lee and Stonewall Jackson, whose deeds will live long in song and story, as long as high character, spotless patriotism, and brilliant military genius, command the admiration of the human race.

After his return to Canada, Colonel Wolseley suffered greatly from the wound in the right leg he had received in the Crimea seven years before. His exertions on foot caused the wound to open afresh, and, under medical advice, he was constrained to proceed to England. Here he placed himself under the eminent surgeon, Sir William Fergusson. There was considerable exfoliation of the right shin bone, and he did not begin to mend until after Sir William had cut out the part affected. Wolseley returned to Canada in the spring of 1863, and resumed his duties as Assistant Quartermaster-General, under Colonel Lysons.

In the Autumn of 1865 the Fenians in the United States, by their threatening attitude, gave cause for anxiety to the Dominion Government, and Colonel (now General) Sir Patrick McDougall, who came out to the Dominion to organise and superintend the local forces, established a Camp of Instruction for cadets, in order to test the efficiency of the training imparted by the Canadian military schools. At his request, the services of Colonel Wolseley were placed at his disposal by Sir John Michel, Commanding the Forces, and he appointed him to command the first Camp of Instruction ever established in Canada. The place selected for this experiment was La Prairie, about nine miles distant from Montreal, on the opposite side of the river.

A General and Regimental staff were placed under Wolseley's orders, and quartermasters and sergeant-majors were appointed permanently to battalions from among the discharged non-commissioned officers resident in Canada. The remaining battalion officers and non-commissioned officers were furnished by the cadets themselves in rotation, except that two cadets were named permanently as sergeants, and two as corporals to each company.

The force was formed into three battalions; and, to avoid all possible jealousy as to posts of honour, they were disposed in the order they would assume, facing the frontier of Canada, to repel an invasion. Thus the cadets of the Toronto school, and the schools west of Toronto, were formed into the right battalion, (three hundred and sixty-six men); the cadets of the Kingston school, and the English-speaking cadets of the Montreal and Quebec schools, composed the centre battalion (three hundred and thirty-four men); and the cadets of French-Canadian origin composed the left battalion (four hundred and five men).

By utilising the small barrack at La Prairie, Colonel Wolseley was enabled to place each battalion under canvas during two weeks, and in quarters one week.

The cadets, among whom were three French-Canadian Members of Parliament, and one Upper Canadian Member, also Lord Aylmer, and several gentlemen holding the rank of Lieutenant-Colonel in the Sedentary Militia, and officers who had served in the Regular Army, fell into the usual routine of camp life with surprising readiness; and though their duties were precisely the same as those performed by soldiers of the Regular Army in camp, their demeanour throughout was beyond praise. Every cadet had an opportunity for showing his ability in drilling a squad or company, as well as for acting as captain and covering sergeant of a company in battalion; and the aptitude and knowledge they generally displayed was a matter of surprise to Colonels McDougall and Wolseley, and afforded a gratifying testimony to the value of the Military Schools which had been established in the Province.

The late General, the Honourable Sir James Lindsay,

then commanding the Montreal Division, marched into La Prairie on the 4th of October, with the Montreal garrison of regular troops, and held two divisional field days, when the Montreal garrison acted as one brigade, and the cadets, with a battery of Royal Artillery temporarily attached, formed a second brigade under Colonel Wolseley. The second field day was held in the presence of Sir John Michel, and, says Colonel McDougall, "I can fully corroborate Colonel Wolseley's opinion that the cadets compared most favourably with the regular troops, an opinion that was shared in and expressed by both Sir John Michel and the Major-General, and that they executed all the movements of a sham fight with the same precision and quickness."

Wolseley performed his arduous duties during the three weeks the camp was established, to the entire satisfaction of his superiors, and Colonel McDougall reported in the following terms :—" I desire to record as strongly as possible my sense of the ability and energy with which the immediate command of the Camp was exercised by Colonel Wolseley, and to which is attributable a large share in the success of the experiment. It was a charge requiring unusually delicate management; but in Colonel Wolseley's qualifications tact is combined with firmness, and both with an intimate knowledge of his profession in an unusual degree."

At length, after many "scares," on the night of the 31st

of May, the Fenian leader, " General " O'Neil, crossed the Niagara river with about twelve hundred men, and, having captured Fort Erie, some three miles from Buffalo, advanced towards Ridgeway, where he threw up breastworks and awaited reinforcements.

On receipt of news of this daring act, the whole Dominion was thrown into a perfect fever of indignation and patriotic ardour. The call to arms was responded to by all classes and conditions of people, and had the necessity arisen, the whole Volunteer Militia force could have been collected in a few days. On the 31st of May, Colonel McDougall, Adjutant-General of Militia, received instructions to call out for actual service fourteen thousand Volunteers, and within twenty-four hours, the companies were all ready, and many had moved to the stations assigned them. On the 2nd of June, the whole of the Volunteer Force, not already called out, was placed on actual service, and, on the following day, the Province had more than twenty thousand men under arms. Notwithstanding that the season of the year entailed heavy sacrifices on those of the Volunteers who were business men, all joined with eagerness ; and, at Toronto, sixty young Canadians joined from Chicago. " Experience has shown," wrote the Adjutant-General, " that, in the event of a regular invasion, a hundred thousand men, in addition to the Volunteer Force, would eagerly come forward in forty-eight hours to aid in defending the country."

When the news of the Fenian invasion arrived at Montreal, Colonel Wolseley—under orders from Sir

John Michel, Commander-in-Chief—started thence for Toronto, where he placed himself at the disposal of Major-General George Napier, commanding the Division. On his arrival he found a Force of regular troops, consisting of a battery of Artillery and the 16th and 47th Regiments, under the command of Colonel Lowry, of the 47th, about to start to attack the Fenians. Wolseley accompanied the column which arrived that night at the Suspension Bridge over the Niagara river; but on reaching Fort Erie, on the following day, they learnt that a fight had already taken place, with indecisive results, at Ridgeway.*

Far different must it have been had the inexperienced commander of the Militia awaited the arrival of the regular troops under Colonel Lowry, or a second column under Colonel Peacock, which, unfortunately, had taken the wrong road.

Wolseley was sent on the following day to Stratford —a railway station near Georgian Bay, on Lake Huron —to take command of a brigade, consisting of a battery of Artillery, a battalion of the 16th Regiment, and two battalions of Canadian Militia.

---

* At 8 a.m. on the 2nd of June, two battalions of Canadian Militia, the "Hamilton" and "Queen's Own" Volunteers, marching from Toronto, attacked the Fenians at Ridgeway, between Forts Cockburn and Erie; but, though there was no lack of enthusiasm and gallantry, the commander was inexperienced, and the ammunition failed. The Canadians got into some confusion, and were forced back, but again attacked the Fenians, and drove them back, many being killed and wounded on both sides. The Fenians now retreated across the river, when many of them were captured by an United States' war-steamer.

But there was no further attempt at invasion by the Fenians, and when Wolseley's brigade was broken up, he returned to Montreal. He had scarcely resumed his duties when, in the Autumn of this year (1866) he was placed in command of a Camp of Observation, consisting of the 16th Regiment, two troops of Volunteer Cavalry, and three battalions of Militia, at Thorold, near St. Catherine's, on the Welland Canal, which the Fenians had expressed their intention to destroy. The large and wealthy city of Buffalo, on the American side, was at this time the centre of the Fenian military organization, and Wolseley had very responsible duties in watching the frontier between Fort Cockburn and the Niagara Falls. He remained at Thorold about a month, exercising his troops, and during this time nearly all the Militia of Upper Canada passed through his hands. Three battalions, of about a thousand men each, were drilled a week at a time, and the work was arduous for Wolseley, who was in the saddle all day and every day.

On the approach of Winter the camp was broken up, and he returned once again to Montreal : but, during the succeeding months, there were constant Fenian alarms, and the Generals and Staff Officers were kept on the *qui vive.* Indeed, in January, 1867, the alarm of threatened invasion was so great that field brigades were established in all the principal military centres, fully equipped, and in constant readiness to turn out should their services be required. Colonel Wolseley was sent to Toronto, were he organized the Toronto Brigade, but, in April, 1867, when matter looked more settled, he proceeded to England, being relieved as Assistant Quartermaster-General, by Sir Henry Havelock.

Wolseley's services in Canada had been so meritorious, and his claims for promotion were so generally acknowledged, that he was almost immediately nominated to succeed Colonel Lysons as head of the Department in which he had acquired such vast experience in the Crimea, India, and China, irrespective of the special knowledge of its working gained in Canada during the past five years. Colonel Lysons' term of service expired in the Autumn of 1867, and, in September, Wolseley returned to the Dominion as Deputy Quartermaster General, being, as we were assured by his predecessor, the youngest officer who was ever nominated to fill that responsible post. He came home to England, on two months' private leave, in 1868, and during his stay, occurred an important event in his life, his marriage with Miss Erskine, who accompanied him on his return to Canada.

In the following year was published his "Soldier's Pocket Book for Field Service,"* which is considered in the Army a standard authority. This invaluable

---

* The preface to the first edition of the "Soldier's Pocket Book" was written in Canada, and dated "Montreal, March, 1869." A second edition of this work was issued in 1871, and a third and revised edition in 1875. Wolseley is also the author of a "Field Pocket Book for the Auxiliary Forces," a work of more recent date.

little work offers—in a handy form, as its name implies —information on every subject of a professional nature, and to every rank in the Army,—from the private, who wants information how to keep his accoutrements clean, or to cook a beefsteak, to the "non-combatant" officer in search for a "form" for indenting for stores, or the General in the field who seeks to solve some knotty point in military law, or in the manœuvring of the "three arms." It is, in short, a most trustworthy and indispensable *vade mecum*, and its value has been universally acknowledged. Much of the information embodied in its pages, with the brevity and conciseness of style becoming a soldier, is original; and the articles on Staff duties, such as reconnoitring, surveying, and other duties of an officer of the Quartermaster-General's Department, embody the results of the writer's own lengthened experience in what was, before the new organization at the Horse Guards, and the establishment of an Intelligence Department, the most important section of the Military Staff.

END OF THE FIRST VOLUME.

London: Printed by A. Schulze, 13, Poland Street.   (L.)

www.ingramcontent.com/pod-product-compliance
Lightning Source LLC
Chambersburg PA
CBHW020856020726
47497CB00005B/1434